THE EMERALD TABLET

THE EMERALD TABLET

DAN JOLLEY

HARPER
An Imprint of HarperCollins*Publishers*

Library of Congress Control Number: 2016936320
ISBN 978-0-06-241165-5 (trade bdg.)

Typography by Torborg Davern
16 17 18 19 20   CG/RRDH   10 9 8 7 6 5 4 3 2 1
❖

First Edition

For Tracy

Always.

PROLOGUE

— 1906 —

The subterranean smell came to Jackson Wright first, thick and damp and dark. His eyelids didn't want to open, but he forced them. When they finally peeled back from his raw, gravelly eyes, he found himself staring at the intersection of four stone arches fifteen or twenty feet above him.

Where am I?

He tried to look around, but . . . *couldn't.* When he strained to turn his head, pain ground into his temples. He tried to search out the cause of that pain, but his hand stopped short, halted with a metallic *clank.* He couldn't move his legs, either. The sharp tang of panic began to rise in his throat.

I'm shackled! Someone's chained me down to . . . what?

Jackson could still move his fingertips. He used them to feel around as best he could. He lay, helpless, bound hand and foot to what felt like a massive stone slab.

What he'd at first thought to be a distant buzzing in his ears clarified: a soft chanting filled the chamber where he was imprisoned. Jackson felt his panic grow. He didn't recognize the words, but it sounded like dozens of voices, and they were coming from all around him.

He couldn't move his tongue. He could hardly even make a sound. *I can't speak!* Terror stabbed at him like a knife to his guts. Was he . . . had someone *drugged* him? Where had he been, that someone could have slipped something into his food or his drink? The last thing he remembered was leaving the house with his father for an after-dinner walk. Everything else was . . . *gone*.

Papa! Papa, help me! The words slammed inside his skull. Desperate. Useless.

The chamber's faint illumination shuddered and flickered like firelight. A writhing, dancing shadow fell across him, and only the metal strap holding his head in place kept Jackson from recoiling—but then his heart leaped.

Papa!

Jackson's father leaned over him, his fine, white-gold hair, hair the same color as Jackson's, all but hidden by the cowl of a long black robe.

Papa, help me! Get me out of here! Papa!

But Jackson saw something in his father's eyes he'd never seen before. Something hard and cold, like chips of ice. Without saying a word, his father moved away, out of Jackson's sight.

Another man approached from the other side of the slab. Tall and narrow through the shoulders, he was draped in a hooded robe identical to the one Jackson's father wore. But this man's face looked like old, white leather, and his green eyes shone with an eerie radiance that turned Jackson's mouth as dry as sand.

Mama! He imagined his mother's gentle, dark eyes. *Mama! I won't run in the house anymore. I promise I won't! Please! Please help me!*

"Zxarna vrahmu otvortse. Dvai shvioutei pivuntxa." As the green-eyed man spoke, the words buzzed and vibrated in Jackson's ears, in his *skull*, as if a swarm of tiny insects had begun digging and gnawing at his brain. His hands longed to scratch, to tear at his scalp, but still he couldn't move. As he spoke, the green-eyed man pulled a stone tablet from inside his robe. The stone was green, not entirely unlike the man's frightening, luminous eyes, and it was crystalline, its color somehow both dark and bright at the same time. It looked like a solid slab of stone, but then the man opened it, and Jackson saw that the odd tablet had pages like a book. Yet the man didn't hold it the way other people held books. He held it in the way someone would hold a live, venomous snake: carefully, and with great respect. Maybe even great fear. *"Dvai*

shvioutei pivuntxa, majia povrunshei taigho shviunta!"

The bizarre language reverberated around the chamber—not an echo, but dozens of voices repeating everything the green-eyed man said. This repetition somehow made the harsh words a thousand times worse.

"Taigho shviunta. Taigho shviunta." The unseen crowd chanted. Jackson would have cried out if he'd been able to make any noise at all . . . because he recognized one of those voices as his father's.

As the incantation continued, Jackson felt the air around him change. He couldn't move his head, but his eyes darted in every direction. His vision went momentarily white as a circle of fire exploded into being eight feet above the slab where he was bound. Its heat made the skin of Jackson's face pull tight. The burning ring rotated slowly above him, an enormous, twisted, ghastly version of the halos he'd seen over the heads of saints in church. *Is this how I'm to die? Like a twig in a bonfire?* Red-orange flames danced and licked around a blinding-white core . . .

. . . and as the crown of fire spun, a broad arc of water surged up through the air from Jackson's left, climbing in the shape of a rainbow over the flames. The water churned and frothed far above him, suspended in midair as it formed another ring, reflecting the fire in icy shades of white and blue and green. The same hard, cold colors he'd seen in his father's eyes.

Jackson whimpered.

Without warning, a blast of arctic wind channeled its way across Jackson's body, running frigid fingers through his hair. The very slab beneath him trembled and shivered, pulsing like a great, stone heart.

Jackson's muscles clenched as he tried again to free himself. It would have been better to scream his throat raw than suffer this paralysis. His heart thundered in his narrow chest, and tears as hot as lava squeezed out of his eyes.

He watched, stunned, as his tears fell *up*. They left his face and streaked straight into the broad, terrible arc of water above him, each drop gleaming like glass in the instant before the impossible current swept it away.

"I am Jonathan Thorne." It took Jackson a heartbeat to recognize the words as English, and another to realize the green-eyed man wasn't talking to him, or to the assembled crowd. *He was talking to the strange green-crystal book itself.* The scratching, hungry echoes of the other language still crawled beneath Jackson's skull as the green-eyed man went on. "I am the opener of the way. I am the leader of the faithful. I am the author of doom and the wielder of power."

Jonathan Thorne pulled a slim silver dagger from the sleeve of his robe and sliced open the tip of his own thumb without hesitation. Jackson's heart nearly stopped at the sight of the blade. In the firelight, Thorne's blood was as black as ink. Thorne leaned over and touched Jackson's forehead, painting something there, Jackson couldn't tell what. Straightening up and using the same thumb, Thorne drew a five-pointed star inside a circle on the cover of the strange book.

"I am Jonathan Thorne," he repeated. "I am the seeker of magick. I am the explorer of the lost paths. I am the One Above All Others, and with this blood I name myself master of a new world of boundless power!"

Slowly, so slowly, Thorne raised the dagger. The knife shifted in his grip, blade pointing straight down. Straight at Jackson's heart.

Jackson's thoughts blurred as panic choked him. *Wake up wake up I've got to wake up! This isn't real. I'm having a nightmare. Why can't I wake up? Why why why? WAKE UP!*

A flicker of movement from Jackson's left drew his eyes, and for an instant, for just a split second, he thought he *had* awakened. Because there was his father, coming back to save him! He tried to cry out, tried to force his unwilling tongue to move. . . .

But he could only watch as his father, with that terrible stony coldness in his eyes, slid off the signet ring Jackson wore on his left middle finger.

No! Papa, what are you doing? Why are you letting this happen?

Jackson's father turned the ring over in his fingers, examining it in the harsh light from the circle of fire overhead. It was simple, gold, bearing the Wright family's wagon-wheel crest: five spokes within a circle. It had belonged to Jackson's grandfather. "You won't need this where you're going, my son," the elder Wright said as he slipped the ring inside his robe.

When his father turned away from him a second time, Jackson felt his heart break.

Perhaps that was why it hurt so little when Thorne raised the silver dagger and plunged it into Jackson's chest.

Death.

Jackson had given a good bit of thought to dying after his pet beagle was run down by a team of horses pulling a mail wagon. He expected to feel his life slide away from him. He imagined his consciousness fading like the flame of an oil lamp as its fuel runs dry.

But instead, the air around him seemed to coalesce, growing thicker and taking on a crimson hue. He could still hear the chanting voices—*"Taigho shviunta! Taigho shviunta!"*—but everything he could see was now a horrible bloodred, as if he was seeing it through some kind of . . . what was it? *A film? A skin?* Blood seemed to flow out of his chest, and the strange membrane grew and thickened with it. Soon it surrounded him.

Suddenly the chanting voices surged, became shouts, and the stone slab beneath him lurched. The ceiling trembled, and dust and bits of mortar rained down; and from somewhere, from everywhere, a vast, deafening *roar* shook the earth itself.

As the bloodred cocoon tightened around Jackson's body, the chanting voices turned to screams.

"Earthquake!" someone screeched.

It was the last word Jackson heard before this world became lost to him.

1

"Okay, guys," Brett said, pushing coal-black hair out of his face. "Lily and me'll lift on three, and Gabe, you push. Got it?"

Gabe Conway squared his shoulders and gripped a length of rebar with pale hands. He wedged the rebar down beside the manhole lid and nodded, while Brett and Lily Hernandez tightened their grips on the lid hook.

Lily nodded, too. Until a few days ago, she'd had shoulder-length black hair just like her brother's but on a whim had decided to get it cut into a short bob. Now she teased Brett endlessly about his shaggy "emo hair."

Brett glanced over his shoulder at Kaz Smith, who was

standing lookout at the mouth of the narrow alleyway, head swiveling back and forth. Beyond the alley, a bank of moonlit clouds had erased the top of the Golden Gate Bridge. "All clear?"

"For now," Kaz whispered. He ran an anxious hand over his buzz cut. "But I hear voices! Just hurry up!"

"One . . . two . . . three!"

The twins pulled, and Gabe pried with the rebar. The sewer cap was even heavier than it looked, but with the three of them pulling, the lid eventually squealed and grated its way free of the manhole. Brett and Lily dropped the hook beside Gabe's now slightly bent rebar as Kaz pattered over to them.

"Okay, everybody down!" Brett barked. Gabe might have been a little irritated at the order if not for the ridiculous grin plastered across Brett's face. Gabe had never seen Brett so excited, and Brett got excited a lot.

Gabe clicked on his flashlight. "Whatever you say, *boss*." He peered down at the rusty ladder riveted to the side of the vertical shaft. "Why don't you take the lead?"

"As if I wasn't going to!" Brett clamped his own flashlight between his teeth and disappeared down the ladder in a flash.

"We're really doing this, huh?" Kaz edged one toe toward the opening. "Can I just repeat that this is a terrible idea? It was a terrible idea when Brett had it, and it's still terrible. What if there are, like, mutated alligators down there? Or flesh-eating mole people? Or . . . or *rats*?" As he was complaining, Kaz clicked on his head-mounted flashlight and started down the ladder after Brett, grumbling the whole way. "I mean, I'm *going,* but these rungs are a case of tetanus just waiting to happen. I don't even remember when I had my last shot. . . ." His voice trailed off as he vanished into the darkness after Brett.

My best friends, disappearing. How appropriate.

Gabe turned to Lily and gestured toward the manhole. "Ladies first."

Lily cocked her head and frowned at him with her huge, dark eyes, black as ink in the dim light. She and Brett had the same eyes. "What's wrong, Gabe? I thought you were excited about this field trip?" That was their code for the adventures they went on: "field trips." Like sneaking into the abandoned drive-in theater to watch horror movies on a laptop all night, or their marathon Ouija board session in the graveyard.

Lily's forehead smoothed out as she seemed to realize what was bothering Gabe. She'd always been able to read him. "Oh. Hey, relax, all right? It's not like you're never going to see us again! My cousin Marybeth moved to freaking Tennessee, but I FaceTime with her almost every day. I think we talk more now than we did when she lived here."

Gabe managed a halfhearted smile. "It's just, you know, I'm tired of all the moving around. I mean, seven cities in twelve years? Who lives like that? You'd think Uncle Steve was in the military."

She smiled back at him. "I bet you'll make tons of new

friends in Philadelphia and forget all about us."

Gabe could always count on Lily to try to boost his spirits when he was feeling down, but he wanted to say so many things in that moment. Things like: *But I'm tired of moving all over the country!* and *I love San Francisco and I don't want to leave.* Most of all, he wanted to tell Lily, *You don't understand. You guys are the only real friends I've ever had.* But he'd never say any of that out loud, and before he even had the chance, Kaz's voice drifted up from below.

"Hey! You're not bailing on us, are you?"

"Duty calls!" Lily said brightly, and scampered down the ladder like a monkey.

Gabe followed. He had to drop the last three or four feet from the bottom of the ladder to the floor of the sewer tunnel, and his sneakers splashed in a shallow trickle of liquid that he tried very hard not to think about. The stink of rot and stale air made Gabe's eyes water. He shined his flashlight around, picked out Lily and Kaz, and started to say "Where's Brett?" but only got as far as "Where's B—" before Brett leaped out of the shadows and shouted "Boo!"

Gabe didn't move or flinch, just closed his eyes and hoped no one could tell how fast Brett's little scare had made his heart beat. Brett's raucous laughter echoed up and down the tunnel. "Solid as a rock, this guy!" Brett bumped him with his shoulder, and Gabe couldn't help but return Brett's grin.

"If we're going to do this, could we please just *do* it?" Kaz waved a hand in front of his face. "It smells like a giant Porta-Potty."

"Fine, jeez, gotta be so serious all the time." Brett unslung his knapsack and rummaged around in it. "Do you not realize how epic this is gonna be?" He pulled out a rolled-up piece of silky cloth bound by a black ribbon. Gabe, Lily, and Kaz gathered around to watch him unfurl it.

Gabe felt a pang when he looked at that piece of cloth. Uncle Steve's occult research was way off-limits and usually kept under lock and key. The only reason they'd found the cloth in the first place was because three-quarters of Steve's office already sat packed in boxes, and in all the chaos of packing, he'd forgotten to lock the door. So what if Gabe and his friends had done a little snooping and poking and prodding? The man had so much bizarre stuff, how could anybody keep from at least taking a look at it?

Besides, Gabe had *not* stolen it. He'd *borrowed* it. Technically it wasn't even him doing the borrowing. Brett had popped open that particular box. And anyway, it wasn't like any of this stuff was *real*. If Brett wanted to add some make-believe to this last field trip, why not play along?

Brett held up the cloth, and Kaz and Gabe shined their lights on it, illuminating a map with the title "The Golden Gates" stitched across the top. Gabe had never seen a map like this before. For one thing, it'd been hand-sewn into the silk with about a hundred different colors of shiny, metallic thread.

For another, it depicted San Francisco, but not the *real* San Francisco. This was more like . . . art. Like an enhanced version of the city from some alternate universe, shimmering with color, all the buildings and streets magnified and twisted and surreal.

"Such a weird map," Kaz said for the thousandth time. "I don't know how you can even tell where we are."

"Everything about this is weird," Lily murmured.

"Would you all just *relax*?" Brett laid the map down across his knapsack and pointed. "Here's us. And the entrance to the secret tunnels is down there. And the secret room is right *there*." He stabbed a spot on the map. "It's, like, only half a mile away. Easy! Now come on!"

Brett's kid-on-Christmas-morning enthusiasm kept his insistence from becoming irritating. Or, at least, *too* irritating. With Brett leading the way, the four of them trooped along the tunnel and deeper under the city, the only noises the splashing of their feet and the sounds of distant traffic above them.

After ten or twelve minutes the traffic sounds faded, and eventually stopped.

"How far underground *are* we?" Kaz wondered, but no one answered him.

Gabe turned the situation over in his mind. Brett had been talking about some sort of secret tunnel system underneath San Francisco for weeks, but Brett talked about a lot of stuff. Like the monster in Lake Champlain, and the haunted island off the coast of Venice, and how the entire city of Paris was full of ghosts because of the catacombs. Except this time things had started clicking into place: first Uncle Steve announced they were moving. Then Brett convinced them all to take a look at the "priceless artifacts" and "important research" that Gabe's uncle usually kept behind locked doors. And then Brett stumbled across this weird map that just *happened* to show the exact maze of secret tunnels below the city that he'd been obsessing over.

Lily had nailed it when she said this whole situation was weird.

And what had been lying there in the box, right underneath the Golden Gates map, but a tiny, ancient-looking crimson book that described a bonding ritual—a ritual that would "tie together the members of a circle in this world, the last world, and all worlds in between." Its cover had the image of a curious-looking knot made of four loops.

"Don't you see?" Brett had waved the map around, his eyes huge, standing there in Uncle Steve's office. He pointed to a spot on the glistening silk sheet where a small square of a room was tucked among the warren of overlapping tunnels. The same quadruple-looped knot engraved on the cover of the crimson book also appeared here, sewn in intertwined threads of several colors. "It's perfect! We find this secret room, we do this ritual thing, and that way we'll be friends forever!"

Kaz had stood in the office doorway, keeping lookout as

usual. "Are you nuts? You want us to go crawling around under the city based on *that*? You'll get us all killed! Or, like, covered in poop."

Brett had flashed a brilliant grin at Lily and Gabe, and clapped a hand on Kaz's shoulder. "We'll steer clear of the sewage, Kaz. Tell you what. Let's just take a look. If we can find these secret tunnels, we'll do the friendship ritual so Gabe knows he'll never be alone no matter what random place his uncle moves him to. If we can't, I'll let it go. Pretend like it never happened. Gabe? What do you say?"

Gabe's mouth had stretched into a massive grin. "You guys are the best. I say let's do it."

And so, on a crisp late-autumn night, the four of them trudged through a dank, foul-smelling sewer tunnel, traveling deeper and deeper beneath the city.

"There!" Brett practically jumped up and down, the beam of his flashlight wobbling all over a buckled brick wall in front of them. "That's it! That's the entrance to the secret tunnels!" He whirled on Kaz. "In your *face*!" Kaz took a step back, startled, so Brett softened his tone and raised a hand. "High five?"

Kaz slapped Brett's hand warily. "Well, you definitely got us *somewhere*. I'm just not seeing exactly where. That's a dead end. Right? Plus it looks like it might collapse at any second."

Brett looked hard at the bricks. "Hmm." He pulled out the map again, flicking his light from the wall to the map and back. "It's . . . huh. I swear, guys, this is supposed to be it."

"How about we take a break?" Lily played her own flashlight along the floor of the tunnel.. "It's dry here, at least."

Gabe took off his own knapsack and sat cross-legged on the floor of the tunnel. Kaz settled down next to him and fished a plastic bag containing a thermos and four cups out of his knapsack. "Tea, guys?"

Gabe grinned. Of *course* Kaz had brought tea. His mom packed him a little thermos of it to bring everywhere. Gabe had spent a lot of time with Kaz's family, and thinking of them reminded him all over again how much he was going to miss living here. The Smiths had a whole flock of kids, so their house sounded like a Chuck E. Cheese's. Gabe envied that. His own house was so quiet it could pass for a library. If he wasn't lecturing at the university, Uncle Steve was holed up in his office, and the house felt so hushed that Gabe was conscious of every step taken, every cabinet door closed.

"I'll take some," Gabe said, holding out his hand.

"You got it." Kaz grinned and handed him a cup, then a small squeeze bottle of maple syrup. Gabe had always loved sweetening things with maple syrup, way more than with sugar or honey. How would he ever make new friends who'd get to know him this well?

"Your maple syrup thing is weird, Gabe," Brett muttered, reaching out to grab his own cup.

"Weird syrup to go along with a weird map and weird

tunnels and weird rituals and weird secret rooms," Lily said as she pulled the silk map closer to better see it. "We're just a bunch of weirdos."

Brett chuckled. Kaz and Gabe shrugged in unison.

Gabe took a bite out of a granola bar he'd been carrying in his pocket. He tried to pass it to Lily, but she didn't notice. She was too busy staring down at the strange silk map and then around the dark passageway they were in. Her forehead was scrunched up, like it was all some big puzzle to figure out. It *was* kind of a puzzle, Gabe supposed. A sort of treasure hunt, even if it only led to some empty room way under the city. But watching Lily trying to piece it together, you'd think a chest of gold doubloons was waiting for them down here.

Though she was supposedly only five minutes older than Brett, Gabe thought Lily was about a century more mature than her twin. Not that she was bossy or boring or anything like that, but where Brett was a loud jokester, Lily was responsible and considerate. Brett was the type to be so busy chattering and goofing off that he'd walk right off a cliff if Lily wasn't always right behind him, watching out for him.

Brett let out a loud belch that echoed down the hall. Kaz jumped in surprise at the noise, then broke into a spasm of giggles.

Gabe grinned and shook his head. Sometimes it was hard to believe that Brett and Lily were siblings, much less twins. But when he turned back to Lily, delight had lit up her smile.

Suddenly, the resemblance between the Hernandezes was impossible to miss.

"Lily?" Gabe asked. "What's up?"

She knocked back her tea, stood, and went to the buckled brick wall. The beam of her flashlight danced up and down along one section. "Guys! Look at this!"

Everyone jumped up to join her. "See?" She pointed. "We were looking at it from the wrong angle. It's like an optical illusion."

Gabe narrowed his eyes. "What're you talking about? That's just a gap in the bricks."

Without explaining further, Lily stuck her whole arm into what Gabe had mistaken for a slender crevice. "It's totally a doorway! And there's empty space behind it! I could tell there was something not quite right about how the shadows were falling."

"*Yes!*" Brett crowed. "Way to go, Lil! You found it!"

"That looks like earthquake damage, guys." Kaz sounded anxious and skeptical, as usual. "This is San Francisco. There've been, like, a billion."

Gabe examined the opening. "No, look. This was deliberate. See? Somebody wanted to hide this doorway."

Kaz huffed. "Okay, then, next question: What kind of maniac builds a secret doorway in the wall of a sewer?"

Lily made a scornful sound, sort of like *pffft*, and before anyone could do anything about it, she wriggled through the gap. Brett whooped and squirmed through after her. Kaz heaved a great, long-suffering sigh. "Creepy friendship ritual it is."

But Gabe saw a gleam in his friend's eye. Old, secret doorways? This was too good. Even Kaz the Skeptic was hooked.

Gabe pushed and pulled his way through the narrow opening after Kaz. He and his friends were standing in a tunnel that was, without question, *way* older than the sewers they'd been walking through. The floor, walls, and ceiling had all been carved from huge blocks of stone. The corridor stretched away into complete, utter darkness.

A chill ran up Gabe's spine, but Brett forged ahead. "Let's go!"

Gabe followed his friends, idly wondering if they should be leaving a trail of bread crumbs or something. He imagined getting lost in these narrow, dank tunnels, and shuddered.

Then Gabe noticed a dark heap in the tunnel ahead of them. "Hey, Brett—what's that up there?"

Brett aimed his light at the thing lying on the floor of the tunnel. It looked like a bunch of brown sticks. And maybe . . . what was that? An overturned bowl?

Gabe's stomach clenched as he realized what he was looking at. "Uh . . . guys? Those are bones."

Lily squinted at them. "What, like a dog died down here?"

Gabe shook his head. "Not a dog. See that skull? Those are human."

Kaz jumped about three feet in the air. "A skeleton!" Everyone else hung back, but Kaz advanced on it, his voice getting higher and shriller the closer he got. "A human skeleton! A *real* human skeleton! Guys, this is a *real dead human person skeleton!*"

Gabe heard Lily's inhaler *whoosh* somewhere in the dark. Gabe was about to ask her if she was okay, but before he could, he heard her comforting Kaz. "It's okay. Kaz, calm down."

Kaz turned to the rest of them. His eyes were as big as silver dollars in the beam of the flashlights. "But . . . but . . . but that makes this a crime scene! Doesn't it? We have to tell the police! Right?"

Brett walked over and crouched down, examining the bones. "Dude, this guy's been dead for a *long* time. I don't think someone's waiting for him at home. We can tell the police when we get aboveground, but let's keep going, okay?" He straightened up and faced them. *"Okay?"*

Gabe stared into the dark, gaping eyes of the skull. *That was a person.* He swallowed hard. "Okay."

Lily nodded, and then finally Kaz did, too.

This is some field trip.

Gabe gave the bones a wide berth as he walked past them.

After a minute or two Brett broke the silence. "I heard these tunnels were used to get corpses out of Chinatown during a plague outbreak," Brett said. "Maybe that's where the skeleton came from. Pretty cool, huh?"

Kaz made a brief choking sound. "Not so cool for the dead guy, man."

"Seriously, Brett," Lily said. "Show some respect. Remember that was somebody's mom or dad . . . or brother."

Brett speared Lily with a frosty glance. "And *you* need to remember you're my sister, not my mother."

Gabe hung at the back of the line and didn't say anything. He tried to tread lightly whenever the twins started talking about family stuff. Their older brother, Charlie, had died in a boating accident the summer before. Gabe knew Brett blamed himself, even though nobody else did. Gabe could hardly imagine what it'd be like to have a sibling in the first place, much less how horrible it'd be to lose one.

The tunnel went through a number of twists and turns, and for a while even dropped down into a cramped little passageway they had to crawl through. Finally the tunnel opened up again, and they stepped out into a huge, circular chamber, too broad for their flashlight beams to reach the opposite wall.

Brett let out a low whistle as he walked slowly toward the center of the room, light swinging this way and that. Behind him, barely louder than a whisper, Lily asked, "What *is* this place?"

Though he spoke at a normal volume, Brett's voice boomed and rolled all around them as he said, "What is it? It's perfect, that's what it is! *This is the secret room!*"

Gabe slowly took it all in. The floor had been divided into

four quadrants. Someone had carved huge, ornate glyphs into all four sections. One of them had no stone laid over it, exposing bare, packed earth. On the opposite side of the chamber, water—*from an underground spring?*—flowed in an arc-shaped trough from one opening in the wall to another. A huge, empty metal bowl on a three-legged stand rested on its side off to Gabe's left. He'd seen drawings of something similar in one of Uncle Steve's books. *That's a brazier. You pile red-hot coals in it.* From his right, a cold breeze came and went like the breath of a wheezing giant.

Gabe swung his light up and spotted a big, square opening in the ceiling. *Air vent.* That drew his eyes along a supporting stone archway. There were four of them, and they met in the center of the chamber, directly above a huge stone slab that had been broken into several pieces. Small holes had been drilled into the slab's corners, and rust stains marred the stone around them. Gabe shivered. He had the same question as Lily: *What is this place?*

But still . . .

Gabe glanced around at his friends.

Whatever it was, this place felt . . . *right.* The chills down his back became a thrill of excitement.

Gabe hopped up and sat on one of the larger pieces of the broken slab. "C'mon, guys." He patted the slab. "Let's do this!"

Kaz came over to him. "This is Brett's show," he said softly. "What's got you so excited all of a sudden?"

Gabe shrugged. "I don't know. I mean . . . if we're doing a friendship ritual, I don't think we're going to find a better place than this."

He felt even surer of his words with each second he spent looking around the chamber. Almost all of the ridiculous occult mumbo jumbo Uncle Steve studied involved the four elements. Earth, air, fire, and water. And wasn't that exactly what this room must represent? The bare earth, the running stream in the trough, the brazier meant to be filled with burning coals, the fresh-air vent in the ceiling. Gabe's grin got bigger. "Come on, Brett! Break out the stuff already!"

Brett and Lily clambered up onto the stone. Kaz followed, shaking his head but not saying anything. Once they'd arranged themselves in a rough circle, Brett pulled out a small penknife and a tiny glass with Wild Horse Saloon engraved on the side.

Gabe raised an eyebrow. "Wild Horse Saloon? Really?"

Brett put the glass on a more or less level spot between them. "The book didn't say what *kind* of receptacle. It just said 'small receptacle.' Slow your roll." Lily elbowed Brett in the ribs, but he ignored her as he opened the penknife. "Pure silver," he said. "Our granddad got this for his retirement, so this'll be our little secret, okay? Now, we ready?"

Gabe looked around at everyone. *If this means never losing you guys as friends, you better believe I'm ready, even if it is just pretend.* He held out his thumb. "Everybody still cool with the elements we picked? Nobody wants to switch?"

"You sure you don't wanna trade, Brett?" Lily asked.

Considering how he'd seen his older brother drown, it had been a big surprise to everyone when Brett told them he wanted to invoke water.

"Nah," Brett said. "Someone's gotta be water, lame as it is. Just hold still, Mr. Human Torch." Brett nicked Gabe's thumb with the penknife, deeply enough to make three or four drops of blood come to the surface of the skin. Gabe let them fall into the glass. Lily held out her hand, and Kaz slowly followed her lead. Seconds later their blood mingled with Gabe's. Brett didn't hesitate when his turn came. Once he added his own blood to the glass, he opened the little crimson book and read aloud.

"In honor of the four elements, we commend ourselves to thee. I name myself Water."

Lily closed her eyes. "I name myself Air."

Kaz gave Brett and Lily a look that said *We're really doing this, huh?* He sighed. "I name myself Earth."

Gabe swallowed hard. "I name myself Fire."

Brett looked at the book again. "Let this joined circle never be torn asunder. Let it endure in this world, the last world, and all the worlds between."

A fresh burst of air howled in through the ceiling vent, making the water in the trough froth for a second. Kaz gasped and put his hands down on the rock beneath them as if he'd felt it move. Gabe wasn't paying much attention to any of that, because all of a sudden his thumb hurt really bad. More than just hurt—it *burned*.

But the wind from the vent died out almost as soon as it had begun, and the pain in Gabe's thumb eased. He looked around at his friends, grateful that they'd agreed to bond with each other, even if it was just in a silly, mumbo jumbo kind of way.

"Well?" Kaz peered at Gabe. "Feel any different?"

Gabe grinned and lightly punched Kaz in the shoulder. "Nope. I still feel like a guy with the three best friends in the world."

"Okay." Brett jumped down off the stone. "Enough with the Hallmark moment! I'm starving! Let's find some . . . Is it breakfast time yet? I want some waffles."

Lily followed her brother. "You and your stomach."

"A man's gotta eat," Brett said, patting his flat belly. He put his arm around Gabe's shoulders. "Come on. Let's find some grub."

Gabe smiled and joked and laughed with his friends as they made their way out of the chamber. But no words spoken or rituals undertaken could change the fact that his time with Brett, Lily, and Kaz was almost over, and it dragged on his heart like a lead weight.

2

Trudging down the sidewalk alone, Gabe felt sadder and more isolated than ever. His friends had already left, Kaz returning to his big, loud, chaotic, wonderful family, and the Hernandez twins to their grandmother, who was watching them while their parents were out of town. Abuelita, they called her. Gabe could practically hear the plump, white-haired older lady playfully chiding Brett and Lily about not speaking Spanish any better than they did, at the same time plying them with cookies and brownies and flan.

Uncle Steve knew how to cook, sort of, but everything he put in front of Gabe was unrelentingly healthy, and definitely didn't taste like love.

Gabe arrived at the steep front steps that led up to their row house. All the lights were on despite it being—he checked his watch—a quarter to one in the morning. That meant Uncle Steve was awake, alert, and definitely aware that Gabe was out *way* past his bedtime.

He tried to open and close the door as quietly as possible, but Uncle Steve had the hearing of a German shepherd. No sooner had the latch clicked back into place than the sound of his uncle's uneven footsteps thumped toward him from the kitchen.

Gabe swallowed hard and did his best to prepare for the inevitable onslaught. Only then did the sight in front of him finally register. Uncle Steve had been busy: the hallway that ran the length of the house's bottom floor was lined on both sides with tightly sealed cardboard boxes. Each of them had been labeled in his uncle's sharp, tidy block handwriting, as if a giant typewriter had thunked words onto the cardboard. LIVING ROOM, one pile read. KITCHEN, the one behind it was labeled. It was happening right in front of him: his whole life uprooted again, his uncle ready to drag him away from everything he'd come to love in San Francisco and drop him in Philadelphia.

Gabe's teeth ground together as Steven Conway appeared at the far end of the hall.

Uncle Steve was tall and built like an Olympic swimmer, with wavy silver-blond hair that fell to his jawline. If you'd dressed him in Robin Hood clothes and given him a big fancy bow, he would've looked right at home on the cover of a fantasy novel . . . except for the prosthetic leg, its metal visible between the hem of his pants and his shoe.

"How could you?" He didn't raise his voice. He didn't have to. Uncle Steve had perfected a tone that made your skin crawl and left you feeling kind of queasy. Usually it also made Gabe drop his eyes to his feet and stumble through an apology, but tonight, to his own surprise, it just irritated him.

"How could I *what*?" Gabe shot back, even though he knew good and well what.

Uncle Steve took a few steps closer, eyes narrowing. He had quite a few permanent lines on his face, but a special one showed up, right between his eyebrows, whenever he got angry with Gabe. "You went into my office. I don't know what you took, but I know someone went through those boxes. You *know* you're not supposed to interfere with my research."

Gabe couldn't help it: he rolled his eyes and grumbled, "Oh yeah, your superimportant hocus-pocus research."

Uncle Steve's eyes narrowed. "Gabe, listen to me. Apart from protecting years of work, I keep the items in my office locked up for a reason. They're dangerous."

"*Dangerous.* Yeah, sure. Bunch of books and papers. *Scary.*" Gabe had never talked back to his uncle like this before. He'd never really told him how he felt being constantly moved all over the country for this imaginary *garbage.* "I only went through your stuff so I could have one last adventure with Brett and Lily and Kaz. I'm never going to see them again after next week, remember? Because of you! The first time in my life I've ever had real, actual friends, and do you let me keep them? No! Of course not! We've got to move again, for no good reason!"

A cloud passed across Uncle Steve's face. So quietly Gabe could barely hear him, he said, "No good reason."

But Gabe didn't stop. He felt a searing wave building inside him, the kind of anger that Uncle Steve had always told him needed to be corralled, controlled, and gotten rid of. *Losing control of oneself never helps anything, and it will certainly never help you.* Gabe couldn't remember how many times he'd heard Uncle Steve say that.

But right now Gabe *wanted* to lose control. He wanted to wad up all the stuff his uncle had ever taught him and throw it back in his face. "Everything we do is about you and your stupid research! What about what I want? Did you ever think to ask me if I was *totally miserable*? No! 'Cause you're always so wrapped up in all this *junk*! You never do anything for anybody except yourself!"

Uncle Steve's blue-gray eyes went wide. He took a breath to speak, but stopped and closed his mouth again. That gave Gabe such an intense jab of satisfaction—*I left him speechless!*—that he was immediately ashamed.

But not ashamed enough to back down.

Uncle Steve ran a hand through his hair. When he spoke, he sounded kind of— Gabe wasn't sure exactly. Stunned? "Gabe, this is all for your own good. Everything I do, every bit of it, is for *you*."

But Gabe was done listening. He spun to his left and started climbing the stairs, very deliberately not looking back. Uncle Steve limped after him, his prosthetic leg thumping on the old, polished wood of the staircase, but Gabe was much faster and was almost at the top landing before his uncle spoke again.

"Gabe, wait. I'll explain if you give me a chance to. Let's talk about this."

Gabe reached the top of the stairs. "You talk, I listen, right? No thanks." He lifted one foot, about to start down the hall to his room, but after a lifetime of conditioning, he couldn't overcome the Uncle Steve Tone when it was turned up to full strength.

"Gabe. *Stop*."

He stopped. Turned and looked down at his uncle.

Uncle Steve sighed. "You're grounded. From now until we leave, the only place you're allowed to go is school." He didn't even sound angry anymore, just tired.

Gabe didn't care. "So you're gonna make my last few days here as lonely and depressing as possible?"

Uncle Steve shrugged. "You brought this on yourself. You knew my office was off-limits, and you deliberately broke the rules. Actions have consequences. Now go to your room, and we'll talk in the morning."

Gabe couldn't form any words. He just made a sort of

growling sound in his throat, stomped down the hallway past the locked door to his uncle's office, and slammed into his room. He thought about shoving his massive, antique chest of drawers in front of the door—if he couldn't go out, he'd make it so that no one could come in, either. But in the space of a heartbeat, all the loneliness and anger and outrage, all the walking and climbing, and the incredibly late hour all piled on top of him at once, and the only thing he felt was *exhausted*.

Gabe skirted another stack of packed-full cardboard moving boxes in the middle of his bedroom floor and fell face-first onto his bed. He would have been asleep thirty seconds later if his phone hadn't buzzed in his pocket.

Group texts stacked up one after another.

The first was from Brett: **AWSM FIELD TRIP 2NIGHT!**

Then one from Lily: **2nite was grrrr8! U guys r the best!**

Finally Kaz chimed in: **I think I might have black lung**

Gabe couldn't hold back a smile. But it was a sad smile, realizing how little time he had left with these guys. Especially now that he could only see them at school.

Part of him wanted to unload on them and stay up texting about what a jerk his uncle was. But it was so late. And it wasn't like it would change anything.

With the phone two inches from the end of his nose, Gabe poked at the keyboard with one finger, too tired to put forth the effort of using both thumbs: **Im grounded. Worth it tho. C u @ school, guys. Nite.**

He dropped the phone on his bedside table and drifted off to sleep while it buzzed and rattled against the wood.

When hazy morning sunlight invaded his room, Gabe squeezed his eyes shut and pulled the covers over his head. He didn't want to get up. He didn't want to go to school. And he especially didn't want to face Uncle Steve. He felt a little bad about what he'd said last night, but he was still angry. He knew his uncle had an early class today, and Gabe hoped that he'd already left.

No such luck. Gabe heard the door to his room swing open. Traces of the Uncle Steve Tone still lingered in his uncle's voice, but mostly he just sounded sleepy. "All right, I'm off to work. Nothing's changed since last night, though. You're still grounded. I trust you can get to school on time?"

Gabe groaned. He knew Uncle Steve wouldn't leave until he got the answer he was looking for. "Yes," he said, his voice muffled by the blankets.

"Good. And I meant what I said about us having a talk later."

Gabe groaned again.

"This *should* go without saying, but until then my office is off-limits. *Strictly* off-limits. Understand?"

"Yes, yes, yes," Gabe muttered.

His door clicked shut, but it took another solid minute before he tossed back the covers and got up.

By the time he'd stood in the shower, pulled on some

clothes, and gotten downstairs to scarf some breakfast, Uncle Steve was long gone. Gabe peered at the clock: seven thirty-six. *Too early for humans. School should start around ten thirty. Maybe eleven.* He had just put his cereal bowl in the dishwasher when the chime of the doorbell echoed down the hallway.

Gabe opened the door to reveal Brett, Lily, and Kaz standing there, all dressed for school, backpacks strapped over their shoulders. Lily gave him a brilliant smile, and Brett and Kaz both tried to look cheerful, but Gabe just couldn't bring himself to grin back. He motioned them inside. "Since when do we walk to school together?"

"Since it might be the only time we have to talk! We couldn't just ignore your text from last night!" Lily said.

"Even though you did a great job of ignoring all of ours." Brett playfully elbowed him in the ribs. "You can't expect to drop a message like 'I'm never going to see you again! Goodbye, cruel world!' and not expect us to check up on you."

That almost raised the corners of Gabe's mouth. "That's not exactly what I said."

Brett peered up the stairs. "Yeah, but we barely have any time left as it is. If you're grounded, we *really* have to make the most of it. Is your uncle here?"

"Nah, he had an early class. Gotta teach all those college students about make-believe and mumbo jumbo."

Kaz pulled his thermos out of his backpack. "I brought you some more tea," he said. "Figured you might want to get in as much as you could."

Gabe took it. "Thanks. This'll go great with lunch." At Kaz's grin, Gabe said, "We should probably get to school. Even though I really don't feel like going today."

Brett threw a couple of brief but meaningful glances at Lily and Kaz. "Well, then . . . why don't we just not go?"

Gabe paused. "You mean skip?"

Brett chuckled. "It has been known to happen, from time to time."

Gabe furrowed his brow at Kaz and Lily. "Are you two okay with this? *You*, Kaz?"

"Just thinking about it is giving me hives, to be honest," Kaz said, absently scratching his neck. "But I'd rather have hives than not give you a proper send-off." Kaz wore his nervousness on his sleeve, but at his core he was as solid as a rock.

"Me, too," Lily said.

Skip school? It was crazy. He was already in big trouble with Uncle Steve. But the longer he thought about it—over the course of a whole six or seven seconds—the more it appealed to him. Hadn't Uncle Steve sort of put him in this situation? It shouldn't surprise him that if he cut Gabe off from his friends, Gabe would do anything he could to spend more time with them. Plus, Gabe could tell that his friends had discussed this before they got to his house. None of them were the type to play hooky, but if *they* were all willing, well . . .

"It's not like it would even matter if I got caught," Gabe

said, thinking aloud. "I'd get even more grounded, sure, but grounded in Philadelphia, where I don't know a single soul. So . . . yeah. Yeah! Forget school today! Let's do something fun!"

Kaz cleared his throat. "Um, I was thinking. We might *not* get caught if the school got some sort of note from a parent."

Gabe grinned, his eyes sparkling with mischief. "Parent *or guardian*, right? Come on. I'll send an email from Uncle Steve's computer and tell them we all got food poisoning. Follow me!"

The four of them tromped up the stairs and clustered outside Uncle Steve's office, which sported a shiny new lock now. Gabe rolled his eyes. *Why not just say "I don't trust you, Gabe?"*

"Okay, who here knows how to pick locks?" Gabe looked from face to face, but his friends all just stared at him.

"It's not like we're hardened criminals," Lily said wryly.

"Oh, come on." Gabe rattled the knob. "People pick locks all the time on TV! How hard could it be?"

Kaz slid his tablet out of his pack and timidly raised a hand. "I think I can help. I'm sure there's a tutorial on YouTube."

Brett clapped Kaz on the shoulder. "Now we're talking! Pull us up some instructions!"

Fifteen minutes later, following several viewings of a short video called "Lock Picking and You" and a house-wide search for a pair of paper clips ("It's not my fault Uncle Steve keeps the paper clips inside the office!"), Brett and Gabe were crouched in front of the door, trying and repeatedly failing to open the new lock.

Lily watched, hands on her hips and one eyebrow cocked. "A pair of criminal masterminds you are."

Brett didn't look up. "I don't see you picking any locks."

She scoffed, "Get out of the way, and I'll show you how it's done!"

Behind her, Kaz leaned against the wall, watching more videos on his tablet, apparently unconcerned with their progress or lack thereof. More or less talking to himself, he said, "Whoa, this ferret's riding a really small bicycle!"

Gabe was too focused on the task at hand to talk. He knew he was supposed to use one paper clip to disengage . . . something. And then Brett was supposed to use the other one to . . . He actually wasn't entirely sure. He glanced at Brett. "Maybe we should watch the video again."

Kaz burst out laughing. "Guys, come look at this ferret!"

Brett's paper clip slipped and stabbed Gabe's finger like a tiny ice pick.

Gabe yelped and jumped up, shaking his finger. He stuck it in his mouth and talked around it, glaring at Brett. "Dude, watch what you're doing!" he cried, except it came out more like "Oo, wash wha oor ooing!"

Brett stood up, shaking his head. "Well, we've done it now." He pointed at the lock. Gabe peered at it, still sucking on his wounded finger, and his heart sank. The paper clip he'd been using had snapped off cleanly, lodged in the lock with no hope of being dug out. Brett went on: "Actually, to be accurate, we *haven't* done it. That lock is ruined. Sorry about your finger, Gabe. Kaz's hyena laugh startled me."

Gabe wrapped his wounded digit in his shirt and squeezed, hoping the pressure would halt the bleeding. He squinted sourly at Brett. "Yeah, you *sound* sorry. What're we going to do now?"

Brett looked around at all three of them before he spoke. "Look, Gabe, your uncle is going to know we tried to break in. The lock will tell him that much."

Lily frowned. "So?"

Brett thumped his fist on the office door. "*So,* we don't really have anything to lose at this point. Let's just break it open."

Kaz's jaw dropped. "What, like we're in some action movie? Tell me you're joking."

Brett gave Kaz his most charming grin. "C'mon, Kaz! Haven't you ever wanted to be a bad boy?"

Those words echoed in Gabe's ears. Wasn't that what Uncle Steve thought he was? Bad? *Well, this'll be exactly what he expects from me, won't it?*

Before Kaz could answer, Gabe said, "Brett's right. Let's do it."

"Guys! Stop!" Lily put herself between Gabe and the door.

"Come on, Gabe. Literally breaking down the door? It's not worth it! Think how much trouble you'll be in!"

"Exactly the same amount as I'm in now," Gabe said, somewhere between glum and sullen. He knew that, as always, Lily was just looking out for him. But she wasn't going to have his back forever: Gabe's remaining hours with her and the rest of his friends were numbered. If he got into Uncle Steve's office and emailed the school, he'd be able to squeeze in a few more. That alone made breaking down the door worth the consequences. "Will you move over, please?"

Lily shook her head, but she stepped aside. Gabe nodded to Brett. "On the count of three." At the end of the very short countdown, Gabe and Brett rammed the door with their shoulders at the same time, and the door sprang free of the wood frame with a splintering crack.

The office was meant to be a bedroom, so it was basically the same size and shape as Gabe's room. Ordinarily it was a treasure trove of strange and bizarre items. Ancient scrolls, polished glass skulls, ornate candlesticks . . . and books. *So many books.* Books of all shapes and sizes, every one of them as old as dirt, and almost none of them written in English.

But now the office had been packed up, stored in Uncle Steve's thoroughly taped, neatly labeled cardboard boxes. The only things left unboxed were the computer sitting on his uncle's desk and half a dozen empty bookshelves. Gabe immediately sat down at the desk and woke the computer. "This won't take long," he said to no one in particular. "I figured out his email password years ago."

Gabe0627. My name and birthday. For just a second Gabe let himself stop and think about what it meant that his uncle had chosen that password. But then he pushed the thought away.

Kaz hovered anxiously in the wrecked doorway and Lily leaned against the wall, arms crossed, but Brett wandered the office, looking around. That was how they'd found the Golden Gates map: Brett wandering and looking.

Gabe had just about finished composing the email on Uncle Steve's computer—being careful not to use his right index finger for fear of getting blood on the keys—when Brett, standing at the corner of the desk, cried out in surprise. "Whoa! Guys, look at this!"

Gabe glanced up to see Brett holding a strange book.

Gabe had never seen it before. The book's cover looked as if it was coated in gold dust, and a slender crimson ribbon was wrapped around it top to bottom and side to side, tying it closed. As Brett turned it in his hands, Gabe spotted several odd runes stamped into the gold. "Where'd you get that?"

Brett pointed at the side of the desk. "It was right here! Behind this paneling."

As Lily and Kaz crowded forward to see the book, Gabe got up and looked at the spot where Brett had pointed. Sure enough, a wood panel on the side of the desk had swung out, like a little secret door. "How the heck did you even find that?"

Brett wasn't listening. He and Kaz had started trying to open the book but weren't having any luck. "What is up with this ribbon?" Kaz said, annoyed. "Is it glued down or something?"

Lily said, "Maybe you shouldn't open it, guys," but Brett ignored her, too. He shoved the book at Gabe.

"Here, maybe you'll have better luck."

Gabe peered at the book. There was something weird about it. He cocked his head, looking closer. In the morning sunlight, the shadow of Brett's arm stretched across the floor of the office. But the shadow . . . ended too soon?

Did the book not cast a shadow?

Gabe shook his head and squeezed his eyes shut. *That's ridiculous. Keep it together, Gabe.*

"Yeah," he shot back, "or maybe I'll put it back where it came from." Gabe was going to say something more, about Brett's snooping around and how he *maybe* shouldn't be doing so much of it, but then his outstretched hand made contact with the book.

Pain shot through his injured finger, and a little smear of blood traced across the cover's surface.

That was when things got strange.

The office seemed to fill with heat. It blazed through Gabe's body, as if the scorching rays of a hot summer sun were suddenly focused on him through a giant magnifying glass. Gabe faltered, grabbing the desk to steady himself.

Lily said, "Gabe! Are you okay?"

But he didn't answer her, because as he watched, astonished, the narrow ribbon binding the book evaporated into a shower of tiny red droplets that diffused in the air and disappeared. Gabe tried to drop the book, but he couldn't. It felt as if the book was somehow gripping *him*. The gold dust on the cover shook loose and rose in the air, revealing a cover of brilliant emerald green. The shimmering motes swirled into four streams, curving and waving like sea serpents.

Eyes wide and voice filled with wonder, Kaz let out a long, drawn-out "Whooaaa. . . ."

"Guys!" Lily's eyes had gone wide, too, but not with wonder. She started edging toward the door. "Guys, I don't like this! *Guys!*"

Gabe could hardly process this amazing and *impossible* thing happening right in front of him. He glanced over and saw Brett watching the swirling gold dust with a broad, toothy grin on his face.

Gabe managed to say "Brett?" before the golden tendrils—again, like serpents—coiled and struck. In a heartbeat, the tendrils flashed out, one for each of them, and flowed *into all their bodies*. They didn't just breathe in the dust. It saturated their skin and sank *through* it, absorbing into them. And then—

—*Gabe found himself somewhere else. Lying on a stone slab looking up at a ceiling where four stone arches met in a cross,* staring through something red. Red as blood. It was blood! Some kind of membrane made of blood enveloped him like a cocoon, and Gabe clawed at it, tore and shoved and ripped until he pulled free and sat up.

As soon as he did, the stone walls around him cracked, crumbled, and fell . . . up. As if gravity had reversed itself, the stones shot straight up into the sky, revealing a cityscape around him that Gabe could barely comprehend. After a moment it hit him: the city was San Francisco.

But not the San Francisco he knew. All the buildings rose into twisted, gnarled shapes, like massive, towering trees that had long ago died of a terrible blight. Movement caught his eye, and he squinted, then wished he hadn't. Gargoyles perched on ledges, actual living, breathing gargoyles, and one by one they turned their heads and glared down at him like vultures zeroing in on a dying animal.

A warm, sickly wet wind blew across him, followed by a roar that made the ground beneath him tremble. Gabe watched as the gargoyles took flight, circling those ghastly towers. High above the towers, framed against a sky swirling with amber and gold, something else flew. Something enormous, held aloft on many-masted wings. No—more than one! Another and another, airborne behemoths, each one a twisted fun house–mirror version of a dragon.

The roar sounded out again, and Gabe twisted his head to try to find the source. He couldn't see what had produced that awful, earsplitting bellow, but he did see a shadow, vast and monstrous, moving through the darkened streets, coming closer and closer.

3

Brett groaned and, after a couple of tries, managed to sit up. His head felt like an elephant had run over it. Actually, it was more like the elephant was standing on his skull at this very second. Scratch that: a whole family of elephants were balancing on his brain, like it was a prop in some messed-up circus trick.

Yeah. That pretty much nailed the sensation.

When his vision finally cleared, there were no elephants in sight, but wherever he was definitely did *not* look like his bedroom. Weird. For a second Brett thought he might be dreaming, but then his mental cobwebs parted and everything came rushing back: Dr. Conway's office, and the Tablet, and . . .

My friends! Brett sprang to his feet. "Guys? Guys!"

A groan from behind him made him spin around. Kaz and Lily were both sitting on the floor, looking as out of it as Brett felt, while Gabe propped himself up on his elbows.

"What just happened?" Lily asked, rubbing her eyes.

Brett helped his sister to her feet, feeling a flicker of guilt as Gabe and Kaz got up on their own. "Looks like we all passed out."

"Yeah," Gabe said, "but why?"

Yeah, why, *Brett?*

He could see the wheels turning in Kaz's head. Counting off on his fingers, Kaz said, "Well, there could be a gas leak in here. But I don't think we would've gotten up from that. Or there could've been a minor earthquake and it knocked us down, and we all hit our heads on the floor. . . . Nah, that sounds dumber the more I talk about it. Oh! We could've picked up some kind of fungal infection down in the tunnels! Are any of you hallucinating?"

"You're hallucinating if you think any of those things make sense," Lily said.

It took effort for Brett to look just as confused as they were. But he had become very good at keeping secrets. Just as he'd become so good at pretending to be as happy and carefree as everyone expected him to be. Sometimes if felt like he was two different people, living two entirely separate lives.

Gabe put a hand on the back of a chair to steady himself,

and Brett jumped over to take his friend's arm. "You okay, man? You don't look so good." He tried to sound casual, but he could feel guilt warm his ears. *I will never forgive myself if any part of this hurts one of my friends.*

Brett had plenty of experience not forgiving himself.

"Nah, I'm fine." Gabe gently pulled his arm out of Brett's grasp. "I'm just confused is all. Look at that." He pointed at the Tablet, now lying on the edge of Dr. Conway's desk. "Am I crazy? Or wasn't that book gold? Y'know, before?"

Lily said, "Hey, you're right. Bizarre."

"It's a tablet," Brett said, more to himself than to anyone else. It'd seemed odd to him, too, but that was what his Friend called it. And now he understood why: the artifact's gold cover was gone, and beneath it was a solid block of glimmering green stone. The material was really strange. It sort of shone, but it was dark at the same time, like it was filled with both shadow and light.

So far he'd done everything his Friend had asked him to, weird as it all seemed. He'd taken the Golden Gates map, and found the special room in the tunnels, and gotten everyone to perform the ritual. He'd even cut Gabe's finger, and made sure Gabe's blood got onto the Tablet. But he hadn't known what to expect.

Brett rubbed the back of his neck, staring at the thing. Had its gold cover disappeared as soon as Gabe's blood touched it? He was about to ask the others what they remembered, from the time when Gabe touched the Tablet to all of them waking up on the floor, when suddenly they had a much bigger problem to deal with.

Dr. Steven Conway stood in the doorway, glaring at them with such intensity and anger that Brett was a little surprised none of them turned to stone. Or dropped dead. Or maybe burst into flames. *If he's back already, that means we were out cold for a couple of hours. . . .* Dr. Conway's silver-blond hair and sharp blue-gray eyes kind of creeped Brett out, and he *always* looked serious, but the look on his face now was at a whole new level.

Without thinking, Brett took a step sideways, blocking Dr. Conway's view of the Tablet.

The man's death-laser stare settled on Gabe. "After everything we talked about last night. It's not bad enough that you're skipping school. You're in here? Going through my things? *Again?*" Dr. Conway hadn't raised his voice, but somehow that only made him sound angrier. "Gabe, how can you be so irresponsible? I tried to tell you how *dangerous* some of these things are. I've been keeping you out of here for your own protection!"

Gabe took a deep breath. *"My protection?"* he said with a blaze of anger Brett had never seen before. "Right. Not like you aren't a total control freak about absolutely *everything*. None of this junk is dangerous. How could it be?"

Brett had the feeling these words had been simmering inside Gabe for a long while. Still, hadn't the Tablet just knocked them all unconscious? The ancient book was clearly a whole lot more than "junk." He had a bump on the back of his head to prove it. Or could Gabe have somehow completely forgotten what happened before they passed out?

"I mean, you expect me to believe that a bunch of moldy papers are going to hurt me?" Gabe continued. "Admit that you just like ordering me around. You're making it all up!"

Dr. Conway took in a sharp, hissing breath. *"Making it up?"*

"You heard me. It's all hocus-pocus. Mumbo jumbo. Total gibberish."

Uncle Steve turned a superalarming shade of red.

It really seemed like Gabe *had* totally forgotten about the Tablet. Weird. Then again, everything about this was weird.

Brett wondered uneasily what Gabe would think if he knew everything Brett did about all this "hocus-pocus." Brett wasn't even sure what he himself thought. He wanted so much to believe everything his Friend had told him, no matter how fantastical it all sounded. Forget fantastic, most of it sounded downright *impossible*. But crazy as the whole thing was, so far everything his Friend had said turned out to be true.

Brett took Dr. Conway's distraction as an opportunity to reach behind himself and pick up the Tablet. Heat flowed up through his hands and arms, filling his body like a charging battery and almost making him drop it. Was this thing really so powerful? Was that why his Friend wanted it so badly? The Tablet looked like it should have weighed about fifty pounds, but Brett could heft it with one hand. He slid the artifact into his backpack, careful not to attract Dr. Conway's attention.

But it seemed like Dr. Conway's whole world had narrowed down and become Gabe-shaped. "How can you think that I'm *lying* to you?" Dr. Conway's voice started to rise. Slowly, but really scarily, like floodwaters. "I wanted to explain to you last night. I thought maybe you were grown-up enough to hear it, but then you stormed off like a child."

"Right, I'm the child, but you're the one who believes in fairy tales?" Sarcasm dripped off Gabe's words. "How can you tell me you believe in this"—Gabe waved one hand at the moving boxes stacked on the office floor—"*garbage*? You act like it's so important, but the truth is, you're a professor of stupid, imaginary stories cavemen told each other around campfires. Stuff to explain why the sky is blue and why snow falls when it gets cold! It's all make-believe!"

Brett had never seen Gabe this angry, or heard him just flat-out call Dr. Conway's work a bunch of crap. He exchanged glances with Lily and Kaz, and a silent bit of communication passed between the three of them: *Let's get out while we still can.* Brett began to edge away from the desk, following his sister and Kaz out of the office and into the hallway.

"You don't know what you're talking about," Dr. Conway yelled, shaking his head. "The fact that you don't understand how these artifacts can be dangerous is *exactly* why I don't want you around them! And as long as you're living under my roof, eating my food, you'll follow the rules I set for you!"

Gabe folded his arms across his chest and stuck out his chin. "You're not my father. We're not even related. Why pretend you care anything about me?"

Dr. Conway's shoulders slumped. He squeezed his eyes shut.

Brett stared at Gabe from the doorway. Overprotective or not, technically related or not, Dr. Conway was Gabe's family. And Brett knew how valuable family really was. Before he could stop himself, he said, *"Dude!"*

That got Dr. Conway's attention, much to Brett's dismay. He speared Brett with that awful, furious stare and jabbed a finger at him, but even then he still spoke to Gabe. "It's them! *They're* doing this to you! Ever since you met them, you've been out of control! Thank God we're moving. You're going to be on a short leash in Philadelphia, young man."

Brett had just enough time to see tears well up in Gabe's green eyes before Lily grabbed Brett's shoulder and hauled him to the front door and out of the house.

They waited on the sidewalk for what felt like hours. Inside the house, Gabe and Dr. Conway kept arguing, and every so often they'd get loud enough for Brett to make out a word, all the way from the street. "Juvenile" was one, along with "irresponsible," "grounded," and "straight home from school."

Kaz shuffled his feet. "Uh . . . guys? Are we going to talk about what happened in there?"

"It's still happening." Lily frowned up at the door of the row house. "Can't you hear them?"

"Not what I meant." Kaz felt the back of his head and winced. "Okay, yeah, I've definitely got a bump on my skull from when I passed out. I mean, we did pass out, right? It had something to do with the . . . What'd you call it? Tablet?" He looked from Lily to Brett and back. "You *do* remember that, right? It wasn't just me who passed out, was it?" His eyes widened in alarm, and his hands flew to his cheeks. "Oh God, was it just me? Did you guys draw on my face while I was unconscious?"

The front door burst open, and Brett whispered *"Quiet!"* as Gabe came rushing down the steps, furiously wiping at his face with the back of his sleeve.

Gabe's expression was dark, but it lightened a shade when he saw his friends waiting for him. "Come on," he said when he reached them. "Let's get out of here."

Brett looked at Kaz and Lily, but neither of them seemed to know what to do, and Brett sure didn't. So they took off up the sidewalk after Gabe, ignoring how red and puffy their friend's eyes were. A couple of times Brett looked back at the house, but he didn't really expect Uncle Steve to try to follow.

Just as well, since Brett had one more item to check off on his list. One more thing to do for his Friend, and then his side of the bargain would be complete.

"So, uh," Kaz started. "Are we going to school?"

Brett jumped at the opening. "No way! Are you nuts?" He checked his phone. "It's only ten thirty! We've got the whole day to ourselves!"

Lily shrugged. "Well, we've already been marked absent, that's for sure."

Brett nodded. "Right! Let's do something fun!"

Sounding more like a depressed old man than a twelve-year-old boy, Gabe said, "Fun. Ha. I bet I'll be locked in my room till I'm eighteen."

Brett nudged him with an elbow and plastered a big, friendly smile on his face. He needed his friend on board; his work for his *other* Friend wasn't done. "All the more reason to take the day off! I mean, you're leaving next week. This is our last shot at a big adventure! The field trip to end all field trips!"

Kaz snorted. "The tunnels and the ritual weren't enough? We still have to tell the police about that skeleton, remember."

Brett frowned at Kaz. "Yeah, I'm sure they'll jump all over a random skeleton from a hundred years ago."

Kaz sputtered, couldn't seem to come up with a good reply, and ended up sticking out his tongue at Brett.

The four of them stopped near a bench at the edge of a small park. Gabe looked back toward his house a couple of times, drew a breath to speak, stopped himself, and finally said, "What'd you have in mind?"

Lily smiled at Brett. "If we were older we'd get busted for contributing to the delinquency of a minor."

Brett dug into his backpack. He tried not to make it obvious that the Tablet was in there, or that he was taking pains not to let his hand brush it. He wasn't quite ready to feel that hot, charging-battery sensation again. "Ah-*ha*!" His hand closed around what he was going for, and he pulled it out triumphantly: the Golden Gates map, rolled back up and tied with the ribbon again.

Gabe groaned and covered his face with his hands.

Kaz's mouth fell open. "You were supposed to put that back in Dr. Conway's office!"

"Guess I forgot," Brett said, trying to sound mischievous. *That's right, I'm just a bratty kid. No other motivations at work. Nothing to see here, move along.* He unrolled the map on the bench and tapped a large, intricate glyph a short distance offshore. "If there's one place in this whole city that's *definitely* haunted, that's got to be it! We have to check it out before Gabe goes!"

Gabe groaned again. Brett wasn't sure exactly what the groan meant—it could have been either *My uncle's going to have me arrested* or *Oh God, not more stupid haunted crap*—so he really poured it on. "Come on, Gabe. I know you said you don't believe in any of your uncle's occult stuff, but this map helped us find that cool chamber, didn't it? There's gotta be something awesome to see out there, paranormal or not."

"I'm pretty sure it was ghost-free back when we went there on our second-grade school trip," Kaz said.

"Yeah, but that was before Gabe got here. Before we got the whole gang together." He wrapped his arms around Kaz's and Gabe's shoulders.

"Alcatraz?" Lily asked as she squinted at the map. She couldn't have sounded more skeptical. "I dunno. Doesn't it cost money to take a tour there?"

Brett struggled to keep his good cheer up as he unslung his arms from around his friends' shoulders and pulled out his wallet. His Friend had told him this would be necessary, so he'd looked up the prices online and brought along his New Bike Fund. He pulled out a medium-sized stack of bills. "Don't worry, Lil. It's Gabe's last hurrah. I've got it covered."

Gabe was already shaking his head. "No way, man! I can't let you spend that much on me!"

Brett put a hand on his shoulder. "Like I said. You're leaving. And yeah, I know we'll Skype and stuff, but this is your big send-off. Don't worry about the money. I got it for my birthday."

Lily's eyebrows almost disappeared into her hair. Brett could tell what she was thinking: they had the same birthday, and she sure as heck hadn't gotten a stack of cash! But he gave her the best "Just be quiet and roll with this" look he could muster, and to his relief she went along with it. Frowning but cooperative.

Gabe sealed the deal when he said, "Well, I *have* always wanted to see Alcatraz."

The four of them filed onto the ferry and, at Brett's suggestion, climbed up to the top level. The air was already cold, and that high up, the wind had some real teeth to it. But up top they could stand along the guardrail and get a postcard view of the city, the island ahead of them, and the water below.

Not that Brett *wanted* a good view of the water. Since Charlie had drowned, Brett hated the bay. The others probably thought he was trying to be brave, choosing water as his element at last night's friendship ritual. But that's only because they didn't get it. They'd *never* get it. Not even Lily.

Brett had been the only one on that boat with Charlie. He was the only one who knew why they'd capsized.

He still couldn't close his eyes without seeing the flash of blood that came when the mainsail crashed against Charlie's head. The terror in Charlie's eyes when he went under the silvery water that last time. Brett had reached for his brother. He'd tried with everything he had to save him. But Brett wasn't strong or tough or brave enough. He wasn't *good* enough.

Charlie went under and never came back up. Brett was left alone with nothing but the cold of the bay around him and the howl of his own scream in his ears.

No. Choosing water last night hadn't been an act of bravery.

It was penance.

Even the idea of going on a boat still made him light-headed.

But he had no choice—and he figured Gabe would enjoy it.

Gabe didn't seem capable of enjoying anything, though. He looked so down, he might as well have had "I feel guilty about arguing with my uncle" tattooed across his forehead.

"I hope we can see the sea lions from the boat," Kaz said, and when Gabe perked up, he continued. "I mean, maybe it sounds lame, but I like watching them even when they're just napping there."

Gabe smiled, and Lily jumped in. "Sea lions are way better than seals. I was down in Monterey one time, visiting my cousin, and we went out to the shore. There's no beach or anything; it's just big rocks, and I climbed out onto one of them, and suddenly there's a seal head poking up out of the water. Just staring at me. And then I noticed another. And another."

Gabe laughed. "They were just floating there?"

"Yeah! I don't know if I was on *their* rock or what, but I counted *fourteen* seals, just floating there in the water, their heads sticking up, all of them giving me the hairy eyeball. It was a little creepy."

Gabe laughed again. Brett looked away. Kaz and Lily had what you call "people skills." They were both so *nice*. Kaz was a worrier, definitely, but just last week he'd given Brett his own rubber boots, right off his feet, because Brett had farther to walk in the rain. Brett had never known a more loyal friend. And Lily . . . she was so sweet to everybody. *Everybody*. Even him. She'd sat and talked with him for five hours straight after they all came home from the funeral and finally ended up singing some ridiculous song from a Disney movie just to cheer him up.

And all the while, Brett knew she must blame him for Charlie's death.

Just like their parents did.

Brett's mom and dad had never said anything like that to him, but he could tell. He saw it in their looks, heard it in their voices. They hated him for what happened to their firstborn son, and he knew Lily must hate him, too. But that was all right.

No one could hate Brett more than he hated himself.

Only one way to change that.

I've got to see Charlie.

That's why he was doing all of this. Brett didn't know if his Friend could really deliver on what he'd promised, but it was worth the risk of finding out. Passing up a chance—no matter how slim—of seeing Charlie again? *That* was something Brett couldn't live with.

Careful not to let anyone see what he was doing, Brett touched the lump on a chain under his shirt: the gold signet ring he'd taken from Gabe's uncle's office. That was what had started all this. Not the map. Not the friendship ritual. He'd found the ring before any of that. Brett had been poking through Dr. Conway's bedroom one evening while the rest of them played Xbox. He'd found a tiny black box hidden inside a drawer, and it—he felt cheesy saying it—"called to him." It wasn't like Gollum's "precioussssss." But he opened the box, saw gold gleaming, and before he even knew what he was doing, the ring was in his pocket.

A seagull flew past. Brett blinked at it and looked around the ferry. He felt his throat going hot; that familiar wet feeling in his eyes. He shook himself. *Don't think about being on the water, idiot. Just don't think about it.*

To distract himself, he fingered the ring through his shirt, making out the lump of the signet, then the slim gold band. He didn't dare take it out just then for fear Gabe would recognize it, but he'd spent enough hours staring at it to know its design by heart. Like a wheel, it was a circle divided by five spokes. Without the ring, he'd never have started having the dreams—the dreams that turned out to be all too real—and he'd never have met his Friend. He wouldn't have gotten any of these instructions.

Without the ring, he wouldn't have any chance of talking to Charlie again.

While Lily and Kaz kept up their chatter, which did seem to be taking Gabe's mind off the domestic apocalypse he'd be facing when he got home, Brett reached into his backpack and, taking a deep breath, pulled out the Tablet. This time he was prepared for the rush of heat, but it wasn't as overpowering as the first time, and his hands stayed steady. That's when he realized that the Tablet wasn't a solid slab of stone, but actually a kind of book sheathed in the strange, crystalline-green material.

Thick, oddly durable-looking pages were bound inside it.

His Friend wanted this thing pretty badly. *What's he going to do with it? How is this going to help me see Charlie again?* Brett could only imagine.

Brett would do anything to see his brother. Anything.

Gabe's voice pulled his attention away from the Tablet's pages. "Brett! You stole that out of Uncle Steve's office?"

Brett could think of zero responses. He tried for a sheepish sort of grin but wasn't sure how well he pulled it off. "Yeah, I guess I kind of did." When Gabe just goggled at him, he went on: "This thing knocked us all out, didn't it? I wanted to get a closer look."

Kaz crowded over his shoulder, peering at the pages. "I'd forgotten all about it. Now that you mention it, I remember we talked about it for a second, but it totally fell out of my head. How weird is that?"

Lily came up behind Brett's other shoulder. "I know what you mean. The whole thing in the office feels really hazy." She frowned. "But how is that possible? It *just* happened."

Brett shrugged. Since he'd met his Friend, he'd learned that nearly anything was possible.

Gabe frowned. "I just remember how angry Uncle Steve was. And still is. Jeez, this is only going to make it worse." But he joined the others, trying to get a look at the Tablet.

Brett had never seen script like the flowing letters that filled the Tablet's thick, slightly yellowed pages. He had no idea what any of the symbols meant—but the ink was a brilliant, shimmering blue, so vivid the letters seemed to hover above the paper. The unnerving blue danced in Brett's eyes . . .

. . . and his gaze slid past the pages to the water rushing by below the ferry. A shiver started around his heart and spread out to the tips of his fingers and toes, all the way to the ends of every hair on his head. Brett's hatred of water, revulsion at the mere *sight* of water, clanged inside his head like an alarm, and yet—

And yet . . .

Brett's eyes widened. Shimmering blue words like waves danced between him and the water.

Beyond them, Brett saw the water. For the first time, he really *saw* it. The tiny curls of the waves, the perfect snow-like whitecaps, the delicate whirlpools that appeared and vanished in the ferry's wake. And if he concentrated, focused his will with enough force, he was *sure* he could see the flowing, shimmering words from the Tablet inscribing themselves onto the water itself. As if the water and the text were different voices but both singing the same song, in exquisite harmony.

"What do you think made it change from gold to green like that?" Kaz's voice, inquisitive as ever, snapped Brett out of his trance. Kaz went on. "And we couldn't get it open before, right? Could we?"

"Check out that funky lettering," Gabe said, one finger hovering over the Tablet as if daring himself to touch the tip of a needle or an open flame. "I've never seen script like that. All sharp and angled. And how'd they get that shade of red? Looks like paint off a sports car."

Lily and Kaz exchanged glances, both of them frowning. Lily said, "Gabe, I think you might've hit your head harder than we thought. That lettering isn't red. It's white and silver. And it's not pointy, either. It's kind of swirly."

Kaz rolled his eyes. "Are we even looking at the same book? I don't know what language that is, but all blocky like that, I wouldn't even *call* it 'script.' Those symbols were stamped on there, like with a bunch of carved rocks or something." When Gabe and Lily just stared blankly at him, Kaz finished with "And the ink is green. Okay, you guys are looking at me really weird. I don't have a booger, do I?"

The bay grabbed Brett's attention, and he pushed his friends' voices aside. Though it sang to him, he didn't like the water. There was something tempting in the strange words that filled its every swell and whirl, but he also saw Charlie's face disappearing under its waves, his brother's mouth open in one last scream.

Brett wanted to get off this boat and back onto land. The ferry was going fast, but he wanted to go faster. As far as he was concerned, they couldn't get to Alcatraz soon enough. *Faster*, he thought, staring at the swirls of glyphs churning just below the cold surface. *Faster*. The bay drew him in again, and when he stared at it just right, the script beneath the surface coalesced into a single symbol. Round and flowing and . . . and powerful. Brett knew it. He could *feel* its power.

Trying to cement this glyph in his mind, Brett traced the symbol in the air with his finger, and almost dropped the Tablet in shock when the symbol *appeared in the air where he'd traced it*, lingering there as if he'd written on the wind itself, first blazing in a searing blue, then darkening into a deep, brilliant gold.

Faster.

There was a surge of pure velocity. Brett's neck whiplashed at the unexpected speed. He tumbled to the deck with everyone else as a sudden wave lifted the ferry and sent it hurtling toward the rocky shore.

4

The ferry lurched so fast and so hard, for a second Gabe thought the deck had come up and hit him square on the side of the head. Only when he started sliding across it did he realize he'd lost his balance and fallen.

Panicked, trying his best not to scream, Gabe managed to grab one of the railing's posts and held on tight. The ferry had tilted sharply toward its bow, and as passengers slid and flailed and screamed around them, it rocketed toward the shore ahead as if fired out of a cannon.

But even as the speed of the ferry registered in Gabe's mind, everything around him slowed to a crawl. A middle-aged man in a business suit tumbled past, feet barely touching the deck, but Gabe could read the time of day on the man's wristwatch. Even, if he squinted, what brand of watch it was.

Lily had grabbed hold of the railing a few feet in front of Gabe, her dark hair rippling in the rushing wind, and Gabe could feel, could almost *see*, each and every current of air, every tendril and wisp of that wind as individual entities.

Beneath him, Gabe heard the grinding of each tooth on every gear as the captain threw the ferry into reverse. He felt the surging mechanical energy—the *fire*—of the engine as it was pushed to its limit. This impossible awareness, this knowledge of the world around him, sank right through the boat's hull and plunged into the icy depths of the bay. Freezing water currents slid across his skin, shivering and twitching with the tiny disturbances of swimming fish. Startled, Gabe forced himself to look up into the sky, but then his gaze was drawn like a magnet to the sun, blazing white-hot in the east. Gabe was suddenly overwhelmed by the heat. It couldn't have been more than sixty degrees on the bay—it never got *really* hot in San Francisco—but Gabe felt as if flames were searing his skin. The sun was burning his eyes, but he was having trouble looking away, too. He'd never noticed how *beautiful* the sun was before. How powerful . . .

He felt so small, so tiny and insignificant, a single particle in the vast mosaic that made up the planet. And yet he *was* a part of it, just as he realized it was a part of him. His mind felt raw, peeled open and restructured, and tears squeezed out of his eyes as he marveled at the majesty of it all.

But just as fragments of a dream disappear on waking, that vast, beautiful, terrible knowledge fled, and Gabe was just himself again, a frightened boy clinging for dear life to a runaway ferry. The rocky shore of the island loomed ahead of them, promising a grinding, painful death, and silently Gabe said, *Stop. Stop. Stop!*

Next to him, Lily stood, let go of the railing, and threw up her arms as if to shield her face from impact . . . and a roaring, gale-force wind sprang up and slammed straight into the ferry's prow. The few passengers who'd made it back to their unsteady feet tumbled to the deck again. Gabe had to grab on even more tightly—for just that moment he felt as if he'd stuck his head into a wind tunnel—but Lily stood there, holding on to nothing, arms up in that defensive posture, solid as an ancient oak tree.

She stayed that way as the ferry slowed and fishtailed to one side. Only when it bumped to a stop against the dock did she lower her arms.

Gabe wondered exactly what he had just seen.

"What just happened?" Kaz asked as he and Brett got to their feet. Other passengers around them did the same, some sort of wobbly, many grabbing on to rails and other people to steady themselves. Kaz shook his head. "What *was* that?"

With some effort, Gabe let go of the railing. Brett stood behind Kaz, the Tablet still in his grip but apparently forgotten. Lily hadn't moved. She just stood there staring at her hands as if wondering what the strange, wiggly objects at the ends of her wrists were.

Gabe swallowed hard. "Rogue wave? Maybe? Brett, are you okay?"

"Fine. I'm . . . fine." Brett's eyes finally focused, and he swiveled his head to look up at the huge, blocky barracks looming above them.

"Was that weird enough for you, Brett?" Kaz asked. "Can we go back now?"

"Are you kidding?" Gabe couldn't have said exactly why, but now that the bizarre crisis seemed to be over, something about arriving at the island filled him with energy and excitement. Suddenly he couldn't *wait* to get off the ferry and start exploring. "We're here! Come on, come on. Let's go!"

"But do you think we have to, like, fill out a report or something?" Kaz asked. "And what if we have whiplash? Or concussions? You guys, do my pupils look dilated?"

"First that thing in your uncle's office, and now this," Lily said, shaking her head. "I didn't think we'd ever top last night's field trip, but so far it's a close call."

"And we haven't even gone inside yet!" Gabe said.

After a park ranger came and apologized for the unforeseen events with the ferry, and apologized again, and hinted sort of broadly that it would be great if no one decided to sue the National Park Service, Gabe ushered his friends off the ferry and onto the dock. His eyes stayed wide as they climbed higher and higher on the island. A glance over his shoulder showed him the bay stretching away from the docks, and the distant city sprawled and gleaming across the hillsides.

Ahead of them, a perky guide led part of the group who'd been on their ferry on a tour. She chattered away at them about the island's history—how it was named La Isla de los Alcatraces, or "Island of the Pelicans," by the Spanish in 1775, and how "*Alcatraces*" became "Alcatraz." She also mentioned how the Native Americans who lived in the area stayed away from the island because they believed it to be cursed.

"Great," Kaz muttered. "Just what we need."

"That ferry ride felt plenty cursed to me," Lily said. She glanced back down the steep hill to the wharf, frowning.

Staying on the edge of the tour group, they moved past the fire-gutted husk of the former Officers' Club and the island's lighthouse. "The oldest lighthouse on the West Coast!" the tour guide chirped. The guide also mentioned how, when the US military decided to establish a fort there, they found the island covered with a layer of bird poop, thanks to the countless numbers of birds that nested here. "They even called it 'Guano Island'!" She paused for laughter, and Gabe thought she'd be waiting for quite a long time.

Gabe looked around at his friends but saw Kaz at the back of the group, standing still and staring at the ground. "Kaz? You all right?"

Kaz lifted one foot, then the other, and looked up at Gabe.

"Guys? Does the ground feel sort of . . . buzzy to you?"

Lily came back to join them. "Buzzy?"

Kaz nodded. "Like, sort of vibrate-y. It comes and goes, sort of regular, like . . . I don't know."

Lily cocked an eyebrow at Kaz. "What, like machinery? There could be some big engine running around here. Maybe you're feeling that?"

Kaz shook his head, clearly troubled. "No, it feels more like . . . snoring?"

Gabe echoed Kaz: *"Snoring?"*

"I don't know! I don't know! I just feel something is all."

Lily said, "Brett, do you feel anything?" She looked around but saw that her brother was standing about thirty feet away, staring at a blank wall. "Hey! *Hermano!* What're you doing?"

Brett shook his head and walked over. "Sorry. Daydreaming. What?"

Gabe said, "Kaz thinks he can feel some sort of vibration in the ground. Said it was like something snoring."

"Snoring," Brett repeated, in his "I'm going to give you endless crap about this" voice.

Kaz sighed.

Lily knelt and put both hands on the ground. She shook her head. "I don't feel anything. Sorry."

"Huh." Kaz shoved his hands in his pockets. "Oh well. Guess it's just me. Never mind, sorry." Gabe looked around for the tour group and saw them about to enter the island's central feature: the cellhouse. His eyes lit up. He was about to urge his friends to hurry up, but Brett beat him to it.

"Come on, guys!" Brett's excitement seemed to match Gabe's own. "Let's go, let's go!"

Gabe had never been anywhere even remotely like the Alcatraz cellhouse. He'd seen movies and TV shows with scenes set in prisons and jails, but walking down Broadway, the main hallway of the building, and looking into the individual cells made his skin crawl. Not because it was creepy, exactly, but because the place seemed so . . . *hopeless*. The drab beige paint, the rows of steel bars . . . he couldn't imagine having to spend a week in this place, much less year after year. Gabe glanced at Kaz, the only one who was actually listening to the audio tour device they'd been handed on entering the building.

Kaz seemed to know what Gabe was thinking. He tapped his earpiece. "This place was designed for the worst of the worst," he said, just a little too loudly. "It wasn't supposed to rehabilitate them. It was supposed to *punish* them."

Gabe eyeballed one of the tiny cells, furnished with little more than a cot, sink, and toilet. "How'd that work out?"

"Inmates kept going bonkers." Kaz pulled off the headset. "If this is where they had to spend at least sixteen hours a day, I can understand why."

Lily walked up to them and ran her hand down one of the bars of the nearest cell. "So, this place was a fort before it was a prison? What happened to the fort?"

From a few paces away, Brett spoke quietly, his voice just loud enough to reach them. "Funny you should ask." Brett was standing next to a window, the Golden Gates map unfurled in his hands. Gabe and Lily and Kaz joined him, and Gabe said, "You look like you found something."

Brett just pointed. Gabe peered over his shoulder at the map, and for the first time realized what part of it meant. There were bizarre illustrations all over the map, and notations in Latin and some other language he didn't recognize. Gabe had thought the odd design over in one corner was just that: an odd design, like the rest. But now that they were all here, standing in the middle of it, the truth jumped out at him: it was a diagram of Alcatraz prison. More than that: a single golden thread wove through the diagram, like a path to follow.

But follow where?

"Oh my God," Lily breathed. "That's here, isn't it? That's this. Us. Alcatraz."

Kaz put his head so close to the map that his nose almost touched it. "So what's with the miniature Yellow Brick Road? Where's that supposed to go?"

Brett set his jaw, glanced around to make sure no one was close to them, and said with a mischievous smile, "We're going to find out." Then he took off toward one end of the cellhouse, moving with determination.

The other three followed after him, if a bit hesitantly. "Wait a minute," Lily said. "Hey! Hang on, *hermano*! If we get caught in some restricted area, they're going to arrest us! And worse than that, they'll tell Mom and Dad!"

Brett didn't look back at her. "Following the map is what got us to the Friendship Chamber, down in the tunnels, isn't it? Relax."

Kaz frowned. "Friendship Chamber? Since when are we calling it that?"

Brett shrugged. "Since I just now decided to call it that. And it doesn't matter. We need to follow this gold thread."

"Says who? Who besides you, I mean?" Lily's dark eyes flashed. "Aren't we going to put this to a vote? Gabe?"

Gabe's head was spinning. That golden thread in the map seemed burned into his retinas, and for some reason he couldn't adequately explain, he was just as eager to see where it led as Brett was. He had the presence of mind to put on a somewhat apologetic expression when he answered Lily. "I kind of want to see where it goes, too."

Lily groaned. "Boys." She speared Kaz with a glare. "I suppose you're on board with this?"

"If I said I wasn't, would you leave Brett and Gabe here, and take the next ferry back with me?"

She rolled her eyes. "Not a chance."

Kaz nodded. "Didn't think so. I'm staying with the group."

Gabe hated that Lily wasn't happy with the plan. The last thing he wanted before he left for Philadelphia was for any of his friends to feel bad about their last few days together—Lily especially. But he couldn't deny it. He *was* dying to find out where the map led.

Paying no attention to his friends, Brett slowed and finally stopped in front of a narrow metal door covered with peeling paint and a sign that read AUTHORIZED PERSONNEL ONLY. He checked to make sure no one was watching, grabbed the handle, and pulled. And with a dull clank the door swung open.

A set of worn concrete stairs vanished down into murky darkness. His white teeth flashing in a huge grin, Brett walked past his sister without a word and headed down the stairs. She growled, but followed him. Kaz and Gabe filed in mutely after her, Gabe glancing around to make sure no one was going to report them for not being Authorized Personnel. Gabe also made sure the door latch worked from both sides, and that it definitely was not locked, before he pulled the door shut with a *clunk*.

The stairway smelled bad. Gabe tried to pinpoint the odor as he descended, and when one of his feet almost slipped on a patch of something slick, he decided it must be mold. He kept waiting for Kaz to complain about developing some sort of respiratory illness, but now that he actually had cause for concern, Kaz said nothing.

Gabe couldn't tell exactly how far down the staircase went. It felt like a long way, though, and when he and his friends stepped out into the tunnel-like corridor at the bottom, it seemed a lot like stepping into another world.

Where the prison above was built of smooth concrete and unforgiving steel, the hallway where they now stood looked more like something out of a medieval European castle. The rough floor, the stone block walls, and especially the dark, dank, open cells with arched doorways all had a dismal, oppressive, Dark Ages feel, as if this were the kind of place where souls were imprisoned and forgotten. Abandoned to wither and die in lightless misery. An odd sensation crept across the back of Gabe's neck, and he realized all the hairs there were standing on end.

"What *is* this place?" Lily wondered, her voice tiny.

"Part of the old citadel," Kaz said, looking around owl eyed. "You asked what was here before the prison was built? Well, we're standing in it."

She stepped into one of the arched doorways. "Yeah, but I mean, what is *this* place? Are these cells? How come they don't have any doors or bars or anything?"

Gabe thought about it. "I bet they were made of wood. And the wood didn't last."

"Come on," Brett said, studying the Golden Gates map. "Follow me." He strode away, his back straight and his steps fast. Ahead of Gabe, Brett disappeared and then reappeared as he moved under the string of dim, widely spaced lightbulbs that dotted the citadel corridor.

Gabe followed after Brett, wondering when, or at this point *if*, the skin-crawling sensation was ever going to leave him. This didn't feel like their journey to the Friendship Chamber, as Brett called it. Gabe couldn't help thinking, or rather *feeling*, as though something a lot more sinister than a dried-up old skeleton was in the fortress with them.

"Wait up," Kaz said. But Brett wasn't slowing down, so Gabe didn't either, and Kaz and Lily had no choice but to break into a jog to pull even with him.

"We're not running a race here, Brett!" Lily called out.

Gabe took a breath to comment—and saw something dark flit across the corridor just ahead of Brett, there and gone in less than a heartbeat. He almost choked. "Brett! Stop!"

Brett simply looked over his shoulder as he walked right past the spot where Gabe had glimpsed the . . . whatever it was. "Come on!" Brett called. "We're almost there!"

Gabe spun and walked backward long enough to ask Lily and Kaz, "Did you guys see that?"

"See what?" Kaz asked.

Cautiously, Lily said, "What did *you* see?"

Gabe faced forward again and, staring into the shadowy cells and recesses around them, heaved a sigh. "Nothing? I guess? Maybe I've just been watching too many episodes of *Ghost Hunters.*"

"Well, my dad does say those shows rot your brain," Kaz said helpfully, before Lily elbowed him in the ribs.

"You're one to talk, Mr. Snoring Earth."

Ahead of them, Brett abruptly turned a corner and

disappeared. "Hey!" Gabe shouted. "Brett! Wait!" But Brett didn't acknowledge Gabe at all this time. Gabe broke into a run.

Brett had turned down a narrower hallway. Judging by the holes in the floor and the walls, the entrance to this passage had once supported a large, heavy door, but now it gaped open. There didn't seem to be any electric lights inside, and the bulbs in the main corridor didn't even come close to penetrating the darkness. "Brett!" Gabe shouted. "Brett, are you in there?"

Brett's voice drifted back to him. "Of course I'm here. This is it. This is where the map leads!"

Gabe pulled out his phone and turned on the flashlight. "Okay, okay! Be right there!" He looked at Lily and Kaz. "Ready to go down the weird, dark, scary hallway?"

Their bright phone lights illuminating their path, Gabe, Kaz, and Lily made their way along the corridor, which curved around to the right. Brett soon came into view, simply standing in the middle of the hall, staring at the rusted metal door to a single cell at the hallway's end. For some reason, he had the strange book from Uncle Steve's office in his hands again.

Gabe approached Brett. "Well? You said 'This is it.' What are we looking at? Where are we?"

Gabe then very nearly jumped out of his shoes when an unfamiliar voice said, "Solitary." Lily let out a short, sharp scream. Kaz tripped over his own feet and sat down hard on the stone floor, but just as quickly scrambled back up.

A boy stood right outside the door to the cell at the end of the hall. He looked to be about ten years old, had very pale blond hair, and wore some sort of school uniform. As soon as Gabe saw him, he knew there was something familiar—*unsettlingly familiar*—about the boy's face.

"No visitors," the boy went on. "No light. No contact. Imagine being in such a place for weeks." The boy spoke in a very proper way. Sort of old-fashioned. Intense blue eyes peered out from under that blond hair and sought out each of them in turn. "Now imagine being trapped in such a place for more than a century."

Gabe started to say "Who *are* you?" but his breath tripped in his throat and fell flat.

Because the boy standing in front of the cell was *glowing*.

5

At first Jackson Wright saw the children like candle flames through a curtain.

He squinted, concentrating. Determined to see them, to see clearly for the first time in *so long*.

The flames grew nearer, brighter, more distinct. One green, one red, one blue, one a dazzling silver. The thick, oppressive substance that passed for air in the Umbra, that had forced its way into his lungs for so many years, *so many decades, more than a century*, began to shift and thin and draw aside.

The blue flame stood closest to him. The red, silver, and green ones approached slowly, as if frightened. *Well, perhaps they should be.*

The red flame spoke. Tentatively, but with bravery behind the words. "What . . . what *are* you?"

Jackson tilted his head a few degrees to one side. "I am a boy. Like you." A lie, but not a lie. Just like he was here, and yet not quite here. Memories flitted across the surface of his mind. Memories pulled from the blue candle flame. *Brett*. And his friends were Gabe, Lily, and Kaz.

Jackson suddenly felt his heart hammering against his ribs. It startled him.

He knew exactly how much time he had spent in the Umbra, the ghastly, dismal, shadow-thick place that had served as his home and his prison. He could count down the years, the days, the seconds—and the *tick-tock*ing of the clock in his head never stopped, *never stopped*.

If only he hadn't been taken. Betrayed. If only the dagger hadn't speared through his heart.

The candle flames finally resolved into the shapes of *children*. And yes, there, in Brett's hand: the Emerald Tablet. One of the other boys had startling eyes of the same searing shade of green. This one had to be Gabe. It could be no one else.

Jackson forced himself to breathe.

In the years of his endless banishment in the Umbra, Jackson had found that this spot was the weakest. This place was where the walls were thinnest between the Umbra and—he scarcely dared to acknowledge the word—*home*. If he had any hope of returning, any at all, it would be in this wretched place, connected with these children. The presence of his grand-father's ring, alongside the Tablet, should be *just* enough to let him dip a toe back into the world. That was why he'd worked so long to lure Brett here.

Jackson's foot touched stone. He could feel how cold it was through the leather sole of his shoe.

Air—*real air*—flooded his lungs.

The children stared at him with a mix of awe and dread. They looked so ordinary—remarkable only for the outlandish clothes they wore. *No girl in my day would have been seen wearing trousers in public!*

Jackson wondered what they saw when they looked at *him*. He lifted his right hand and peered at it. He had forgotten the pale skin, the fine bone structure, the faint webwork of blue veins visible beneath the skin.

It took him several seconds to realize that the cold, hard light flowing from his body was out of place. He still wasn't human, but he was almost home. He was *so close*.

The girl, Lily, crept up to the green-eyed boy's shoulder, her own eyes, like Brett's, deep and inky black in the dim light. "You don't sound like a boy," she said. "You sound like . . . like a professor or something."

So simple, their thoughts. Jackson knew how fortunate he was to have made contact with children. Extraordinary children, despite their appearances, but children nonetheless. And while he might still have the appearance of one their age,

Jackson Wright was no longer a child. He knew how easily these young ones could be manipulated; he had been in Brett's head for some time, visiting him in dreams, whispering and cajoling through the Umbra's veil. He had bent Brett to his will, and now the other three would follow.

Anything to keep them away from the mainland. The Dawn must be allowed time to do what it did best. To seek out its target. To perform the ritual. The Dawn must not be interrupted. *And then I can come home. Finally!*

Since Jackson's arrival, Brett had simply stood there, holding the Tablet, staring. His eyelids twitched now and then, and his brows drew together, but he hadn't said a word. Jackson wondered idly what thoughts must be galloping through Brett's mind. Fear? Excitement? Validation that the specter from his dreams was, in fact, real?

But none of the others knew about their connection. Jackson had made sure Brett kept that bit of information to himself. Time to make some new friends, then. "My name is Jackson Wright. If I may ask, what are your names?"

To Jackson's mild surprise, Brett spoke up first, his voice as dry as dust. "Brett. Brett Hernandez." With the hand not holding the Tablet, he indicated the girl. "This is my sister. Lily."

The short one cleared his throat. "I'm Kazuo Smith. But everyone calls me Kaz."

Finally the boy with the green eyes took his turn: "I'm Gabe Conway."

Jackson fought to keep one of his eyebrows from arching. *Conway, you say? I think not. Not with those green eyes.* But that was conversation for another time.

"It is a great pleasure to meet you all." Jackson gave a little bow. It made Lily giggle, but Jackson couldn't tell whether she found the gesture amusing or was on the edge of hysteria.

Lily spoke up. "I, uh, I think we'd better ask Gabe's question again. What exactly are you?"

Jackson paced back and forth in front of them, relishing the sensation of his feet on solid ground. "Let me answer your question with a question. Have any of you noticed any strange occurrences in the last day or so? Anything for which you can provide no explanation?"

Kaz exclaimed, "Yeah!" and it was as if a dam had burst. "There was a book and it had a gold cover, and after we touched it we all passed out, and when we went on the ferry to come here there was a . . . a rogue wave or something, and the ferry almost crashed, and then I kind of thought the, uh . . . the ground was . . . um, never mind about the ground." Kaz paused for breath. He pointed at the Tablet in Brett's hand. "That's the book. It turned green while we were passed out. I should've mentioned that before."

Kaz had opened up like a punctured blister, but the other three children, even Brett, regarded Jackson with unmistakable suspicion. Gabe and Lily, in particular, eyeballed him as if he were a hornet's nest, a bundle of swarming, stinging pain only waiting for the slightest provocation to explode. Jackson sighed. In his day children were not so mistrustful.

The thought sent a sharp pain through his chest. Not a physical pain. It was more like the stab of heartbreak. He had forgotten many things about this world over the long decades in the Umbra, but the sight of his father's face as he pulled the signet ring from Jackson's finger remained just as fresh and clear and agonizing as the day it happened.

I was a fool to trust my father all those years ago. These children would be even greater fools to take the word of a stranger at face value now. The thought gave him no comfort: if his nature had been more suspicious as a boy, he might not have been robbed of a normal life. He might not have been sentenced to more than a century in the Umbra.

And if Brett had been warier, Jackson wouldn't be here now. . . .

Lily nervously kicked a pebble across the floor. It bounced and came to rest against Jackson's shoe. Taking another deep, glorious breath, he continued. "I am not surprised you've noticed some oddities. The truth is this: you are all becoming attuned to the vibrations of the universe. This ability, this talent, is known as the Art. As your understanding of it grows, each of you will be able to use the Art to alter the very fabric of reality. This Art is a form of magick."

Jackson recalled when he had first learned that magick was real. He remembered the wonder he'd felt. The *possibility*.

But times must have changed. Brett's tanned skin had taken on a grayish tone, and beads of sweat began to run down his temples. Was he physically ill, or were these merely the boy's anxieties exerting themselves? The small one, Kazuo, appeared to be on the verge of vomiting, and Gabe stared into space, frowning. Perhaps letting the truth of Jackson's words sink in.

Only Lily seemed unfazed. She stared at him, hawk-like. He would need to keep a careful watch on that one.

Gabe glanced around at his friends before turning that unnerving green-eyed gaze on Jackson. "So, what do you want with us?"

Jackson tried to choose his words carefully. The boy, Gabe Conway, if that was what he insisted on calling himself, was by far the most important one in this group. The one whose trust he must win at all costs. Jackson tried to temper his voice so that it would sound soothing. "The four of you have been bound together through an ancient and unbreakable rite." Jackson's eyes slid over to Brett, who still appeared weak and shaky, and down to the Tablet he held. *I wonder if Brett will ever comprehend how thoroughly his strings have been pulled?* "You have also unlocked the sacred text of *Tabula Smaragdina*. The Emerald Tablet of Hermes Trismegistus himself. A keystone text to the magickal arts."

Lily's brow furrowed. "Tris . . . I'm sorry, who?"

Kaz spoke to her under his breath: "Sort of an Egyptian,

uh . . . god of magick or writing . . . sort of guy."

An unexpected flash of anger shot through Jackson at such a clumsy summation of so powerful an entity. He tamped it down. "As I was saying. The four of you can see things other people cannot see, and the things you can *do* . . . you cannot yet imagine. You have opened the Tablet, have you not?"

Gabe nodded guardedly.

"And you could see the writing on its pages, no? Allow me to guess: you each saw something different. Correct?" No one spoke, but Lily sucked in a quick breath, and Brett hugged the Tablet to his chest. "You each saw the hidden language of one specific element. You are bound to these elements, each of you. Bound to an immutable element of the terrestrial plane."

Lily looked at Kaz, but he shrugged his shoulders helplessly. "He lost me after Hermes Trismegistus."

"Speak English, would you?" Lily said, a quaver in her bold words. Jackson almost smiled. She was afraid of him, display of bravery or not. *Good.*

"Keep that courage about you," Jackson said. He tried to grin, but this seemed to make Lily even more frightened, so he dropped it. "You will all need to be brave to face what is coming."

Gabe turned to Brett. "Is *this* why you wanted to come down here? Did you know about this—this *freak show*?"

Brett blinked. Swallowed hard. "Did I *know* about this? I just wanted to see where the gold thread went!" He waved a hand vaguely at Jackson. "I didn't know we were gonna run into Ghost Boy here!"

Jackson scowled. He could feel the encounter going wrong. "Listen to me! You *have* to listen. The four of you have a destiny. A destiny that you *must embrace.*"

Gabe's eyes narrowed as he turned from Brett to Jackson. "Look, *Ghost Boy.* We don't understand what's going on here, and until we've wrapped our heads around this a little better, why don't you just back off with all the elements and destiny and crap, okay?"

And, like the cracking of a brittle twig, Jackson snapped. He saw the cold, hard light blaze from his body to flare against the ancient walls. "You *fools!*" His voice was like thunder. The four children stepped back in shock, even Brett. "You have glimpsed the power you possess, you have been *told* of the danger and the destiny that await you, and you waste precious seconds on *nonsense?*"

Gabe's green eyes flashed with anger. It made Jackson pause. Part of him wanted to apologize, console them, explain everything in a clear, calm way that would make them all understand. *Or at least understand what I* want *them to understand.* But he saw the situation slipping away from him and knew he was powerless to stop it. He had spent far too long in the Umbra, far too long without any human contact, and it had *damaged* him.

But . . .

He didn't want to admit the real root of his mounting despair. He should be in control here! He should be moving these children like pawns on a chessboard! And yet, as they took quaking steps backward, he wanted to cry out to them, make them understand the truth:

I've been so lonely!

"You cannot leave!" Jackson meant for it to come out as a request, but his voice quaked with anger. Lily turned pale, and Kaz looked like he was fighting back tears. "Stay here!" Jackson asked, but what he heard wasn't a question. It was a demand.

A threat.

"Get away from us!" Gabe yelled. For a heartbeat, just for an instant, his voice sounded like the crackling of flames. Jackson's skin abruptly tightened as a wave of heat rolled down the corridor.

"Let's get out of here!" Lily shouted. Kaz fled immediately, but Lily had to grab Gabe by the arm before he seemed to hear her. As she pulled Gabe back she said, "Brett, come on, let's go!" Then she sprinted after Kaz with Gabe close behind her.

But Brett lingered. Jackson fought for self-control, fought against the unreasoning tide of chaos and anger that threatened to overwhelm him. Brett was his friend. Brett would understand.

"Where is he?" Brett whispered, fear mingled with desperation. "You promised. You *promised*. Where's Charlie?"

No! No, no, no, he wasn't ready for that question! Not yet! And the anger must have shown on his face, because Brett quailed away from him, threw one hand up to protect his face as the light from Jackson's body flashed and flared. Grotesque shadows danced along the length of the corridor, and Brett turned and ran.

Jackson's eyes brimmed with tears. "No!" He hoped Brett would stop, stop and come back to him, but Brett ran every bit as fast as his friends had. With a wail that mortified Jackson even as he heard it escaping his lips, he cried, "Don't leave me alone! *Not again, please!*"

But only Brett's footfalls answered him.

A solid, freezing calm washed over Jackson. These children were his lifeline. Jackson knew he couldn't let them get away. Not yet. Not before his plan had time to unfold.

He sprinted after Brett. If he could make one of them stay, surely the others would cooperate. They weren't the kind of children to abandon one of their own, were they? No. The soles of his shoes rasped against the stone as he ran after them. Far ahead of him he could hear frightened, confused cries. Someone had taken a wrong turn. *Good. Yes. Run in circles, so I can catch you!*

As he ran, Jackson's awareness of his surroundings grew. This prison, this *Alcatraz*, echoed and hissed and thrummed with anguish, whispered echoes reflected by the deepest scars of human suffering. Alcatraz was cursed, he realized. Might that have been why he could step through the veil here? Why he felt so—the knowledge pained him—why he felt so at home inside these walls? Jackson Wright *belonged* here.

Because who, in all the worlds, had ever been so cursed as he?

6

*E*scape!

The thought rang inside Gabe's head with each pounding footfall.

Out the little hallway, take a right in the big hallway, straight up the stairs! Simple!

But then why did Kaz, twenty panicked paces in front of him, leave the narrow corridor and turn left? Lily, just ahead of Gabe, adjusted course and almost bounced off a wall—"Kaz!"—and went after him.

"Kaz went the wrong way!" Gabe called over his shoulder to Brett. "We've gotta grab him and—" The words snapped off cleanly. Brett wasn't behind him, and Gabe skidded to a stop.

Oh crap, that Ghost Boy got Brett! Wait, no—there was Brett, sprinting right at him.

"What are you *doing*?" Brett shouted. "MOVE!"

Gabe had no time and no need to ask what had happened, because Ghost Boy was right behind Brett, running full tilt, cold light streaming and pulsing off him as if in time with the beating of a phantom heart. "Stop!" he wailed. "You have to stop!"

Gabe took off again just as Brett caught up to him, and they exited the narrow hallway together. Gabe hung a left. "We've gotta get Kaz and Lily!"

Brett nodded, not questioning, and the two of them ran deeper into the old citadel's halls, their shadows long and eerie in front of them, cast by Ghost Boy's pale light.

Gabe got lost almost immediately, at least as far as keeping track of which way led out. He could hear Kaz's frightened voice ahead and Lily's more reasonable words trying to calm him, but they must have been running, too, because turn after turn, corner after corner, Kaz and Lily stayed just out of sight.

"How do we get out of here? *We've got to get out of here,*" Brett breathed next to him, huffing and puffing.

"I know, I know!" Gabe risked a glance over his shoulder. Ghost Boy wasn't quite at their heels, but the icy freak show light he gave off was getting stronger by the second in the hallway they had just left. "Come on!"

With Gabe still in the lead, he and Brett rounded a corner

and ran straight into Lily. She and Gabe hit the stone floor in a tangle of arms and legs, and he found his face shoved into the crook of her neck. An involuntary part of his brain offered up the opinion *Wow she smells fantastic*, but he didn't even have time to feel what should have been a tidal wave of embarrassment. Immediately he sprang to his feet and hauled Lily back to hers, and spotted Kaz hiding, or at least trying to hide, inside one of the doorless cells.

"Come on let's go let's go LET'S GO!" Gabe shouted, and Brett grabbed Kaz by the arm and hauled him out of the cell while Gabe and Lily took off down the hallway ahead of them.

"Do you know where you're going?" Lily demanded, and Gabe opened his mouth to say "I have no freaking clue!" when—he could scarcely believe it—he spotted a narrow, bright line beneath a metal door in the wall ahead. *Sunlight?*

Gabe banged into the door and, with every bit of strength he had, shoved it open. Bright, glorious sunlight and a delicious wave of salty ocean air washed over him, and he would have taken maybe half a second to enjoy it, but Brett and Kaz rushed past Lily and slammed into him from behind. All four of them stumbled out into the light, onto a narrow, stone-paved walkway that appeared to run around the back of the prison.

Gabe pointed. "The dock's that way! Run!"

"Please. Please don't!"

Ghost Boy's voice stopped him in his tracks. Gone was the weird, otherworldly menace. Now all Gabe heard was a scared little boy. He didn't want to turn his head and look, but he couldn't help it. And in the process he realized Kaz, Lily, and Brett were all doing the same.

Ghost Boy—Jackson Wright, he'd said his name was—stood in the doorway of the prison. *Maybe he can't come out into the sunlight! Maybe we're safe out here!*

But Jackson Wright *could* come out. And as soon as he walked out onto the path, Gabe really, really wished he hadn't, because when the sun's rays hit him, Jackson's body turned completely transparent.

No. That wasn't right. It wasn't as if the boy turned invisible. It was as if Jackson Wright had suddenly become a window. A portal that appeared in the real world but offered a view of a very different one. And to Gabe's horror, it was a world he recognized.

As Jackson Wright moved, Gabe could see a gold-and-amber sky swirling around towering, warped, grotesque buildings. A gargoyle took flight and soared across the space where Jackson's eyes should have been, and someone screamed, maybe Kaz. And even though his conscious mind was too pants-wettingly freaked out to make a rational decision, his feet at that moment found a mind of their own. Gabe turned and tore away from Ghost Boy, all three of his friends right behind him, and only then did he realize that the scream had come from his own throat.

The stone path emerged from a thicket of bushes onto the

steep trail leading up to the cellhouse's front entrance. Gabe was happy to let the incline work in his favor and practically flew down the hillside. A glance behind him confirmed that his friends were still with him and, better yet, that Jackson Wright was not.

They didn't stop until they reached the wharf, where Gabe sagged against a low concrete wall, gasping for air. Brett and Lily were both winded, but they recovered a lot more quickly than he did—especially after Lily broke out her rescue inhaler and took a huge pull off it—while Kaz wheezed and coughed and wheezed some more.

Gabe went over to Kaz, who was bent over with his hands on his knees, and squatted down, putting their faces on the same level. "You okay, buddy?"

"I can think of a lot of words to describe myself right now." Kaz got out the words between gasps. "Terrified. Horrified. Suddenly insecure on a freaking *cosmic* level." He finally straightened back up. "But 'okay' is not on the list."

Kaz wobbled over to a bench and sat, his head hanging down between his shoulders. Gabe sat next to him. Every time Gabe closed his eyes, the image of the twisted city he'd glimpsed through Jackson Wright was right there, front and center.

I've seen that place before. The sky, the towers, the . . . creatures. Right after we touched the book. The "Tablet."

Gabe didn't want to believe it. Didn't want to think he could have seen into some other world, and especially not a world as horrible as that place. Just the thought of it made him feel . . . *contaminated.* As if the city itself were toxic.

Maybe he'd imagined it?

But any hope that the strange, distorted city might not have been real evaporated when Lily shook his shoulder and said, "Did you *see* that?"

Gabe raised his head and dimly noted that Brett was standing several steps away from the rest of them, staring back up at the prison. "See what?" Gabe asked, knowing the answer.

"That ghost kid." Lily hugged herself, shuddering. "I could see *through* him. To some other place. It was *terrible.*"

Gabe stood and faced the wharf. The ferry they had come in on was slowly making its way back to the mainland, and appeared to be empty. Another ferry had just come to a stop at the dock, and as he watched, passengers began to file onto it.

I bet none of them ran into weird ghost kids.

Fatigue washed over Gabe. He found himself wishing he could go back to the way things were just yesterday. Before the world went completely nuts. *Blissful ignorance. Can't appreciate it till you've lost it, I guess.*

"Come on," Gabe said. "Let's just get out of here."

Kaz groaned but stood. Lily beckoned to her brother, and Brett followed her. Sticking close together, and casting frequent glances back up at the prison, they left Alcatraz Island and boarded the ferry.

Finally drained of fear, since there had been no sign of Jackson Wright the ghost boy coming after them, Gabe felt his emotions swiftly spiraling downward. This whole day was a mistake. They never should have messed around with things in Uncle Steve's office. And they definitely shouldn't have ditched school and come out here. Gabe had wanted another adventure with his friends, absolutely, but this? *Whatever this is, we're in way over our heads.*

They settled into some indoor seats on the ride back. Gabe had no great desire to get close to the water again, and no one else seemed to, either. It would have been easy to let his eyes glaze over, just stare into space like . . . well, like Brett was doing. Usually the first one to tease or crack a joke, Brett seemed to be dealing with all this weirdness by getting really quiet. Gabe hoped he wouldn't shut down completely.

After a couple of minutes Kaz spoke up, sounding as if he'd lost most of his panic and regained all of his worry.

"So . . . are we gonna talk about this?"

Lily waved a hand vaguely in the air. "I don't even know where to start."

"Well, how about that kid?" Kaz shuddered. "What *was* he?"

Gabe slowly shrugged. "Beats me. Could it have been— I mean, did we just see a ghost?"

Lily thought about it. "But we saw something else *through* him. I've never heard of any ghost story like that."

"Dead isn't gone," Brett said, barely louder than a whisper.

Brett's eyes glistened, and Gabe realized his friend was a hairbreadth away from tears. "'Dead isn't gone'? Brett, what does that mean?"

Brett shook his head and looked down at his feet. "Sorry. Just—ghosts. Thinking about it. About . . . Charlie." Lily sucked in a sharp breath, while Brett turned his face away and fell silent.

Gabe knew he'd just walked all over the sorest of sore points for the Hernandez twins, and he knew when to back off.

Kaz leaned over to Gabe and murmured, "Are they okay?"

He glanced at Brett, then at Lily, who suddenly seemed to have decided the bay outside the window was the most fascinating thing on Earth. Gabe shook his head quickly at Kaz: *leave them alone.* Kaz understood and sat back in his seat, only sneaking a few furtive glances at the twins.

Gabe stood and wandered over to the windows on the opposite side of the cabin. Beyond the city, a wall of fog had gathered along the tops of the mountains and rolled down into the city like a slow-motion avalanche. Buildings and roads and hills disappeared into it. As he stood there, taking in the sight, Ghost Boy's words rattled and pinged in his head like pebbles in an empty tin can.

Each of us is connected to an element?

That reminded Gabe of the whole fire, water, wind, and earth setup from the hidden Friendship Chamber. Then there was Uncle Steve's insistence that the stuff in his office was actually dangerous.

Gabe had never thought much of the books and artifacts in Uncle Steve's office. He'd been sincere when he'd called them "hocus-pocus": a bunch of made-up stories that kept Uncle Steve permanently distracted and that he seemed to find infinitely more interesting than he'd ever found Gabe. But was it possible that, all this time, those objects had held real power?

And that Gabe and his friends had somehow *unlocked* that power?

Am I losing my mind?

The truth was, Gabe had been feeling sort of off ever since he'd touched the "Emerald Tablet." Every time he even thought about the glimpses of the warped version of San Francisco he'd seen—twice now—a hollow pit formed in his belly. He didn't know why, but seeing that place felt like . . . what would he call it? *An omen?* Like a sign of terrible things to come. But seeing the city's evil twin didn't have anything to do with the elements, did it?

Did it?

Gabe turned back to his friends. "What that Jackson kid said. *Have* you guys felt anything else weird lately? I mean other than the stuff with the book."

Kaz blinked at him. "And being chased out of an old prison by a ghost?"

"Yes, Kaz, aside from that. I mean, like he said. Stuff with the, uh . . . the elements."

Lily said, "Well . . . ," and stopped. Shook her head.

Kaz eyeballed her. "'Well'? Well what?"

"When we were on the ferry, on the way out to the island, and everything went crazy with the, uh, rogue wave? Well, right before we stopped . . ."

Gabe flashed back to the sight: Lily, standing as solid as a tree on the deck, her arms thrown up defensively just before the ferry slowed down.

"I kind of felt like, um, I might have had something to do with that. Like, with that big gust of wind. We were going *way* too fast, so I imagined running into a wall of air, like something from a hurricane, that would slow us down. I thought about it enough that I could kinda *feel* it. Then I guess it sort of happened. I don't know how."

"Wind. And air was the element you chose for the friendship ritual."

What was the element Gabe had chosen for himself? *That's right, fire.* He had a sudden memory of the sensation of the sun beating down on him; the flames searing into his skin.

Could it be a coincidence?

Kaz stared at Lily, and at Gabe, and for just a second at Brett. But Brett was still checked out. Jumping to his feet, Kaz waved his hands and bugged his eyes out at them. "Do you guys hear yourselves? Do you know how absolutely insane this sounds?"

Gabe shrugged. "Then how do you explain it? Mass hysteria?"

"Yes! Maybe! Who knows, it could have been something with that weird green book! It made us pass out, didn't it? Maybe it also made us hallucinate!"

Wearily, Lily said, "Kaz, I want an explanation just as much as you do. But didn't you say you felt something weird with the ground on the island?"

Kaz stuck out his chin. "So? You're talking about . . . what, 'feeling the air'?"

Lily spread her hands. "So if the book makes us hallucinate, why isn't it doing it all the time? Why me one time, and you twenty minutes later, and not Brett at all, especially when he's the one lugging it around in his backpack?"

Gabe pursed his lips. He walked over to Brett and felt intense relief that his friend's eyes had dried. Now Brett just looked exhausted. "Hey. I think we ought to take another look at the Tablet." Gabe couldn't help picturing the word with a capital *T* now. Brett motioned toward the backpack sitting at his feet, not looking at Gabe or anyone else. Gabe took that as permission, opened the backpack, and pulled out the Tablet.

Whoa. It feels . . . hot? But no. The heat faded, so quickly he couldn't tell whether he'd imagined it.

One thing he wasn't imagining, though, as he moved it around under one of the cabin's interior lights. The Tablet *didn't* cast a shadow. Another layer of weird to go with everything else.

He sat down next to Brett and beckoned Kaz and Lily over.

"What are you doing?" Lily asked.

"Just checking."

"Oh yeah, great idea," Kaz grumbled as he took a seat next to Gabe. "Let's all get another dose of Mystery Mind Fog."

Gabe's hands trembled a little. He clenched his fists until the shaking stopped. Then he opened the Tablet to one of its thick, yellowed pages covered in the same brilliant red-orange, spiky script he'd seen before. It wasn't even script, really. More like glyphs and symbols. Even though he couldn't make heads or tails of them, Gabe thought they looked familiar somehow.

He flipped back to the very first page of the book—and, letting out a yelp, almost dropped it.

Fire danced across the page. Actual fire. Not red-orange writing, not glyphs or symbols. Flames licked up from the page, dancing and crackling.

"Gabe?" Lily sounded alarmed. "Gabe, what is it? What do you see?"

"Fire," he croaked. "The page is burning . . . and none of you guys see it, do you?"

Kaz slowly shook his head. Lily did, too. Brett didn't even turn around.

"All right," Gabe said, staring into the flames. "What do you see?"

Kaz took several seconds to answer. "It's made of stone.

Granite, I think. And moss is growing in a couple of cracks in the surface."

Lily reached forward, her hand turning and curving above the Tablet. She smiled. *How long has it been since any of us smiled?* It felt like a lifetime. "It's *air*. I can see it! There's a little bit of fog, and it's spinning and flowing and—" Tears started in her eyes. "Guys, it's beautiful. Even more than the silver script I saw before. I wish you could see what I'm seeing."

That almost settled it. Almost. "Brett?"

Brett turned and glared at the surface of the book as if it were a venomous snake. "Water," he spat. "It's water, okay? It's like looking into the freaking ocean. Satisfied?"

Gabe felt a flush of heat rise inside him, his heart beating like crazy. "You guys get it, right? We're all seeing the same elements we chose last night." *Are we all losing our minds?* But Gabe knew that this wasn't insanity.

It was magick.

Magick was real.

Kaz exploded out of his seat, suddenly furious. "No! No! This is stupid! It's worse than stupid! It's impossible! This can't be happening! It's like you said to your uncle, Gabe—this stuff is all made up! It has to be! Don't you understand?" He jabbed an accusing finger at the Tablet. "It's that thing! That book! It's, it's, it's *radioactive* or something! Messing with our heads! No wonder we're all seeing things! You need to get rid of that book, Gabe! Throw it overboard! Do it! Do it now, or we'll all die of radiation poisoning!"

Gabe wasn't about to throw one of Uncle Steve's priceless books into the bay, but Brett made the decision for him. Stabbing a dangerous glare at Kaz, Brett took the Tablet out of Gabe's hands and stuck it back into his backpack, which he then held close to his chest. He didn't say the words "Come and take it, I dare you," but he didn't have to.

Kaz sat back down, trembling.

Gabe leaned his head back and closed his eyes. Kaz was right. Even the most far-fetched scientific explanation must be more likely than some sort of supernatural nonsense.

But, much as he would've liked to, he couldn't deny how he felt. This *was* like something out of one of Uncle Steve's creepy old books.

Something has changed.

As the ferry approached the mainland, Gabe scanned the city's skyline, remembering gnarled, twisted towers where clean glass skyscrapers now stood.

They headed straight back to Gabe's house. It was a somber group. The silence that had fallen after Kaz's last outburst followed them off the ferry and stayed with them through the cable car ride and the hike up the sidewalk. But they all agreed, or in Brett's case didn't disagree, that *something* was wrong with them, and Uncle Steve seemed the best person to approach about it first. No one wanted to say it, but Gabe was pretty sure they were on the same page: if this was something supernatural, well, a professor of the occult ought to know what to do about it, right?

Or, if Uncle Steve thought that they'd all been dosed with something, he could drive them to the ER. Either way, Gabe knew his uncle would be furious with them. Skipping school was just adding insult to injury. But there was no way around that, and Gabe realized that he really did want to apologize now. He would've given an awful lot to have had Uncle Steve there when everything happened on Alcatraz . . . and, much as he didn't want to admit it, he really *should* have stayed out of his uncle's office. Glancing up, Gabe saw dark, angry storm clouds gathering overhead and hoped they weren't a sign of more awfulness to come.

As they climbed the steps to his house, Gabe tried to rehearse in his mind what he'd say to Uncle Steve, but when he unlocked the door and stepped inside, every shred of thought vanished. He gasped and steadied himself against the doorframe, his knees suddenly weak.

"Oh my God," Lily said at his shoulder.

Gabe had never seen anything like the sight that greeted him when he pushed the door open. The foyer and hallway had been demolished.

The floor had exploded upward in multiple places, leaving craters that made the place look like a mine field. Big patches of the ceiling were charred black. All of Uncle Steve's carefully packed cardboard boxes had been shredded, the contents strewn everywhere, so that the few undamaged sections of the floor were covered with ripped clothes and blackened papers. Gabe's jaw dropped as he walked through, taking in the damage. And that was before he reached the kitchen. Some force had been unleashed there, so immense that it had reduced the whole rear quarter of the building to an impassable mass of rubble. The back door was just . . . *gone*.

Why aren't the police here? And fire trucks? Did none of the neighbors even hear this?

"Uncle Steve? UNCLE STEVE! ARE YOU HERE?"

The echoes that came back to him were all wrong. The place was wrecked so thoroughly, it didn't even feel like his house anymore. A million questions jockeyed for position in Gabe's reeling mind, but his worries about Uncle Steve trumped them all.

"Gabe!" Kaz called out from the foyer. "Gabe, c'mere and look at this!"

"In a minute!" Gabe said, dashing past Kaz and Lily and Brett. He took the stairs two at a time up to the second floor. The damage was just as bad up there, if not worse—as if multiple grenades had gone off under the floorboards—but after checking every room, Gabe came to a conclusion: his uncle wasn't there.

Thank God. He wouldn't have survived if he had been. No one could have survived this.

Gabe came back down the stairs, trying not to think about what he would've done if he'd found his uncle's body. "What is it?"

Kaz pointed at one of the craters in the floor. "Look in there."

Gabe walked over and peered into the hole. A symbol had been carved onto the subfloor: an odd, curving glyph similar to ones he'd seen in the Tablet, but dabbed in a silvery ink. "How . . . what . . . ? This looks like it's been here for months."

"I know," Kaz said. "But who would crawl around carving weird symbols under the floor?"

Gabe had no idea. For the sake of his own sanity, he decided to focus on something else and looked over at Lily. "Is this what you were seeing? In the Tablet? Silver writing, all swirly and whatnot?"

Lily nodded. "It's the right color and shape, for sure, but something about it's off."

Gabe frowned and squatted down next to the hole. He knew what Lily meant. He hadn't seen the Air language in the Tablet, but the blazing script he *had* seen glowed with life. This symbol carved into the wood was just . . . sitting there. Inert. He wasn't sure why, but he had the strong feeling that this glyph was *dead*. Used up. Drained of whatever energy it had once held.

Gabe went to two other holes in the floor, and to his rapidly diminishing surprise, found similar glyphs beneath them, too.

"How did these even get here? Were they here when we moved in?"

Lily said, "There's more." She led Gabe over to a section of wallpaper that had come unglued from the buckled wall. Lily pulled it back even farther, revealing yet another dead, silver symbol, carved into the plaster.

Gabe grabbed his head with both hands and squeezed his eyes shut. Whoever had done this—*what*ever had done this— to his house, they were obviously a lot more dangerous than some ordinary burglar, and it all tied back to that stupid Emerald Tablet, and *where was Uncle Steve?* "We've got to find him," Gabe said in a strangled voice, and he must have looked even more upset than he felt, because Lily immediately took his arm as if he might faint dead away.

Brett drifted by, his eyes unfocused. In a daze. Gabe couldn't help it: he felt a flash of irritation that his strongest friend, a friend whose help he could really use right about now, was so . . . *absent.* "Brett."

Brett swung his head around at the sound of Gabe's voice. "Huh?"

"Dude, could you, like, at least *try* to focus here? My house is a war zone, and my uncle's missing!"

Brett blinked, and the damage to the floors, walls, and ceilings finally seemed to register on him. He rubbed the back of his neck with one hand and nodded. "Sorry. Yeah. What do you need? What can I do?"

"We should keep looking around," Kaz said. "See if we can find something that'll tell us where Dr. Conway is, or who took him."

Gabe nodded. The room swam around him, and he blinked fast, trying to get rid of what he suddenly realized were scalding-hot tears. "Let's start with the office."

Gabe led his friends up the stairs and into his uncle's office. The whole room looked like a set from one of the horror movies the four of them loved to stay up late and watch together. Just like downstairs, the carefully packed moving boxes had been torn to shreds, and the empty bookcases were little more than piles of kindling. Picking through the debris, Gabe noticed something: every single one of the "artifacts" Uncle Steve had collected was missing. His computer was still there, knocked off the desk onto the floor, for what little that was worth.

From a far corner Kaz made a tiny gagging noise.

"Kaz?" Gabe went over to him. "You okay?"

"I'm okay, yeah. But I can't say the same for whatever that used to belong to." Kaz pointed, and when Gabe saw what he was pointing at, he almost gagged himself.

Lying in a pool of golden liquid was . . . a leg? That was the best Gabe could do to describe it: it looked like a large dog's hind leg that had been ripped off the body. And more than that, he was pretty sure it had been *skinned*. Its muscle tissue and veins and tendons were all visible, running down to a set of wickedly sharp claws. Gabe leaned over to take a closer look, got a nose full of ripped-off-skinless-dog-leg funk, and jerked backward.

Kaz said, "Yeah, I should've warned you about the smell. Do you think this came off whatever tore the house up?"

"I don't know. I can't even . . . I don't know how to make sense of this."

Oh yes you do. You're going to have to admit your uncle was right all along. This is supernatural.

Gabe couldn't deny it any longer. Nothing from the real, normal world could have done this to his house.

Lily said, "Gabe, let's not think the worst, all right? Your uncle's not here. He might not have been here when this happened. Let's not assume something bad happened to him when we don't know for sure, okay?"

Gabe tried to latch on to what she was saying. Deep down, he knew his uncle loved him and that Steve was only so infuriatingly overprotective because of that. And even though Gabe never told him so, he loved his uncle, too. Uncle Steve was the only family Gabe had ever known.

And Lily was right. Uncle Steve might not have been there at all when this happened. He might have gone back to the university. Or to get groceries. Or . . . or *anywhere*. He could come stomping through the front door any second now and demand to know what Gabe had done to his house while he was gone.

From the desk, Brett cleared his throat. "Guys? I've got some bad news."

Gabe stumbled over to Brett, his legs working on autopilot, dread heavy in his gut. There on the floor under the desk lay Uncle Steve's prosthetic leg, charred and bent and ruined. Gabe clapped a hand over his mouth to keep himself from crying out. There was no question, then: Uncle Steve *had* been here when the attack happened, and whoever did it had *taken* him. It wasn't as if Uncle Steve would go somewhere without his leg!

They took him . . . or . . . . Gabe thought about that other leg, lying severed and skinless in the corner.

They took him . . . or they ate him.

Gabe's knees went weak. While he steadied himself on the edge of the desk, Lily knelt and picked up something partially hidden underneath more ruined papers. It was an old framed photograph, one Gabe had never seen before, of four people in out-of-date clothes and hairstyles. A crack in the glass ran directly across Uncle Steve's face.

"Who are they?" Lily asked.

Gabe pointed at each person in turn. "That's my dad. That's my mom. And that's Uncle Steve, except with a better haircut, and that's . . . I don't know who that is." The person he didn't know was a middle-aged woman with long, graying hair and very light-blue eyes.

Kaz said, "Here, Brett, give me a hand with this, would you?" Gabe watched absently as Brett and Kaz gathered up the components of Uncle Steve's computer, his mind on a desperate loop: *Don't think the worst. Don't think the worst. Don't think the worst.*

Please don't be dead.

The computer booted up, despite being sort of battered. Kaz peered at the monitor. "Holy crap."

Gabe blinked. "What?"

"Look! Your uncle was in the middle of writing an email!" Kaz moved out of the way and let Gabe peer at the screen.

FROM: dconway@supermail.com

TO: greta.jaeger@brookhavenmed.org

RE: Moving again

Doc,

It's not safe to keep Gabe in SF anymore. I've got the house warded to a fare-thee-well, but the Dawn's getting closer and closer. I can feel it in the air—you know what I'm talking about.

I can't begin to tell you how frustrating this is, either. I am SO CLOSE to getting answers about Aria's location. But as always, safety is the most important thing. I

Lily said what Gabe was thinking: "What, that's it?"

"That's as far as he got," Kaz said quietly. "I wonder what this 'Dawn' is?"

Brett leaned over to look at the screen. "And who's Aria?"

Gabe's head fairly spun. He felt crushed under a whole

mountain of guilt, for one thing. All this constant moving from city to city—Uncle Steve had always told Gabe that this was for his own benefit, but Gabe had never believed it. But looking around at the wreckage of their house, it was impossible *not* to believe it. And it wasn't just that.

"Aria's my mom." Gabe said.

"But, uh, isn't she, you know . . . ," Lily said carefully.

"Yeah." Gabe cleared his throat. "She and my dad died in a car wreck when I was three." What could Uncle Steve have possibly meant by "close to getting answers about Aria's location"?

Kaz had pulled out his phone and started tapping. "Well, here's something. That email address belongs to a hospital on the edge of the city. This Greta Jaeger person must work there."

"And she obviously knows more about what's going on than we do," Lily said. "You guys thinking what I'm thinking?"

His eyes haunted, Brett said, "We need to go there."

Gabe turned and leaned against the edge of the desk, his mind going in what felt like a million different directions at once. He only half-heard Lily when she started speculating about what Uncle Steve could have been involved with. "You guys, this isn't, like, a regular burglary. Something crazy happened here. It must be connected to what happened on the ferry and with Ghost Boy," she said, echoing his thoughts from a few minutes earlier.

Gabe wasn't really listening. He was too consumed with the sudden thought that all this, everything bad that had happened, was one hundred percent his fault. He should have listened to his uncle. He shouldn't have gone snooping around in the office. He shouldn't have let Brett talk him into skipping school and going out to Alcatraz. *I should have been here! I could have . . .*

Could have done what?

He didn't know, and that made him even more miserable. When the doorbell rang, its sound came as a welcome relief from all the shouting and screaming inside his head. "Let me go see who that is," Gabe told his friends. "You guys figure out how to get to this hospital, okay?"

Lily nodded. Gabe left the office and half walked, half jumped down the stairs, but paused on the landing. *Wait a minute.* What if it was whoever did all this, coming back for him now? Not that somebody like that would ring a doorbell, but still . . . Except, then, what if it was a neighbor? How would he explain his house looking like an exploded mine field to Mrs. Binkowski from next door?

Through the leaded-glass window in the front door, he could see the familiar outline of police officers' hats and felt a flood of relief. *Somebody must have heard all this and called the cops after all! They can put out a missing person's report! They can help us find Uncle Steve!*

Gabe almost had his hand on the doorknob when an unwelcome voice spoke up behind him. "I wouldn't do that if I were you."

Gabe yelped and spun around to find Jackson Wright standing not ten feet away, watching him with a grave expression. Ghost Boy didn't look as solid as he had in the depths of the prison, but to his relief Gabe couldn't see through him to that horrible other place, either. "You *followed* us? *Did you trash my house?* Where's my uncle? What'd you do with him?"

Jackson's expression didn't change at all. "Regretfully, you cannot help him."

Gabe's lips stretched back in a snarl. He wondered what would happen if you punched a ghost square in the nose. "Where is he?"

"As I said, you cannot help him. But I can help you."

Gabe gritted out, "Oh yeah? How?"

"Well, to begin with, I advise you not to let in the local constabulary. They are not what they appear to be."

Ghost Boy sounded so smug it made Gabe want to scream. "You know what I think? I think you can take your help and shove it." He turned and grabbed the door handle.

"You mustn't!" Jackson shrieked, his smug composure suddenly gone, and lunged for Gabe. But when his outstretched hand touched Gabe's shoulder, it passed right through him, leaving Gabe with nothing but the sensation of cold air on his skin.

Gabe waved a hand at Ghost Boy as if shooing away a mosquito. "Get away from me!" It worked better than Gabe had expected: Jackson Wright evaporated, vanishing like a tiny puff of smoke. Grimly satisfied at that, Gabe opened the door and looked up at the two burly policemen standing there. According to the metal tags on their uniforms, their names were Duffy and Holmes.

Gabe didn't give them a chance to speak. He just let all the words pour out in a flood: "Officers I'm really glad you're here somebody totally ransacked our house and my uncle Steve was here but I think they took him because he has a prosthetic leg and I found the leg upstairs can you help me please you've gotta help me!"

While Gabe panted, Officer Holmes eyeballed the damage to the foyer and let out a low whistle. "Well, there's something you don't see every day. How'd this happen?"

Gabe shook his head. "I don't know."

Officer Duffy gave him a reassuring smile and pulled out a pad and pen. "All right, son, we'll get this taken care of. First off, what's your name?"

"Gabe. Gabe Conway. My uncle's name is Steven Conway."

"And can you tell when this happened?"

"This morning! Everything was okay when I left a couple of hours ago, but I just got back and found it like this!"

Officer Holmes also pulled out a pad and pen. Thunder rumbled in the charcoal-gray sky. "All right, Gabe, just bear with us. We've got to make sure we have all your personal information, and then we can take a look around. Now, you live here with your uncle?"

"Yes. Yes, sir."

"Just the two of you?"

"That's right."

Both officers scribbled on their pads. "And how long have you lived in San Francisco?" Officer Duffy asked.

Gabe thought that was an odd question to ask, but he wasn't about to act difficult when these guys were going to help him find Uncle Steve. "Only a year. We were about to move."

"Oh? That's helpful. Okay, now, is Steven Conway a blood relative of yours?"

"Huh? Uh . . . no. He adopted me after my parents died."

Officer Holmes nodded. "Fascinating. Fascinating. All right, now, have you seen something that looks kind of like a stone tablet? Green in color? Or it might have been gold. Seen anything like that, Gabe?"

Gabe came within a hairbreadth of saying "You know about the Tablet?" For a fraction of a second his mind raced with the possibility that the police already knew all about this, about everything that had happened. And that meant they would know what to do!

But then his stomach went cold. Ghost Boy's words rang in his ears: "They are not what they appear to be."

"Why're you asking about that?"

Officer Duffy's eyes took on a hard gleam. When Gabe desperately looked to Officer Holmes, the man's face was no friendlier.

"Why don't we step inside and get out of the rain, Gabe? We can talk all about it."

Ghost Boy was right!

Gabe took a step back and slammed the door as hard as he could, throwing the dead bolt the moment that the wood touched the frame. No sooner had he done that than the cops started pounding on the door: "Gabe! Open up, kid!"

"What's going on?"

Gabe spun to see Lily, Brett, and Kaz at the bottom of the stairs, watching him with wide, frightened eyes. "These guys aren't cops!" he hissed. "Run!"

"Run where?" Kaz demanded. "The back door's caved in!"

"Back up, go back up!" Gabe gestured frantically. "Go go go!"

And go they did, though Lily shouted over her shoulder, "This is crazy! We're gonna be trapped up here!"

"You got a better idea?" Gabe shouted. "No? Then upstairs it is!"

Gabe rushed up the staircase after them, but just as his feet hit the landing, the front door *exploded*, spraying wooden shards and splinters all over the foyer. When the sawdust cleared, the two cops stepped inside and—Gabe's flesh crawled as he saw it happen—a line of glyphs suddenly sprang to life in a semicircle on the floor around the doorway, gleaming first silver and then a brilliant gold. Officer Duffy had already taken a running step toward Gabe before Officer Holmes saw the glyphs and tried to haul him backward. But it was too late, and the glyphs . . .

. . . *detonated*. A tremendous explosion ripped through the foyer, throwing both cops back out the door as if they were rag dolls.

In that instant, once and for all, Gabe Conway became a believer in magick.

So that's what Uncle Steve meant about the house being warded!

The explosion had carried Duffy and Holmes all the way across the street and slammed them into a parked car, but as Gabe watched, they both began to stir. Gabe was pretty sure the car had taken a lot more damage than they had.

"I can't believe that just happened," Kaz breathed at Gabe's shoulder.

Gabe spun to find all three of his friends there with him, staring out at the quickly recovering cops. "What are you doing down here? I told you to go upstairs!"

"Yeah, that was a great plan," Brett said, showing a tiny bit of his old spark. "Pin ourselves down with no escape route. Besides, you just blew up the cops."

As if in response to Brett, Officers Duffy and Holmes heaved themselves up off the street. Holmes put two fingers in his mouth and produced the loudest, shrillest whistle Gabe had ever heard, and two creatures straight out of Gabe's wildest nightmares leaped from a patch of shadows across the street and charged straight for the ruined front door.

The creatures were vaguely canine, but skinless, just like the severed leg they'd found upstairs, and *huge*, like small horses. But worst of all, they didn't have faces. Gabe stared in horror. The things had mouths, huge and gaping wide and filled with gigantic fangs and giant black tongues that lolled out, dripping horrible saliva. But the mouths were the heads' only feature; they had no noses, no eyes, not even any ears.

Gabe took in all this in the space of two hammering heartbeats before he roared, *"Get upstairs GET UPSTAIRS NOW!"* He would have physically dragged his friends back up to the second floor, but he didn't have to, because they'd all seen the same thing he had and were already sprinting up the stairs. Gabe followed, running as fast as he could.

Behind them, the skinless nightmares burst into the house. One of the creatures *sprinted up the wall*. The other one ran along the *ceiling*, just as if it were on solid ground.

Gabe tore after his friends, and all four of them rushed into Gabe's room. Gabe slammed the door and locked it, and said, "Help me!" as he started pushing the chest of drawers. Brett and Lily both came to his aid, and they slid the heavy piece of furniture in front of the door.

Snarls reached them from outside, so deep and thick they sounded more like massive diesel engines than animals. Gabe backed away, joining his friends in a knot in the middle of the floor, as two sets of daggerlike claws pierced the bedroom door and ripped it off its hinges.

Lily and Kaz both screamed, but Gabe shouted, "The bed! Turn the bed over and get behind it!" It was the only thing he could think of to do, but it must have sounded like a decent plan to Brett, at least. Brett ran to the king-size bed and he and Gabe, working together, flipped it onto its side so that its legs pointed toward the door. All four of them got behind it and wedged themselves into a corner.

With a huge *bang!*, the eyeless, skinless terrors slammed the chest of drawers out of the way. Before Gabe could take a breath, they began tearing the bed apart. Great wads of mattress stuffing filled the air as the monstrosities tore through it in their frenzy to reach Gabe and his friends. Their awful weight crushed Gabe backward against the wall and pinned him painfully against Kaz, who let out an awful sound somewhere between a scream and a sob.

"Hunters!" That was Officer Duffy, his voice coming from the hallway outside the room. "We need them alive!"

"Well," Officer Holmes amended. "Some of them."

7

Thanks to the storm's crazy lightning, Brett saw every detail of the massive claws that ripped through the box springs right in front of his nose. When the monsters finally got through the bed and dug into his guts, Brett was sure he'd be able to see that, too. *Awesome.*

Despite the mortal danger, Brett couldn't help thinking that this was all his fault. He pushed the thought away. His Friend had told him he'd have to suffer to see Charlie again. But any amount of suffering was worth it.

It had to be less than Charlie had suffered.

The creatures—"hunters," the fake police had called them—growled and roared ravenously as they tore at the bedding, but an immense peal of thunder masked the sound.

One of the hunters jammed its muzzle into the hole it had just ripped open, horrible teeth snapping as the stench of sulfur blasted Brett's face.

"Keep the green-eyed boy alive," he heard Duffy say. "And the girl. Kill the other two."

Brett couldn't believe this was actually happening. It was like something out of a movie. A really gory movie his grandmother definitely would *not* approve of him watching.

He did his best not to think about how those savage teeth would feel as they tore into his flesh. He and Kaz and Lily all dug their fingers into the frame of the box springs, desperate to hold it in place. Brett didn't think they could keep the hunters off them for more than a few seconds, but those seconds were precious. *If they want to kill me, I'll go down swinging! And as long as I'm breathing, I won't let them touch my sister!*

Brett turned his head and was about to say "Hold on! Don't let go!" when he noticed that Gabe wasn't holding on at *all*.

Instead, Gabe had shrunk back into the corner as far as his body would allow and was making small, vague gestures with his hands, as if to ward off something. "Stop," Gabe murmured. "Stop. Stop! Get away!"

"Gabe!" Brett shrieked. "What are you *doing*? Help us!" But it was as if Gabe couldn't hear him, and Brett almost came up off the floor as the hunters finally tore the bed away from them. Both creatures dropped into a crouch, teeth bared and dripping, ready to bite and crush. The impostor cops stood just behind them, awful grins on their faces. *The kind of grin you get when you're about to eat something you've been looking forward to for a long time.*

Brett shuddered when he realized the hunters were waiting for a command.

Officer Duffy nudged Officer Holmes with an elbow. "This is the best part, don't you think?"

"Stop," Gabe said, a little louder.

Officer Holmes's grin threatened to break his face in half. "After what that one's uncle did to my prize alpha? This is payback."

At the top of his lungs Gabe screamed, "STOP!" The ensuing flash was so bright that, for just a second, Brett thought the house had been struck by lightning.

The overhead bulbs and the lamp on Gabe's nightstand all exploded, the glass pulverizing into the finest dust, and fat blue arcs of electricity jumped out of the sockets and *danced around Gabe's hands.* Lily and Kaz both shrieked and scrambled away from him, but Brett stayed where he was, staring. The blue-white energy swirled and churned and in the blink of an eye turned red-orange. The red-orange of flames. An inferno like a tiny sun crackled and spun in place between Gabe's hands. Its fiery glow was reflected in Gabe's eyes. Gabe rose to his feet, drew in a great breath, and bellowed in a voice like the roaring of a forest fire.

"GET AWAY FROM US!"

A cone of flame blasted across the room, too blindingly bright to look at, too hot to do anything about but turn and shrink away.

When Brett felt the heat fading, he chanced a look at what was left of Gabe's bedroom. A massive V-shaped scorch mark marred the floor, the vertex of its angle pointing straight at Gabe. The bed itself was nothing more than a few blackened, smoldering splinters crumpled against the far wall. The hunters writhed on the ground, bodies smoking, yelping and mewling in pain. Brett watched as they righted themselves, bolted straight toward a window, and crashed through it, out into the storm.

Brett wasn't sure what had happened to the cops.

A huge gust of wind blew what felt like a solid sheet of water in through the ruined window, and some remote part of Brett's mind registered that as a good thing, since flames were dancing across the ceiling. No matter how badly it had been damaged, Brett didn't think Gabe or his uncle would want their house burned down.

"Whuh . . . what happened?"

That was Gabe. Staggering, almost unconscious from the looks of it. Brett scrambled up and steadied his friend.

"A better question," Kaz said, pointing out into the hall, "would be: 'Why don't we get out of here?'"

Brett followed Kaz's pointing finger. Holmes and Duffy lay on the floor of the hall, skin blackened, clothes in shreds . . . but both still alive, twitching and groaning in pain.

"Come on, help Gabe," Lily said. "Let's get away from this place."

With a cautious Kaz leading the way, and Brett and Lily supporting a still-woozy Gabe, the four of them stepped past the semiconscious cops and sprinted down the stairs.

Brett was the last one into the cable car. He had to brace himself as the car lurched into motion.

Long, rolling, crackling crashes assaulted the city, punctuated by wall-shaking booms, and sheets of rain battered the windows. He checked the time. It was two-thirty in the afternoon but might as well have been eleven o'clock at night, judging by how dark it was. Streetlights did little to penetrate the gloom.

They'd run flat out for ten blocks once they got out of Gabe's house, only slowing once they got to a busier street. That was when Brett realized how soaked he was. The rain was completely nuts—the kind of downpour you can't imagine lasting for more than a couple of minutes.

They'd stopped to buy cheap plastic ponchos, but those hadn't done much good.

Brett caught up to the others, huddled in a tight cluster at the back of the car. The storm had driven most people inside, and they nearly had the car to themselves. Brett was grateful for the isolation.

The thought he'd had in the bedroom at Gabe's house kept coming back to him. *This is all my fault.* Jackson's instructions had seemed so simple at the time. But even with Ghost Boy's warnings, Brett hadn't pictured anything like this. Gabe's home destroyed, Dr. Conway missing, and now they had some sort of demonic creatures after them? And those fake cops—would there be more?

How did the fake cops know about the Emerald Tablet, anyway? The Tablet was right at the center of the deal Brett had made with Jackson. Go with his friends to Alcatraz, deliver the Tablet to Jackson, and then he'd get to see Charlie again; that's what they'd agreed. Granted, things had gotten a little weird at Alcatraz, and he hadn't managed to give Jackson the Tablet, but that wasn't Brett's fault. So where was his brother?

It was creepy, too, how Jackson behaved totally differently in real life from the way he had in Brett's dreams. In the dreams, Jackson was just a normal kid. Well, maybe not *normal* normal, since he was . . . Brett didn't want to say "a ghost." Formerly alive?

A deceased citizen?

Life-challenged?

Brett fought back a giggle but sobered up quickly as he remembered all the weird things Jackson had said to them down in the underbelly of the prison. He was glad to have proof his Friend was real and not a figment of his imagination, but in person Jackson was kind of, well, *scary*. And angry.

Why was he so angry?

In any case, Brett intended to keep a very close eye on the Tablet until he got what was promised to him.

He sidled up next to Gabe. His friend seemed to have recovered from the . . . thing that he did back at his house with the fire. Brett didn't have the words to describe what he'd seen. What he'd *felt*. But his skin was still stretched a little more tightly than usual from being so close to such intense heat. Kaz might still not want to believe it, but even he was getting to the point where denying what was happening made a lot less sense than accepting it. They'd all seen it: *Gabe could control fire.*

And if that was true, did it mean Lily controlled air and Kaz controlled . . . what, rocks? *Is that why he thought he heard the ground snoring, back on Alcatraz?* Brett stared out at the downpour. *Why did I have to choose water?* Doing penance for Charlie's death by choosing the element for the friendship ritual was one thing, but being *bound* to it? Having it *become a part of him*? It was like something straight out of his nightmares.

This had all gotten way out of control. Brett wanted to see Charlie more than anything, but he didn't think he'd be putting his friends and sister in danger. If he had, he'd never have agreed to any of this.

As it was, he already had more guilt than he could handle.

"Dr. Jaeger will have answers," Lily was telling Gabe. That was the lady Gabe's uncle had been emailing before whatever happened at the house happened. "She'll explain what's going on and tell us what to do."

Gabe barely seemed to hear Lily. He aimed some words at no one in particular. "Ghost Boy knew those cops were no good."

Brett's head snapped up. "*What?* You talked to Jackson again? When? Where?"

"He showed up at my house. Right before I opened the door to those cops. He told me not to, and I ignored him." Gabe looked up at the ceiling. "And if you're listening now, you could've *told* me about the no-face-having monster dogs! That would've been okay!"

Brett squeezed his eyes shut. Jackson had told him he couldn't appear anywhere but Alcatraz. *How many lies did he tell me?* Unless there was another explanation. What if his Friend was getting more powerful? Maybe that meant he could do other things Brett didn't know about. Maybe Jackson was still planning to deliver on Charlie! That had to be it. Their plan had just hit a little snag, that was all.

Kaz pulled out his phone and tapped at it. "Dr. Jaeger's hospital's about half a mile's walk from the end of the cable car line."

"That's nothing!" Brett grinned. "It'll take us, like, five minutes to walk there!" This grin was the real deal, now that he realized Jackson was still looking out for him. The deal was *on.* "Our ponchos will keep us dry. Well, mostly, anyway."

Kaz stared forlornly out the window at the waterlogged city.

"We'll probably catch pneumonia, the way this day is going."

Brett sighed.

It turned out to be slightly more than a half mile from the cable car stop to the visitor's entrance at the Brookhaven Medical Institute. None of them was happy about that, Kaz least of all, because he'd stepped in what he'd thought was a very shallow puddle and sunk in up to his knee. "I used to like these shoes," Kaz had moaned. "They were good shoes. Now I'm going to have to take them out behind the woodshed and shoot them."

"You don't have a woodshed," Lily observed flatly.

"I don't have nice shoes anymore, either."

Brett had expected to hear nothing but how Kaz was *definitely* coming down with pneumonia, but when they arrived at Brookhaven, they all forgot about everything else. At first glance it looked like a huge, high-end hotel, with fancy brickwork and a sculpture garden off to one side. But then they got closer and took in the seventeen-foot-high, razor-wire-topped chain-link fence and the bars on the windows. A tasteful sign beside the main entrance sealed the deal: BROOKHAVEN INSTITUTE FOR PSYCHIATRIC REHABILITATION.

Lily said it first: "This is an insane asylum!"

"It doesn't matter what it is," Gabe said. "Uncle Steve's email to Dr. Jaeger mentioned warding. Those were the protections around the house. *Magickal* protections. We've got to find out what she knows."

The four of them headed in through the main entrance. Brett didn't like the looks of all the security around the place. What kind of patients did they have that they needed razor wire to keep them in? But they had to talk to Dr. Jaeger. If she knew what happened to Dr. Conway, Brett would be able to fix whatever kind of mess he'd accidentally landed his friends in.

Kaz looked around, goggle-eyed, as they crossed the lobby. "This is just like the place where they kept Sarah Connor in *Terminator 2*!"

Kaz was always referencing old movies Brett had never seen. Brett just kept his mouth shut.

A tidy little area, sort of like a combination reception desk and nurses' station, sat beside a very large, imposing, unquestionably locked door. A woman in scrubs looked up from filling out paperwork as they approached. "What can I do for you?" she asked. Brett thought she looked suspicious of them. Like she was thinking, "What the heck are *you* doing here? Maybe I should call your parents?"

"We're here to see one of your employees," Gabe said. He was the best out of any of them at talking to adults.

The nurse cocked an eyebrow and reached for a phone. "Oh? Who? I can let them know you're here."

"Greta Jaeger."

The cocked eyebrow sank down into a frown. "Excuse me?"

Gabe's confidence seemed to take a hit, but he soldiered on: "Greta Jaeger? She's a friend of my uncle's."

"Oh, I highly doubt that, young man."

That stumped Gabe. Lily stepped up beside him and said, "I'm sorry, what do you mean by that? Gabe here, his uncle has been emailing Dr. Jaeger. She has a Brookhaven email address."

"*Doctor* Jaeger?" Now the nurse was the one who looked surprised. "She might well have been a doctor at some point, but I assure you that she's not a doctor *here*."

"Wait, are you saying that she's a—" Brett began to ask.

"Patient. Yes."

Brett turned to his friends. They looked every bit as shocked as he felt.

The nurse continued. "Now, I don't know if this is supposed to be a joke or if you're just extremely ill informed, but if you think I'm going to let four children waltz in and talk to a *murderer*, you could not be more mistaken."

Brett felt all the blood drain out of his face and into the pit in his stomach. He looked over at his friends and saw the same reaction there.

Murderer?

What?

Brett knew the name for the thing they all sat under. *Porte-cochère.* He'd had a huge crush on a girl named Melinda Stockard last year, and since she was taking French, he'd decided to learn a little bit himself. It turned out she liked some guy from her neighborhood who went to a snooty private school, but a few

French words had stuck with Brett, anyway. Especially since French wasn't *that* different from Spanish. Not that his Spanish was that great, much to his grandmother's dismay.

A *porte-cochère* was a covered area where cars could pull in out of the rain and drop off passengers. Sort of like a glorified carport. The one outside the Brookhaven Institute was particularly big and fancy, and had a fountain in the middle of it. He, Gabe, Lily, and Kaz all sat on the edge of the fountain, watching the rain fall and wondering what to do next. The rain wasn't coming down quite as hard as it had been, but it was still plenty hard, and as steady as if someone had turned on a giant faucet somewhere in the sky above them. Brett wasn't looking forward to the walk back to the cable car stop, but none of them had enough money for a taxi.

"I don't know," Gabe was saying in response to some question from Lily that Brett hadn't heard. "We can't get in to see her, but we can't just give up, can we? This is all we've got. Maybe we go to the FBI?"

Kaz let out a bitter little laugh. "Do you even know where the FBI *is*?"

Gabe shrugged. "They've got field offices, don't they? There's got to be one somewhere in San Francisco."

"Yeah," Lily said glumly. "We go there and tell them what?"

Brett drew a breath to speak—he thought maybe he could try a joke—but something caught his attention. He couldn't tell what at first. It was like . . . a buzzing? An echo? Something he heard and felt at the same time, somewhere deep in his brain. Not a buzzing, but . . . a flow. Like the rush of a stream over rocks, drawing him to the surface of the fountain's pool—

—which was *vibrating*. Brett turned around to get a better look.

His stomach went queasy.

A glyph floated there under the water's surface, just like it had on the ferry, and a stab of panic shot through his gut. *What do I do, what do I do?* But even as that thought ran through his mind, Brett's hand lifted, half by itself. He *knew* what to do. Brett's index finger traced the shape of the glyph in the air— and he yelped and jumped up from his seat.

"What?" Lily demanded. "Brett, what's wrong?"

He used the same index finger to point at the water.

His friends looked where he was pointing, and Kaz yelped even more loudly than he had. Gabe said, "Oh my *God.*" Lily came over to Brett and took his hand. Hers was trembling.

A *face* floated there, just under the water, where the glyph had been. An older woman with long, stringy gray hair. Her cheeks were sunken, and her skin bore thousands of wrinkles, but her eyes gleamed with ferocious intelligence. Intelligence and *purpose.*

The woman's lips moved. Brett expected to hear words, but instead what sounded like *whale song* floated faintly up to him.

"Who *is* that?" Lily whispered.

"I think," Gabe leaned closer to the water. "Oh, wow.

That's gotta be Greta Jaeger. Remember the photo in Uncle Steve's office?"

"She looks a lot older now." Kaz peered over Gabe's shoulder at the water. Brett got the feeling that was as close as Kaz was willing to get. "But I guess spending a few years in an insane asylum would age a person pretty fast, huh?"

"It looks like she's trying to talk to us." Lily turned her head to put an ear nearer to the water's surface. "That sound could be, like, really distorted words, couldn't it?"

Brett let out a low, pained groan as the realization struck him. "Guys . . . I think I'm going to have to put my head in there. In the water."

Lily drew back. "What? No! Brett, you don't have to— I mean— What if she pulls you in?" Lily knew how he felt about the water.

Brett shook his head. "I don't get the feeling that she's dangerous." He swallowed hard. "I just *know* this is what I'm supposed to do."

Gabe nodded. "Because your element is water."

Brett wasn't exactly pleased that he was the only one who could do this, but he was the one who'd gotten them into this mess. He had to do everything he could to get them out of it. "Wish me luck." Before Lily could protest any further, Brett took a deep breath, leaned over the fountain, and stuck his head below the surface.

He blinked a few times, surprised that the water didn't

irritate his eyes. On the contrary, suddenly Brett felt as though he could *truly* see, for the first time ever. And right in front of him, as if she were there in person, was Greta Jaeger.

"H-hello?" Brett felt the air bubbles escape his lips and knew all he should have heard was a *glub-glub* sound, but instead his own voice sounded as clear as if he were on the stage of a concert hall.

"Hello, Brett." Greta Jaeger's voice was low and kind of smoky. "The rain told me your name. The rain tells me many things." Greta's eyes slid sideways, as if she were looking at another person in the conversation. "Yes, I understand. We don't have much time."

A thought crossed Brett's mind: *This lady is a patient in a mental hospital who says she talks to the rain. What am I doing?*

Greta Jaeger's gaze came back to Brett. "I felt you tap into our element earlier today when you called up that wave in the bay."

Brett surged up out of the fountain, gasping. *I called up that wave?* He hadn't wanted to admit it to himself, but deep down, he'd known all along. *I almost crashed the ferry. I almost got us all killed!*

Lily was there at his shoulder, rapid-fire: "Well? Is it working? Can you hear her? What's she saying?"

"She knows my name." Brett coughed. "She says the *rain* told her."

Lily, Gabe, and Kaz all started talking at once, asking

question after question; but Brett waved them silent and plunged his head into the fountain again.

Looking over Brett's shoulder, Greta said, "Good heavens, you have a full circle! How is that possible?"

What? Full circle? Brett managed, "Huh?"

"Your companions. I can see them there. You've all been bound to the elements. And that means you're all in terrible danger."

Brett came up, blowing water out of his nose, trying to suck as much air into his lungs as possible. He really, righteously hated the water, but he had to know more. He didn't wait to hear any more of his friends' questions before dunking his head again.

It still wasn't easy to talk underwater, but Brett persisted. "Why did the nurse say you were a murderer?"

Greta drew back, hesitant. "Listen to me, Brett." Her voice grew even lower, more intense. "Now is not the time to get into that."

"It's the perfect time! How can we trust you if we don't know the truth?"

Greta looked over to the side again. She nodded curtly before turning back to Brett. "There was a terrible accident. It was tragic, but many different people were to blame."

Brett was about to say something else when Gabe's head plunked down into the fountain next to him. Gabe looked around wildly, at both him and Greta, and tried to talk; but his words actually did come out sounding like *glub-glub-glub*. Gabe pulled his head back out, and Brett followed him, filling his lungs.

"What was that about?" Brett demanded.

"I just wanted to talk to her." Gabe wrung water out of his hair and sneezed violently. "For all the good it did me. I guess you're the only one who gets to use the Magic Fountain Phone."

Brett shrugged, took another deep breath, and went back in. As soon as he opened his eyes, he saw the shock on Greta Jaeger's face. "What? What's wrong?"

"Your friend. That was the first time I could see his face clearly. He looks just like his father!" She turned away, talking to the rain again. "Yes, yes. That explains everything."

"Explains what now?"

"Brett, I need you to tell me what led up to this moment. When did all these events begin for you? Please, don't leave anything out."

It took a lot of resurfacing and gasping, but Brett laid out an edited version of all the events of the last couple of weeks, from the map in Uncle Steve's office and the bonding ritual underground all the way through the fake cops and the nightmare beasts. He left out the parts about finding the signet ring, and his Friend, Jackson the ghost boy. Ghost Boy had made it clear from the start that their connection had to be secret, and Brett couldn't risk telling anyone, not while he still needed his help to find Charlie.

Greta Jaeger just listened, and as he spoke, Brett realized talking underwater was getting easier. As if the air in his lungs was lasting longer and longer each time.

When he finished, Greta nodded thoughtfully. "The Emerald Tablet . . ." She trailed off. Brett was about to prompt her to continue when she said, "You must be very careful with it. You have no idea how dangerous it is."

Brett noticed his vision getting a little dark around the edges. He ignored it, determined to learn as much as he could. His head had started pounding, but he ignored that, too.

"But how do you even know about it?"

"Your friend. Gabriel. His uncle, Steven, is an old friend of mine." Greta's eyes got sort of unfocused. Like she was reliving old memories. "I was close with Gabriel's parents, as well. We all stood together against the Eternal Dawn."

"The Eternal Dawn?" Brett remembered the name from Dr. Conway's email. "What's that?"

Her eyes snapped back into focus and narrowed. "A cult," she spat out. "Catastrophic. Apocalyptic. Left to themselves, they would destroy the world as we know it."

Brett started to say something else . . . and realized something was wrong. *Really* wrong. He almost took a deep breath. Almost pulled the water into his lungs, and in a rush he knew:

The water *wanted* him to.

It wasn't getting easier to hold his breath.

The water was just making it *feel* that way.

How long have I gone without breathing?

Too long . . .

Brett's vision darkened even more. He felt light-headed, and almost blew out what little air his lungs still held when he realized the water was *pushing in*. Squirming, like a living creature, into his nose, into his mouth, trying to slide down his windpipe.

Let me in.

Brett heard the voice as the faintest of whispers. Tiny, but insistent . . . and growing louder.

Brett. Let me in.

Dimly he saw Greta's eyes widen in fear. "Brett! Don't give in to the water! You have the power to control it, but the element has a will of its own! A *desire*! You must stand strong against it or it could kill you! Or worse."

Brett tried to come up for air, but his body wouldn't cooperate. No, it was nicer to stay down under the surface. He should accept the water, invite it in, allow it to fill him. A part of him *wanted* to.

Three sets of hands grabbed him and forcibly dragged him out of the fountain. Brett slumped to the pavement, coughing and blowing water out of his nose and his mouth and maybe even his ears. Then he saw that a few tendrils of water had actually *followed him out of the fountain*, glassy tentacles reaching for him, trying to pull him back under. After a couple of seconds they retreated, disappearing under the surface. Brett wasn't sure his friends had seen them, and at that moment didn't care. He just lay there on his back, panting, and—

And suddenly he was *somewhere else*. Still lying on his back, staring up at the sky, but it was no sky he had ever seen before. Not blue, but a deep, disturbing amber. Unbelievably tall black Gothic towers stood silhouetted against that bizarre golden sky, and . . . *things* flew around them. Huge, impossible things.

What am I looking at?

Gradually, he became aware of the sound of shouting. Then slowly it resolved into the voices of his friends, all calling his name. The amber sky and the terrifying black towers faded, replaced by the *porte-cochère*.

Brett had never felt more relieved. Gabe helped him sit up and lean back against the edge of the fountain. "Are you okay?"

Brett blinked and absently patted himself down. "I think so. Wow. That was *horrible*."

Lily crouched beside him. "What happened? It looked like you got, like, *stuck* in the water."

Brett was about to say "That's exactly what happened" but stopped himself and squinted. "Hey." He pointed over to the edge of the *porte-cochère*, where a grassy lawn stretched out between the institute and the street. "Is it . . . it's raining *harder* over there. Do you guys see that, too?"

Before anyone could answer him, Brett got to his feet and walked over. Gabe and Kaz and Lily quickly joined him.

In a patch maybe twenty feet by twenty feet, the rain

drilled down so hard that it had knocked some of the grass loose, exposing bits of bare earth. Bits that connected and made lines and loops and angles. The rain was *writing* on the ground, and as Brett watched, a time and an address became clear. And another line below that:

You'll find answers here. Don't be seen. Be careful. G

Beside him, Lily turned to Kaz. "Have you seen enough yet, Skeptic Lad? Still think there's a logical explanation for all this?"

But Brett didn't catch Kaz's answer, because a flash of movement drew his eyes up to a window on the institute's top floor. A window where a gray-haired figure stood, watching him, one hand raised in either greeting or good-bye.

8

Gabe pulled the collar of his jacket tighter around his neck as a frigid wind whistled around them. He, Kaz, Brett, and Lily all huddled in the doorway of a closed bank on the edge of the Mission District, trying and not succeeding at staying dry. Thunder still rolled and crashed above them in a relentless barrage.

They had spent the last half hour, partly on the cable car and partly on foot, listening to Brett tell them everything that Greta Jaeger had said.

Gabe had been deeply, profoundly unhappy about having to move out of San Francisco, but at least relocating to a different city and getting settled in a new school was something he understood. This? Elemental magick and strange creatures and doomsday cults? *What am I doing?*

But he had the answer to his own question. His home was destroyed. His uncle had been kidnapped.

As unbelievably, wildly impossible as everything that had happened today was—it hardly mattered next to that one line in Uncle Steve's email.

I am SO CLOSE to getting answers about Aria's location.

Gabe had barely dared to let himself think about what that meant. After all this time, could his mother be *alive*?

He had to figure all this out. He *had* to.

"So, yeah," Brett said. "That's the last of it. She said if I don't control my element, it could, uh, take over. Do bad stuff to me." He glanced around at his friends. "I guess that applies to you guys, too?"

"A cult." Kaz folded his arms, his face sour. "Of course it's a cult. And not just any cult! A magickal doomsday cult! The only thing that would make it better is if aliens figured in somehow."

"Have I gone on record about how dumb it is for us to be here?" Lily gestured at the dark, hulking building up the street. Its massive, blocky shape was an eyesore amid the brightly colored row houses and enormous, intricate works of graffiti art they'd passed on the way. "We're literally here because of the ravings of a crazy woman. A crazy *murderer*, assuming that nurse knew what she was talking about."

"But this is the only clue we've got." Gabe wished that wasn't the case, but as Uncle Steve was fond of saying, If wishes were horses we'd all ride. Gabe had always thought Uncle Steve's old-fashioned sayings were *extremely* lame. But now, thinking about them just made Gabe miss him. "We can't trust the cops. And we can't ask anyone else. The stuff we've seen today is nothing *but* crazy."

Lily shrugged, frowning. "I can't argue with that."

"Still no sign of those hunter things." Kaz peered up and down the street. "Either we're sneakier than I think we are, or there aren't many hunters to go around." He looked again. "Actually, I haven't seen *anybody* in the last twenty minutes. Guess we're the only ones too dumb to be out in the rain."

Gabe squinted at the building to which Greta Jaeger had directed them: the Liberty Street Theatre. Brett knew the place already. He'd told them on the way that he'd been planning a field trip there, to do a little urban spelunking. "The place has been abandoned since the forties," he'd said. "I'm kind of amazed it's still standing."

Kaz turned to Lily. "It's getting pretty late. Shouldn't we tell our families where we are?"

Gabe frowned, and Lily seemed to read his thoughts. "We can't tell them the truth," she said.

Kaz shook his head. "Considering what we've seen so far, along with what Crazy Lady told Brett, the less our families know about all this, the better off they'll be. But if we don't tell them *something*, they're going to call the police. Right?"

Solemnly, one by one, the four of them nodded. Lily took over the nuts and bolts, sending texts to Kaz's parents and her and Brett's grandmother, telling them that they were staying over at each other's houses. Gabe pretended not to notice when Lily realized he had no one to text—that the strictest parent out of any of theirs wasn't around to make excuses to. Gabe half-expected Brett to come up with some words of support, but Brett had fallen silent again, just staring at the theater.

"All right." Gabe stood up when the last of the texts had been sent. "Let's see what this place is all about."

Kaz peered at the theater. "What do you think's in there?"

Brett gave him an elaborate shrug. "*Really* wish I knew. But I don't have Clue One."

"I hate when people say this on TV," Lily said quietly, "but *there's only one way to find out.*"

Keeping close to the buildings, as much to minimize the soaking they were taking from the storm as to try to remain unseen, Gabe led his friends up the street to the theater. He tried the front door and found it locked. *Of course.* He pointed them around the side of the building to a narrow alleyway, where they took not-very-effective shelter under a fire escape.

"Okay," Kaz said, rainwater dripping off the hood of his poncho, "what now?"

"Now you get away from this place!"

Everyone jumped, and Lily clapped her hands over her

mouth, as Jackson Wright materialized right behind them. He looked the same as he had in Gabe's foyer. Glowing faintly. *Intensely* creepy. And, judging by the expression on his face, kind of irritated.

"I know you are fools, but I did not realize you were all utterly mad." Jackson's words came out even more stiffly than usual. "You ignored my warning about the constables, but you *must* listen to me here. The danger in which you will place yourselves if you venture into this theater cannot be overstated. I speak not of faux policemen and diabolical canines. If you find a way into this house of horrors, you will face the full might of the Eternal Dawn. It would be suicide. Plain and simple."

"Nothing you've ever said to us has been 'plain and simple,'" Gabe shot back. "Look, Greta told us this is our one shot at getting some answers. And maybe saving my uncle."

Jackson's eyebrows tried to climb up into his hair. He laughed, an icy sound that made parts of Gabe shrivel up. "You take counsel from *Greta Jaeger*? I shall wager she neglected to mention *why* she is incarcerated in that odious place."

When Lily spoke, there wasn't even a trace of fear in her voice. Gabe envied that. "The nurse already told us. She said she was in there for murder."

"*Multiple* murders," Jackson said. "Two victims. Nine years ago. Does that sound familiar, Gabriel?"

Jackson's words seemed to echo in Gabe's ears as his stomach sank several inches lower and clenched like a fist. Jackson went on, confirming his worst fears: "Greta is in that institution because she is the one who killed your parents."

Someone gasped. Lily? Gabe looked over—no, it was Kaz. Lily and Brett both just looked angry. Gabe took a step backward and steadied himself with one hand on the theater's rough stone wall. *My parents were* murdered? Uncle Steve had always told him they died in a car wreck.

But it's not like that'd be the only thing Uncle Steve hid from me.

But wait, Uncle Steve's email had made it sound like Gabe's mother might still be alive! And if that were true, then maybe Jackson Wright didn't know what he was talking about? *Or he's lying to my face.* Gabe wouldn't put it past him. How did Ghost Boy even know so much about this Eternal Dawn?

Gabe's confusion slammed around in his head and his heart and quickly turned to anger. He faced Jackson. "What exactly are you, anyway? Why should we believe a single word you say?"

Jackson sighed and rolled his eyes. "Apart from how I *clearly* told you the truth about those constables at your door? Fine. I will enlighten you." He moved closer to Gabe, and his faintly glowing eyes narrowed to slits. "I am someone who has stood very close to the edge of the precipice you now stand upon yourself. Someone who knows what the Dawn and their agents are ready and willing to do."

Gabe snarled. "What a bunch of garbage." Jackson took a

step back, which gave Gabe a fierce stab of satisfaction. "You just say a bunch of stuff that doesn't mean anything! Look, either tell us what you know, straight out, or go back to wherever you came from!"

The look of shock swiftly fled from Jackson's features, replaced by his usual unbearable smugness. "Knowledge is dangerous. You will learn that soon enough, but for now I am attempting to keep you safe. *Again.* So listen to me, all of you: *do not go into the theater.*"

Gabe scowled at Jackson for several long heartbeats. "All right, *all right.* We'll take your advice this time."

Jackson folded his arms across his chest. "Good. I expect I shall see you all again . . . *very* soon."

His translucent body faded, becoming wispy, smokelike, and Brett yelled, *"Wait!"* But where Jackson Wright had stood, there was only darkness and rain.

Gabe turned to Brett. "What? What were you going to ask him?"

Brett averted his eyes again. "I—I just, I didn't know why he wasn't being straight with us. Seemed like he knew a lot more than he was saying, y'know?"

Gabe felt relieved. Brett might have seemed aloof before, but clearly he was paying attention. Gabe started walking toward the back of the theater. "Come on. Let's see if the back door's locked, too."

From behind him Lily said, *"Huh?"*

Kaz grabbed his elbow. "Hold on! You just promised Ghost Boy that we'd stay away from this place!"

Gabe looked down at Kaz but didn't stop walking. "Listen to yourself. This morning you didn't even believe in ghosts." Gabe tried a smile to soften his words. And maybe to make himself feel a little better. Or at least less awful. He'd always loved his uncle, and still did, but how much had Uncle Steve kept from him? How much of Gabe's life was a bald-faced lie? He intended to find out.

Gabe made it to the back door, which was of course locked up just as tightly as the front one. He turned to face his friends. "Look, that Jackson kid *was* right about the cops, but if getting inside here helps me find out what's happened to Uncle Steve, I don't care how dangerous it is." He paused, looking each of them in the eye. "But this is about me and my uncle. If you don't want to come with me, I totally understand."

Brett and Kaz looked at each other. Gabe couldn't blame them for their uncertainty. Lily, on the other hand, nodded slowly. "Let me talk to Kaz and my brother for a minute, would you?"

Lily led Brett and Kaz away from him, and the three of them put their heads together. Gabe stood and waited, grateful for the poncho, though he wondered if his soaked-all-the-way-through feet would ever be warm again.

Gabe found himself hoping his friends would come with him. He knew he had to face whatever lay inside the theater, but—especially if it turned out to be as dangerous as Jackson Wright made it sound—he really didn't want to do it alone.

After about two minutes his friends came back. Gently, Lily said, "Gabe, if you really want to do this, we've got your back." Kaz and Brett both nodded.

It took Gabe a moment to get the words out, working around the sudden rush of warmth her words gave him. Even in the icy rain. "This is why I didn't want to move away." He fought like crazy to keep from tearing up. Brett and Kaz would *never* let him hear the end of that. "You guys are the best."

"So?" Brett asked. "What'll it be, *jefe*?"

"I don't trust Ghost Boy. I want to take a look inside this place."

Kaz nodded. "Then we're with you."

It hadn't taken more than a puff from her asthma inhaler and a running start for Lily to monkey-climb up to the fire escape. She was barely heavy enough to pull down the extendable ladder, but down it had come, and one unlocked third-floor window later, all four of them stood inside the Liberty Street Theatre, peering through dense shadows and trying not to breathe too loudly.

They were in what might have been one of the theater's business offices or maybe an actor's dressing room. The place was pitch-dark, but with the help of their phones' flashlights, they found a stairwell and descended to the main floor.

"This doesn't make any sense at all," Brett said once they reached the theater's lobby. He shined his phone's flashlight around. "Shut down for ages, and everything looks brand-spanking-new?"

Gabe couldn't argue. If he'd walked in off the street, he would have thought the theater was open for business. The plush red carpet was clean; no dust had settled on any surface; the lobby sported polished wood and brass finishings that gleamed as if freshly shined. Even the glass at the concession stand was clean and free of fingerprints. "Come on." Gabe pointed to the big doors that opened into the theater proper. "Let's keep going."

The four of them walked down the main aisle, past row after row of plush, scarlet upholstered theater seats, toward the stage, above which hung a massive glass globe, easily four feet across. The globe glowed with a faint golden light, and something like smoke swirled inside it.

"Don't tell me that's some ancient version of a disco ball," Lily said, regarding the globe with suspicion.

Kaz piped up, "What's a disco ball?"

Before Gabe or anyone else could answer him, a sound echoed through the theater, loud, unmistakable: a massive lock disengaging. Then another, and another, followed by the metallic creaks of multiple doors swinging open.

This place wasn't going to be deserted for much longer.

"We've got to hide!" Gabe whispered. "Come on!" He

sprinted the rest of the way down the aisle and around the empty orchestra pit, and clambered up onto the stage. Huge, heavy red curtains hung on either side of it, and he led his friends behind one of them, deep into a pool of shadow. The curtain didn't quite touch the stage, and once he'd made sure everyone was hidden behind him, Gabe flattened himself and peered out through the gap.

The sight that greeted him turned his blood to ice water.

Figures in black, red-lined, hooded cloaks had begun to file into the theater from side doors that Gabe hadn't noticed at first. Their robes were plain except for a single image woven in gold: a rising sun with outstretched rays glinted above each of their hearts. Some of the cloaked figures wore featureless silver masks, blank but for eyeholes. Others' faces were simply concealed in the shadows of their hoods. There were dozens of them. Maybe hundreds. "Jackson was right," Gabe whispered over his shoulder. "We *shouldn't* have come in here!"

Brett tapped him on the back of the neck and pointed. On the far side of the stage, in full view of where they were trying to hide, another door had swung open, and something huge and rectangular was emerging through the doorway. Gabe scrambled to his feet and, glancing around wildly, stabbed a finger at a narrow ladder on the wall behind them. "Up!" he whispered. It was the only direction they could go. "Come on!"

Moving as fast and as quietly as he could, Gabe mounted the ladder, which soared up into total darkness. After two or three minutes that felt like ages, Gabe and his friends arrived at a narrow catwalk suspended far above the stage. It felt solid enough, and didn't creak when he stepped on it, so Gabe crept out to the middle. If they were going to be stuck up here, he intended to get as good a view as he could. He had to avoid a number of tools and lights lying on the metal walkway; the last thing he needed was to knock something off and have it clang to the stage below. He wanted to tell his friends, "You don't have to come out here with me if you don't want to," but he also didn't want to risk being heard; and Lily, right behind him, showed no hesitation at all as she followed him out to a good vantage point.

Peering straight down, Gabe felt yet another gut-punch when he saw the large rectangular object being pushed onto the stage. It was a series of metal dog cages, piled onto a rolling platform. Frightened whimpering emanated from inside them. *What are they going to do with those dogs?* He was pretty sure he didn't want to know—but he didn't think he'd have a choice.

A black-cloaked man took the stage. His voice boomed out over the assembled audience. "Greetings, noble brethren. After over a hundred years of toil, dawn is breaking at last." Gabe couldn't stop his eyes from rolling. *Oh, jeez, he sounds just like Jackson.* "Finally, the Great Work is near completion. The crucial nature of this ritual cannot be overstated. Therefore, Primus herself shall lead it."

At the name Primus, the crowd fell even more silent than

it had been. Then they began to *hum*. Very softly, a deep, dark note that rolled out through the theater, a single tone of respect and reverence from a throng of voices. Gabe wondered if this was the Eternal Dawn's version of a drumroll. Whatever it was, it made him want to stick ice picks in his ears.

A woman in the same kind of black, hooded cloak slowly, majestically mounted the stairs to the stage. Her robe was embroidered with more gold than the others. The humming continued until she reached the stage's center and faced the crowd, at which it cut off abruptly, leaving an overwhelming silence as profound as the depths of the ocean. The woman could have whispered into that void and been heard all the way at the back of the theater.

"My brothers and sisters, the Emerald Tablet has at long last been unlocked. Dawn is indeed upon us!" A murmuring from the crowd, then . . . excitement. Anticipation. "And we have captured the descendant of the blood who unlocked it."

With one voice, the crowd breathed out, "The blood has power."

Wait a minute. Wait, wait, wait a minute! Gabe's mind raced as he struggled to catch up. *They've* captured *someone? The book got all weird and turned green when* I *touched it. With my bloody finger! I unlocked the Tablet—or at least I think I did. Who else has the same blood that I have? Who did they capture, thinking they're me?*

The woman—that had to be Primus—went on. "We will

need the Emerald Tablet to complete the Great Work. Our interrogations of the captive bore no fruit. Therefore, we will need more hunters to search the city." She cast a glance at the dog cages, and the whimpering grew louder.

More thoughts spun out of control in Gabe's head. *My mom had the same blood as me. If my mom is still alive, could she be the captive they're talking about?*

Kaz reached across Lily's back and touched Gabe's arm. He didn't make a sound, but he mouthed the words exaggeratedly: *We should go!*

Gabe didn't know what to do, but he couldn't bring himself to move. *What if Mom is here? I have to know!*

From inside her cloak, Primus produced a piece of red chalk. Kneeling, she turned in a slow circle, inscribing an ornate, complicated series of glyphs and runes on the floor. Gabe could tell she had practiced this many times before. There was no hesitation, no wasted motion. The circle just flowed out of her.

When she finished, a trapdoor opened in the stage and a strange machine rose up out of the floor. It was ancient looking, with tarnished knobs and gears and a single huge lever protruding from one side. Primus stepped out of the circle. She took hold of the machine's lever and nodded in the direction of the dog cages.

Every square inch of Gabe's skin puckered into gooseflesh.

Another cultist stepped forward and opened the cage doors, one by one. There were five dogs—five medium-size, filthy, fur-matted mutts—and as if in some kind of canine trance, they stepped out of their cages and walked across the stage toward the circle.

"They look like strays," Lily whispered. If she hadn't been so close to Gabe's ear, he wouldn't have heard her. "They're defenseless. What're they going to do to them?"

Gabe was afraid he knew. The contents of his stomach threatened to rise.

Primus pulled the lever. A hole irised open in the glowing globe, and some of that swirling, golden, smoky essence curled out like a tentacle. The first of the strays stepped into the chalk circle, and the smoky tendril lanced down, striking the dog like a snake.

Just like the swirls of gold dust from the Tablet struck us!

The dog threw back its head and howled, and the smoke enveloped it, hiding it from view entirely. Gabe was glad of that. He didn't think he could take actually watching what happened to the poor animal, especially when the sounds started. Wet, ragged, ripping sounds that made Gabe want to retch up everything he'd eaten in the last week.

When the smoke cleared, a skinless, faceless hunter stood where the dog used to be, snarling and snapping its slavering jaws. Another cultist came forward, holding a—Gabe cringed—holding a *branding iron*. The cultist pressed the brand against the hunter's muzzle. Then he stepped back and shouted a command. "Heel. Obey your mistress." The hunter growled and gnashed its teeth, but moved to stand behind Primus. Orderly. Obedient.

Gabe risked a look over at Lily, and caught Kaz wiping away a tear. Lily's knuckles turned white as she gripped the catwalk's rail.

Below them, one after another, the remaining stray dogs were transformed into hunters. Gabe's stomach rolled into a tight little knot as he realized the new pack of hunters were standing directly below him. *Don't look up don't look up don't look up!* He hoped against hope that the creatures' lack of noses meant they couldn't smell very well.

The opening in the globe sealed itself shut. The hunters waited quietly, but from the twitching of their weird, barbed tails, they seemed to be filled with excitement. Primus inscribed another chalk circle on the stage. When she finished and stood, the globe flashed and pulsed and thrummed, its vibrations traveling throughout the theater as if it was revving up.

"Now," Primus addressed the crowd, "on to the great ritual of Exchange that we have awaited for generations." She gestured with both hands, and more cultists scrambled to the four corners of the theater. They started setting up what looked like altars. One was topped with a brazier of fiery coals, one with a basin of water, one with a small cairn of stones. Gabe realized with a jolt how similar the setup was to the underground chamber where the four of them had bound themselves to the elements.

Primus's voice rang out like a bell. "Bring out the descendant of the blood!"

The doors at the back of the theater opened, and four cultists came in, bearing a stretcher between them. A stretcher with someone strapped to it. Gabe's heart whirred in his chest.

The stretcher passed under one of the theater's ornate chandeliers, and Gabe caught a glimpse of all-too-familiar white-blond hair.

Uncle Steve!

Gabe went light-headed with relief to see his uncle. But this surge of elation didn't last. They'd found Steve, and he was alive, but he was also in the grip of a bunch of insane fanatics!

"What are they going to do to him?" Kaz whispered.

After seeing what the cultists had done to those poor dogs, Gabe didn't intend to wait around to find out. He kept an eye on the stage, scanning the catwalk for weapons. The poles at their feet—"gaffs," he thought they were called—wouldn't be much use against those hunters and a theater full of cultists, but they were better than nothing.

The cultists carried the stretcher up onto the stage. Now Gabe could see that Uncle Steve was unconscious, or maybe drugged. He just lay there motionless, though they'd strapped down his arms and his leg anyway. Primus glided over to him.

"This man, Steven Conway, unlocked the Emerald Tablet. It has been testified that the Tablet can be activated only by a descendant of our Great Founder, Jonathan Thorne."

"He who shall bring the dawn," the crowd chanted.

"And so we are faced with a unique and precious opportunity," Primus continued. "The Principle of Balance tells us that Steven Conway can be sent to Arcadia in exchange for the Great Founder himself."

"Blood for blood," the crowd said with one voice.

"The blood has power, and with it the Great Founder can finally be returned to us from Arcadia after all these years!"

Gabe had been trying to figure out how to get his friends and Uncle Steve out of here, but Primus's words tied his brain into knots. Watching the scene below was like turning on a movie an hour into its running time. He already knew that the world was different than he had ever imagined: full of magick and elements and strange cults. But with every sentence, Primus underscored how little Gabe truly knew. Arcadia? This Great Founder? Gabe didn't have a clue what any of it meant. Now more than ever he wanted his uncle. He *needed* him.

Uncle Steve was within sight, but still so far away. And Gabe now understood why. *It's all a mistake. A colossal mistake!* The Eternal Dawn must have tracked the opening of the Tablet to the Conways' house, and the only person they'd found there was Uncle Steve. They must have assumed he'd been the one to unlock it. But Uncle Steve hadn't opened the Tablet: Gabe had.

All of this—every single bit of it—is my fault!

Meanwhile, the crowd applauded and cheered. Through the din Gabe heard the same words chanted over and over:

"Blood for blood! Blood for blood! Blood for blood!" His mind reeling, Gabe tried to steady himself by reaching out for the catwalk's railing—and misjudged the distance. Only by a fraction of an inch, but it was enough. Lily and Kaz sprang forward to try to catch him, but it was too late.

With a sickening lurch, Gabe fell off the catwalk and plummeted toward the stage and the pack of hunters waiting below.

9

Gabe had just enough time for his depressingly short life to flash before his eyes before he landed on something that felt like a really huge, really soft pillow.

Except he hadn't landed. He was suspended facedown, no more than ten feet below the catwalk, staring at the hunters sitting placidly below. Gabe clenched his jaws shut as tightly as he could to keep from screaming. Before his brain could begin to make sense of what was happening, he began to rise, swiftly but gently, as if he were being hoisted by a thousand tiny ropes. After a few long seconds he landed back on the catwalk next to Lily.

Lily wobbled, and slumped down on her backside. Her eyes

swam in and out of focus. Brett slid a steadying arm around her shoulders.

"How did you *do* that?" Kaz whispered.

Lily blinked. "I don't know. I just . . . I saw Gabe falling, and I reached for him, and when I did, I . . . I *felt the air*. Trillions and trillions of molecules of it, and I just gathered up a bunch of them and slipped them underneath him." She looked Gabe in the eye. "I knew I could do it. I *knew*. And I think that made it happen."

"How scientific. I almost forgot that that's *totally impossible*." Kaz sounded as if he was trying to pack as much sarcasm into his words as he could, but the attempt fell flat. Kaz's tight, tortured expression confirmed it. He'd taken his best shot at playing the skeptic, but now even he had to admit it: logic was out and magick was in.

Gabe sneaked a look at the stage below them, expecting to see every eye (and eyeless face) turned their way, but no one seemed to have noticed his fall. He felt a spike of intense relief at that, but it faded almost instantly when he caught sight of Uncle Steve, still unconscious and strapped down on the stage below. The cult members had put together another altar, and his uncle's stretcher lay on top of it.

The leader, Primus, started speaking in a language Gabe had never heard before, and that was saying something. Uncle Steve's studies covered three continents, and Gabe had been exposed to dozens of languages, including dead tongues like

Latin and Sanskrit. The words coming out of Primus's mouth, however, didn't sound like anything Gabe had ever heard. They didn't even sound human.

"Zxarna vrahmu otvortse. Dvai shvioutei pivuntxa."

In response, the crowd started chanting. *"Taigho shviunta. Taigho shviunta."*

Primus continued. Gabe thought he felt the temperature in the theater drop a degree with each syllable she spoke. *"Dvai shvioutei pivuntxa, majia povrunshei taigho shviunta!"*

How on earth was he going to get Uncle Steve out of this?

The crowd got more animated. *"Taigho shviunta! Taigho shviunta!"*

"What are they saying?" Brett whispered, and Gabe was about to reply along the lines of *Maybe we shouldn't be talking so much since we're trying to hide up here* when he looked down at the hunters again.

All five of them were sitting stock-still, heads lifted, "staring" straight at him with their featureless faces.

Kaz had noticed them, too, and said, "Umm, guys," but it was too late to move. The hunters broke out into bone-chilling howls and screams, and bolted straight up the walls, making a beeline for the catwalk.

The crowd's chanting cut off. Primus's voice, in English this time, sliced through the air. *"Do not stop! We cannot let the ritual be interrupted! The hunters will handle whatever disturbance lurks above!"*

The crowd started chanting again—*"Taigho shviunta! Taigho shviunta!"*—as the first of the hunters reached the catwalk. Gabe snatched up one of the pole-like gaffs and tried to swing it like a baseball bat, but it banged off one of the catwalk's support struts and almost made his hands go numb. Instead, as the hunter leaped at him, Gabe held the pole like a spear and jammed it into the hunter's mouth. Sulfur-stench breath washed over Gabe as the beast howled in surprise and pain, and pitched off the catwalk's edge—but instead of falling, it hooked a claw into the edge of the walkway and ran *upside down* back along the catwalk's length.

"I scared one away!" Gabe shouted. "I think! Grab those poles and jab 'em in the snout!"

Kaz and Lily picked up two more gaffs, while Brett grabbed a big monkey wrench, and the four of them tried their best to make a stand. If the catwalk hadn't provided such a narrow path, the hunters would have overwhelmed them instantly, but as it was, the creatures had only two ways to approach. Several painful pokes in the nose and mouth sent the rest of them scurrying away.

Or so Gabe thought. He'd been so focused on the ones right in front of him, he hadn't paid any attention to the ones that had retreated. When he caught sight of them, he only had enough time to say, "Guys, *hold on!*"

Because two of the hunters had been busily gnawing through the catwalk's main supports.

One of the supports snapped in half, and the catwalk tilted, almost dumping all four of them off the end. Kaz gripped the railing with both hands, his gaff forgotten, and screamed at Lily, *"Do that thing! That thing where you levitated Gabe!"*

Lily apparently had just enough presence of mind to savor Kaz's change of heart. "You mean that *impossible* thing?" She might have given Kaz more of a hard time, but at that moment the other main support gave way, and the entire catwalk dropped like a stone.

For about fifteen feet.

Before Gabe's stomach could even catch up with him—it seemed to have stayed in the rafters—Lily's eyes turned a solid grayish white. She concentrated, and the catwalk trembled, slowed, and floated down toward the stage below.

Brett's head snapped up. "Look out!"

The hunters leaped for the descending catwalk, but Brett, Kaz, and Gabe managed to swat them away. They landed on their feet, though, like giant cats, obviously unhurt and even more bloodthirsty.

As soon as the catwalk dropped below the fly curtains and into full view of the crowd, the cultists broke off their chanting again. Some of them even jumped out of their seats and ran for the exits. *Not enough of them, though.* Gabe saw dozens of silver-masked weirdos head for the stage, ready to pounce on them once they landed.

Primus broke into English again: "Stop them! They cannot

be allowed to interfere!" Then she picked up the alien chanting, Gabe was pretty sure in midsentence. Another cultist, the one who'd announced Primus when she first came to the stage, took over.

"You remember what happened the last time a ritual like this went wrong! Protect the Primus and the Sacred Circle *at all costs*!"

The catwalk touched down on the stage, but Gabe didn't think they had anywhere to run. The hunters had regrouped behind them, and a couple dozen cultists, braver than the rest, had taken the stage and advanced on them with daggers and billy clubs.

Lily knew she could catch me. And that's what made it happen.
That thought echoed in Gabe's mind.

The whole world seemed to slow down around him. Kind of like when his life flashed before his eyes, except a lot more interesting this time, because *he knew he could do it, too.* Because he already *had* done it. Who grabbed energy out of the electrical sockets in his bedroom and set the room on fire? *He did.* That was no freak bolt of lightning. He'd done that himself. And maybe he didn't know exactly how, but maybe he didn't have to. *After all, I don't know how the internet works, but I use it every day!*

Gabe tried to remember the way it had felt on the ferry. When his mind seemed to flow out of his skull and feel the water and the air and the rocks all around him. Except this time . . .

This time I'm going for fire, just like I did back in my bedroom.

The blazing brazier on the stage pulsed and throbbed like a heart. The power of the theater's electric lights flowed through the wires as if they were veins and arteries. Small pinpoints of power jumped out at him from the cultists themselves, coming into focus as glowing, burning rectangles. *Cell phones*, Gabe realized. *Freaking cell phones!*

"We can do this, guys! *We can do this, because we've done it before!* Lily saved my life with air! Brett must have caused that massive wave on the ferry! I blasted the hunters with fire back at my house! *We can do this!*"

Voice shaking, Kaz wailed, "*I* haven't done any of that! What am I supposed to do?"

Gabe's eyes fell on the stone cairn on top of the altar the cultists had set up. "Those rocks! Kaz, do like Greta Jaeger said! *Take control!*"

One of the cultists, a huge, burly man holding a knife so big it qualified as a sword, rushed straight for Kaz and bellowed like a roaring bear. "We'll cut you into confetti for this!"

Kaz shrieked and threw out his hands—

—and the rocks flew out of the cairn like bullets from a machine gun. They slammed into the huge cultist with resounding, crunching thumps, one to the kidneys, one square in the rib cage, and one straight into his ear. The cultist staggered, eyes unfocusing, and the last stone caught him solidly in the hip. That impact knocked him off balance and sent him hurtling from the stage. He crashed into the orchestra pit, the huge knife falling from limp hands, and groaned feebly.

A frightened, collective gasp echoed through the other cultists. As one, they took a step back, suddenly unsure.

Kaz looked at Gabe. His eyes had turned solid, stony gray, and a massive grin spread across his face. "Well, what do you know?"

Gabe whirled to Lily and Brett. "See? *See?* We can do this! We can take control!" He faced the hunters. Unlike the cultists, they didn't act scared at all. Gabe filled his lungs with air, and when he let the words loose, they whooshed and crackled and roared like an inferno:

"I am bound to *fire!*"

Gabe's vision became tinted in fiery orange, as if brilliant light was flowing from his eyes. He could almost feel the heat. Whatever the hunters saw made them back up a step. He lifted an arm, and slender bolts of lightning sprang from every electrical socket in the theater and converged on Gabe's hand . . .

Which *caught fire.*

Gabe extended one finger toward the pack of hunters—"Shoo!"—and sprayed a cone of flame across the back of the stage. The hunters scattered, howling and yelping, leaving trails of smoke behind them as they fled.

Beside him, Lily's eyes again turned gray white, and her voice howled through the theater like the coldest, most cutting winter wind: "I am bound to *air*!" A blast like a tornado picked up ten cultists and scattered them toward the back of the theater, each body flying through the air like a tossed rag doll. Gabe watched, wincing, as the cultists came to bone-cracking halts against walls, doors, and ornate support columns.

Brett's words seemed to come from far away. Deep, distorted, as if spoken from the bottom of the ocean. *"I am bound to water."* Gabe looked up at the ceiling, where the sprinkler system burst to life, filling the theater with water. Water that twisted and curved in midair. As Gabe watched, the water coalesced into rock-hard projectiles of ice that rained down on a dozen more cultists, bashing noses and jaws and slicing upraised hands until they battered the consciousness out of their targets. The cultists all went down in heaps.

But that still left at least fifteen cultists out there amid the seats, and every one of them produced some kind of weapon and charged toward the stage. Kaz shouted, "What do I do? I'm out of rocks!"

Gabe put a hand on Kaz's shoulder. "Kaz. You're bound to *earth*. What do you think this building is sitting on?"

Kaz gaped at him for a second. Then—whirling and growling through gritted teeth—Kaz raised both arms like a conductor demanding more volume from his orchestra.

His voice emanated from somewhere directly below them, enormous and raspy and impossibly deep, like the plates of the earth's crust grinding together. "I. AM. BOUND. TO. *EARTH*!"

The building trembled. Dust cascaded from the ceiling, mixing with the water from the sprinklers, as the floor beneath their feet bucked and shook. Gabe had never heard the noise a rock slide made before, but he felt sure it sounded very much like this.

A wall of stone burst up through the floor of the theater, right in front of the charging cultists. Gabe winced as he heard the sound of multiple faces crashing into the unforgiving rock. But Kaz wasn't finished. He thrust out his hands and curled his fingers like claws, and the rock wall *curved*, surrounding the injured cult members in a cage of stone.

Panting, Kaz let his hands drop and sagged into Gabe. "Oh my God," he breathed. "I want to do this all day, every day, for the rest of my life!"

But a voice cut through the cries and whimpers from the dismantled cultists: Primus, still speaking the alien words. Gabe shook his head, clearing it—in the middle of all the chaos, he'd honestly forgotten about Primus—and focused on her, just in time to see her raise a slim silver dagger, poised over Uncle Steve's chest.

Ice-cold with terror, Gabe screamed, *"Stop her stop her SOMEBODY STOP HER!"*

He broke into a run, but Brett slid past him, riding an ice-slick trail across the stage. As he moved, Brett shucked off his backpack, shouted, "Catch!" and flung it to Kaz, who caught it with both hands. Without that extra weight, Brett zoomed toward the altar faster than an Olympic speed skater. Gabe tried to follow, Kaz and Lily right beside him, but the hunters came out of nowhere, four of them darting between Gabe and his uncle.

Lily shrieked, *"Bad dogs!"* and made a huge sweeping motion with her arms. A gale-force wind picked up the creatures and tumbled them through an open side door. The wind slammed the door shut behind them, and Kaz made a crushing motion with one hand; the foundation beneath the door buckled, crimping it shut. Gabe heard the hunters howling as they threw themselves against the door from the other side but couldn't get through.

Gabe sprinted past Kaz and Lily. He saw Brett crash into the altar holding up Uncle Steve's stretcher just as Primus screamed, *"Netch shvee oetveer!"* and plunged the silver dagger into his uncle's chest.

Gabe gasped as if his own chest had been stabbed.

"NO!" Gabe drew back a hand and made a motion like throwing a punch, and a fireball the size of a cinder block streaked across the stage and struck Primus square in the stomach. The impact jerked the dagger out of Uncle Steve and knocked the woman away, leaving her shouting and frantically slapping flames out of her robes.

Gabe took one running step toward the altar before what felt like a ton of slimy bricks crashed into him. Lily hadn't gotten rid of all the hunters after all. The fifth one had just knocked Gabe sprawling toward the stage's edge. As the hunter stalked closer to him, Gabe shouted to Brett at the top of his lungs, "HELP MY UNCLE! PLEASE!"

Over the hunter's skinless shoulder, Gabe could see Uncle Steve begin to convulse, and even as Brett tried to pull him off the altar, blood began to spread out of the wound. But it wasn't normal bleeding. Instead of simply pooling onto the floor, the blood slid along the length of Uncle Steve's body, enveloping him like a bizarre red cocoon.

"What—what is that?" Kaz asked in horror.

Gabe had no idea. It was as if the blood had a mind of its own.

Brett had been applying direct pressure to the wound, trying to stop the bleeding. But instead of slowing, the weird blood membrane flowed up over his hands, and then his wrists. Gabe watched his friend try to pull away from the blood, but it seemed to grip him fast. Whatever it was, Brett was just as stuck in it as Uncle Steve.

From somewhere on the other side of the altar, Primus's scream rang out: "A *null sanguis!* The ritual is corrupted! Run, Brethren! *Run!*"

Gabe knew the Latin words "*null sanguis*" translated roughly to "no blood." What did that mean?

He didn't have time to consider it because, with a shock, Gabe realized the blood membrane was the same thing he'd seen when he first touched the Emerald Tablet back in Uncle Steve's office. After he'd passed out, in his dream he'd been chained to a stone slab and looking up at a film of blood.

Gabe got back onto his feet, blasted the hunter away from him with a burst of flame, and tried once more to reach his uncle. But by then it was too late. The blood membrane had almost completely enveloped Uncle Steve and Brett and begun to *grow*, expanding like a massive, grotesque balloon. Vaguely, Gabe was aware that many of the cultists who remained in the theater were bolting for the exits. Primus was gone, too.

His path finally clear, Gabe lunged across the stage toward the altar, arms outstretched, ready to plunge them into the membrane. *I'll haul them both out myself! I can't lose my uncle* and *Brett! I've got to help them, I've* got *to!*

But he never reached the cocoon. Kaz grabbed him around the waist and hauled him backward.

Gabe shoved Kaz away. "What are you *doing*?"

"What are *you* doing?" Kaz demanded as Lily rushed over to join them. "They could both be dead in there! You want to die, too?"

Lily grabbed Kaz, her eyes wild. "Is Brett in there? *Is Brett in there?* We have to get him out! We *have* to!"

Kaz's eyes flashed gray, and when he clamped his hands on Gabe's and Lily's upper arms, the sudden strength in his grip made them both gasp. Kaz's voice was deeper and more, well, gravelly than Gabe had ever heard it. "Of course we'll help them! But we can't help if we're *dead*! And we're *gonna* be dead if we don't get away from *that*!"

As Kaz dragged him and Lily away, Gabe blinked and looked past Kaz at the blood cocoon. He couldn't see Uncle Steve or Brett at all now. The membrane swelled and swelled, until it was more than half the height of the massive theater—and off to one side, a tiny bubble-like protrusion appeared. It detached itself from the larger mass, hit the ground, and split open . . . to reveal a boy. A blood-and-goo-covered boy, but definitely a young human male.

Lily shouted, "Brett? *Brett!*"

Gabe's heart almost broke at the relief he heard in Lily's voice. Because, while he couldn't tell who the boy was, he knew with complete certainty that it wasn't Brett Hernandez. He thought that deep down maybe Lily knew it, too, but her grief and desperation were making her grasp at any possibility that her brother was safe.

Then something *enormous* pushed against the inside of the main mass. A roar erupted from it that shook the building all the way to its foundation . . . and a gargantuan, leathery wing burst through the red membrane, its clawed tip brushing the theater's ceiling.

10

For a long, agonizing moment, all Gabe could do was stare. Bit by bit, the horrendous sight started to make sense. The *thing* that had emerged from the membrane had no skin, he could tell that for sure, just sinewy muscle, like the hunters. And okay, that was definitely a head, because a mouth split the featureless muscle and bone, revealing teeth as long as a grown man's arm. The mouth got worse: another, slightly smaller set of teeth was nestled just inside the first one.

A horrifying sense of déjà vu swept through Gabe. *I've seen this thing before.*

A second wing unfurled. Another set sprang free after the first one *and another one after that*, until six wings trembled and twitched in an undulating coordination that made Gabe's stomach clench with recognition.

This is one of the creatures I saw flying around the towers in that horrible version of San Francisco! Did that mean . . . had he seen the place Primus was talking about? Had he gotten a glimpse of this "Arcadia," where all these terrible things were coming from? And if this mammoth creature was from Arcadia, why was it *here*?

A shrill scream from off to his left finally made Gabe tear his eyes away from the monstrosity. He'd been so busy staring at it that he hadn't registered how terrified the cultists were. They bolted in every direction, shrieking at the tops of their lungs. One of them bellowed, "It's a null draak! Run for your lives!"

Run. Yes! Snap out of it, Gabe!

He spun, looking for Kaz and Lily, but almost lost his footing when the enormous creature—the "null draak"—slammed one clawed foot into the theater floor. It roared, louder than a freight train, a horrible sound that made Gabe's insides quiver like jelly.

A hunter growled somewhere behind him. While Gabe had been distracted by the null draak, the hunters had broken through the door. But instead of coming after him and his friends, the hunters seemed to be focused on the massive creature.

With good reason, it turned out. The null draak casually stretched out one wing and swept up two of the hunters, flinging them against the far wall. They yelped in pain and limped away into the shadows.

This thing wasn't messing around, but Gabe forced himself to focus on what had happened to Uncle Steve and Brett. They'd vanished as soon as the null draak appeared. *Where are they?* He searched the debris of the room and caught sight of the kid who'd popped out of the side of the cocoon just before the monster. If the boy came from wherever it was his uncle and Brett had gone, then maybe he'd know how to get them back.

The null draak's gargantuan, sightless head swung away from him, and Gabe darted toward the mystery boy. He already knew it wasn't Brett, but through the blood and membranous goo, it looked like . . . *Jackson?* But he wasn't translucent and glowing anymore. Now he just looked like a regular, flesh-and-blood, blond-haired dork.

As he ran, Gabe scooped up the blood-stained dagger Primus had used on Uncle Steve. Three hunters stood between him and the kid. They were focused on the null draak, but they got more interested as Gabe got closer. The beasts' fangs dripped with some hideous, unspeakable liquid as they stalked toward him.

But already the electricity thrumming along the cables inside the theater's walls seemed to call out to Gabe. *Beckoned* to him. He had only to *will* it to come to him and he knew it would.

A half-circle-shaped wall of blinding fire surged up between him and the canine monsters, and the hunters yelped and scattered backward, unable to get through the barrier of pure, destructive energy.

So this is what real power feels like. A smile spread across Gabe's face. If anyone had been there to see it, he or she might have said that it was not a nice smile at all.

"Gabe!" That was Lily's voice, somewhere over to his right. He craned his neck and tried to spot her, but the flame-wall was too bright to see past. "Gabe, *behind you!*"

Gabe heard the *click-click-click* of hunters' claws on the hardwood floor behind him. *I thought the null draak had taken care of those two!* Gabe swung the fiery wall around to block them, except that left him unprotected from the first three. He snarled, trying to extend the wall, but the edges frayed and fizzled. Apparently his mad fire skills had a limit. That sense of power he'd found so delicious left him in a heartbeat, replaced with the certainty that he was about to get torn to shreds.

"Guys! I could use some help here!"

"We're trying to get to you!" That was Kaz. "There's kind of a giant dragon in the way is the thing!"

He was about to swing the flame-wall toward the first three hunters again when the null draak let out a bone-shaking roar. The massive beast whipped its eyeless head toward the hunters. Zeroing in on the cluster of three, it took a great breath and breathed a cloud of *something* onto them. Acid? It must have been acid, because the three hunters dissolved into a foul-smelling, soupy mass, along with the floor underneath them and part of the wall nearby.

Holy freaking crap, it's on our side!

The eyeless face swung toward him. Drew in another breath.

Or not.

Gabe had no idea whether his fiery wall could protect him from whatever kind of super-disintegrator murder acid the null draak was about to spew at him, and he had no intention of finding out. He was about to throw himself completely off the stage when Kaz's voice rang out again, this time from the back of the theater.

"Hey! Dragon-breath! Over here!"

The null draak was still turning toward Kaz when a chunk of rock the size of a sofa slammed straight into the side of its muzzle. The impact would have propelled the rock all the way through an average house, would have crushed a full-size SUV beyond recognition, and would definitely have turned a human into a puff of red mist.

But the boulder bounced off the null draak's head. It was hard to tell, since the thing didn't have any eyes, but Gabe thought it looked really, *really* annoyed.

"Gabe!" Lily shouted this time, from right next to the exit doors. "Come on! Run!"

But what about Uncle Steve and Brett? Gabe knew the answer. He just didn't want to admit it to himself. His uncle and his friend were gone, and for now he had to concentrate on not getting dissolved by a giant acid dragon. Gabe leaped off the stage and hustled up the aisle toward his friends.

Out of the corner of his eye, Gabe saw Jackson Wright finally get to his feet, still up on the stage near the multiwinged monster. Jackson wiped blood and goo out of his eyes, raised his hands, and—Gabe blinked—created a shining, spinning orb of golden light about the size of a beach ball.

Even in the midst of all the fear and adrenaline and over-size skinless monsters, this surprised Gabe enough to make him stumble.

The orb spun and crackled in the air in front of Jackson Wright, and instantly every bit of the null draak's attention clamped down on it.

Like a cat with a ball of yarn.

"A null draak in the middle of San Francisco." Jackson sounded every bit as condescending and insufferable as he had the last time they'd spoken. "Well, you've really done it now. He'll make 1906 look like a picnic in the park."

Lily's jaw fell open as Gabe reached her. "Is that *Ghost Boy*?"

"What, now he's real?" Kaz threw his hands up. "Okay, you know what, I quit. None of this makes any sense. I'm officially done with logic."

Watching Jackson keep the null draak distracted with the glowing orb, Gabe felt a wave of rage sweep over him, just as hot as the flames he'd used to keep the hunters at bay. He wasn't sure exactly how, but one way or another, he knew Jackson had caused every bit of this disaster, and Gabe promised himself the prissy little dweeb would pay for it.

Just not yet. First they had this mountainous, sword-toothed *dragon* to deal with.

"Okay, let's go let's go let's go!" Kaz practically hopped up and down. "All the hooded weirdos have cleared out! Let's make tracks!"

"You can't!" Jackson shouted. He flung the golden orb away from him, and the null draak spun in place to go after it, gouging huge furrows in the stage and the theater floor as it did. Jackson came pounding up the aisle toward them. "You brought this creature here! You're responsible for its disposal!"

Gabe scowled. "*We* didn't bring *anything* here! None of this is our fault!"

"Perhaps not." Jackson produced another gleaming golden orb and sent it rocketing down the length of the theater.

What element is that supposed to be? What's he doing?

The null draak roared and batted at it with one enormous, black-clawed foot. Jackson went on: "But if you just run away and turn it loose, you'll be the ones who let it destroy the city."

"What are we supposed to do to that thing?" Lily waved her hands. "I can make big winds! I don't think that's going to do much more than tick it off!"

Kaz nodded. "Yeah. I put everything I had into socking it in the jaw with that boulder, and it just laughed."

Jackson's eyes shimmered and turned an unsettling shade of gold. "You haven't given it *everything*." The null draak roared and spun toward them, but Jackson went on in the same calm, obnoxious tone. "Gabriel. Send a fireball at our bellicose friend."

The null draak's wings were trembling less now, and extending farther and farther from its body. Gabe realized it was in the process of drying them off and limbering them up. And when it finished that, it could burst out of the theater and take flight. Gabe still wanted to run away. Run away; find some dry, warm, brightly lit corner to hunker down in; and try his level best to forget that any of this had ever happened. But looking at the null draak, and at the faces of his friends, something changed, deep down in Gabe's most basic makeup. Who else in San Francisco knew what was going on? Who else could do what they could do?

No one.

Jackson's right. This is up to us.

Gabe reached for the power flowing all around him, wound up for another punch-like gesture, and unleashed a fireball.

Just as he did, Jackson thrust out one of his own hands. A flash of golden light infused Gabe's burst of flame, and the fireball *split into six*. All six fiery missiles streaked straight at the otherworldly beast, each targeting one of its six wings, and each one hammered home. The null draak *screamed*. Flames coated its wings, and it beat them frantically against each other, slamming and writhing until the fire went out.

"What was that?" Gabe demanded. "What did you *do?*"

"You're welcome," Jackson said smugly. "Now come on. Lily, isn't it? Let's see what we can accomplish."

Jackson's golden light flashed again as Lily focused her power. What would have been a powerful wind became something like the eyewall of a hurricane, tangling the null draak's wings and sending the creature crashing into the back wall. The stage collapsed under the monster's weight. The draak screamed again.

"Come on!" Jackson bellowed. "I witnessed what you did, Kaz, caging those Eternal Dawn vermin! Cage this monstrosity now! Pin it to the earth!"

Breathing hard, his eyes gone stony gray again, Kaz gritted his teeth. Golden light sheathed massive pillars of stone as they erupted through the theater's floor. The pillars shimmered and twisted and turned to metal, curving over the null draak's body and tightening until they became bars as thick as the trunks of redwoods.

Panting, Kaz almost collapsed, and only didn't because he grabbed hold of Gabe. "Is that it?" Kaz sucked in great gulps of air. "Did we do it? Is it trapped?"

As if in answer, the null draak unleashed its loudest roar yet and flexed its grotesque, skinless muscles against its earth-born prison. The bars creaked . . . groaned . . . *began to bend* . . . and as Kaz cried out, they snapped, leaving only ragged, metallic stumps protruding from the ruined floor.

Jackson let out a series of curse words that Gabe had never heard before. "All right, clearly it's too strong. We *have* to run for it. And that probably won't do any good, because now that we've angered it, it will surely track us down. Oh well, I suppose San Francisco had a good run."

As if on cue, half of the theater's ceiling buckled and collapsed. Waves of pounding rain hammered down on the null draak, and a column of water descended from the ceiling. No, not a column. The liquid cylinder twisted and became something more like a corkscrew, easily ten feet across at its narrowest point.

Lily clutched Gabe's arm. Even the null draak seemed taken off guard by the spiraling, watery tower.

In hushed tones Kaz said, "But Brett was the one who could do water stuff. If he's gone, then who . . . ?"

The tower touched down on the stage, spraying water all over the theater, and a figure stepped out of it onto the splintered floor. A figure with long, gray hair and wearing hospital scrubs. Gabe recognized her instantly. "It's Greta Jaeger!" he gasped.

Jackson rolled his eyes. "Oh, splendid."

Greta spread her arms wide, fingers splayed, and the towering column sprouted dozens of smaller coils. Every one of them moved as if with a mind of its own, but every one of them went after the null draak. Some harassed it, knocking it off balance, pulling at its wings; others took a more straightforward approach and slammed into it like watery battering rams. At the same time, Greta Jaeger glanced at Gabe and his friends, then turned her face up to the pounding rain. Streams of rainwater began to clump together around her, growing more and more solid and coalescing into glistening masses of pure water. It was amazing—like some kind of movie special effect come to life right in front of them. As the shapes developed, Gabe realized what she was doing.

"Wait—that one looks like *me*!" Lily pointed. "And that's you, Kaz! And Gabe, and even Ghost Boy here. We're all over the place!"

She wasn't exaggerating. As Greta's whips of water kept beating the null draak, the rain had manifested dozens and dozens of mirror images of Gabe and his friends. The null draak lunged forward and brought its teeth together on one of the images of Gabe, snapping it in half, so that several gallons of water splashed onto the floor. The creature reared back, tossing its head in one direction and then another.

"She's got it confused," Gabe whispered. "Does this mean it won't come after us now?"

With another ear-splitting roar, the null draak's patience appeared to run out. Extending its multiple sets of wings, it took advantage of the enormous hole in the ceiling and leaped up in the air. Gabe, along with everyone else in the theater, was knocked off his feet by the unearthly downdraft as the null draak rose up through the ceiling and winged away.

Kaz had covered his head with his arms. Muffled, his face still pressed to the floor, he asked, "Is it over?"

Lily helped Gabe to his feet. "Of course it's not over," she gritted out. She whirled on Jackson. *"Where's my brother?"*

11

Brett's first hazy thought when he regained consciousness was, *What's wrong with the sky?*

He was lying on his back on a surface made of . . . a bunch of small, round, hard things? Cautiously he sat up. *Yep. Cobblestones. Where are there cobblestones?*

The fog in his brain cleared enough for him to take in his surroundings with something like objectivity. He sat in a small courtyard bounded on three sides by brick buildings. Except the bricks weren't the right color. Instead of red, or gray, or any other color he'd ever seen, they looked more like . . . *honey?* Definitely some shade of yellow that bricks weren't supposed to be.

Also, the sky was all *kinds* of wrong. *Skies are blue! Or gray, or maybe white if it's about to snow.* They definitely were not freaking *orange*, and they didn't have weird bloodred streaks torn in them. Brett had seen this kind of sky only once before— on Alcatraz as he'd looked through the outline of Jackson into that messed-up version of San Francisco.

He couldn't quite get his eyes to focus properly. That's how it felt, anyway. From the courtyard to the buildings, right down to individual bricks, it was as if nothing had any hard, defined edges. Things just sort of . . . faded. *I must have hit my head when I landed.* He felt his skull but didn't find any telltale knots or bumps or cuts. *Okay, then why does everything look like I'm dreaming?* And it wasn't just the bizarre, persistent blur that kept throwing him. Even beyond the bricks, the colors were all wrong. Objects seemed deeper, richer. *It's like I'm in an oil painting.*

Brett got to his feet, and that involved yet another thing he couldn't explain. He popped up to a standing position with almost no effort, as if his body had suddenly decided to weigh less than it usually did. It made him think of the footage he'd seen of astronauts bouncing around on the moon's surface.

A dread-filled voice from behind him made Brett spin around. "Oh no. Oh *no*. What are you doing here?"

Standing there in the courtyard, not ten feet away, was Gabe's uncle, Steven Conway. Brett took a second to come up with something to say, and in that second several gears ticked over in his head, one of which was the very clear memory of Dr. Conway's mangled, ruined prosthetic leg lying on the floor of his office. Brett's eyes darted down to Dr. Conway's ankle, the one that normally revealed a flash of metal between the hem of his pants and the top of his shoe, and saw what appeared to be normal, healthy skin.

No WAY.

"Dr. Conway, did you—is that—did you *grow your leg back*?"

Steven Conway looked down. He lifted his leg and wiggled his foot around. His voice definitely held a note of wonder as he said, "Well . . . how about that?"

More than elemental magick or hooded cultists or blood cocoons, the sight of Dr. Conway's flesh-and-blood leg made Brett's brain want to turn inside out. "How is that *possible*?"

"Never mind." Dr. Conway took Brett's arm and started leading him out of the courtyard. "Come on, we need to move. It's not safe here."

"But—"

"Later."

All the questions Brett had jumbled up in his brain and wedged themselves into a logjam. Unable to pick one, *any* one to ask, Brett just kept his mouth shut and let Dr. Conway haul him by the arm. The memory of fighting off the hunters in the theater with his friends danced behind his eyes. It didn't seem real. None of this seemed real.

When they reached the street, the scene became even stranger. *Oh my God . . . the horses!*

Dozens of them lay across the cobblestones, every one of them dead. Most of them still had some sort of tackle buckled onto them, and a couple were still fastened to carts, which had overturned when the horses fell. *Those poor animals! What happened to them?*

The city where they stood looked sort of like San Francisco, but . . . somehow off. It took several seconds for Brett to realize what was wrong. Or, not wrong exactly, but *absent*. There was nothing modern. No streetlights, no satellite dishes. No electronic billboards. It was like standing inside the world's biggest museum, all of it dedicated to the turn of the twentieth century. Gas-burning lampposts dotted the cracked sidewalks. Every street was paved with the same old-fashioned cobblestones.

What had happened here? At least half the buildings looked as if they'd been hit with bombs. Roofs had caved in, storefronts had crumbled, and great, ragged crevasses ran through the streets.

"What hit this place?"

"I'll explain when we get to safety."

Brett frowned. "But it doesn't look like anybody's here. What are we trying to get away from?"

As he said those words, a series of shadows streaked across the street, and Dr. Conway jerked his head up to stare straight overhead. Brett followed, and saw a swarm of . . . *somethings*.

They were too high up, and their edges too blurry, for him to tell what they were as they swooped and twisted above him and Dr. Conway. Once again Brett felt a rough hand grab his arm. "In here. Now."

He let Dr. Conway drag him into one of the less-destroyed buildings along the edge of the street. They waited, barely breathing. The shadows darted and flitted across the ground outside for six or seven long moments. When they finally left, Brett gulped in some air and looked around.

"Holy cow," he whispered. "Is this a candy shop?"

Dr. Conway let go of Brett and gave the place a once-over. "Used to be, yes, I suppose."

Brass-and-leather stools were lined up in front of a marble counter, on top of which sat big glass cases. A few of the cases still had candy in them, just sitting there in big heaps, waiting to be fished out with the pair of shiny tongs that hung behind the counter. Brett peered at one of the piles. The candy was sort of amber colored—*Is everything in this place some shade of yellow?*—and oblong, maybe an inch and a half in length. It also sported a healthy coating of dust.

"That must be hoar hound," Dr. Conway said from right behind him. "Common treat for kids of this time. You wouldn't like it. Even without the, ah, 'dust jacket.'"

Brett brushed aside what he thought had been an attempt at humor. "What do you mean, 'of this time'? Where are we?"

Dr. Conway beckoned Brett farther back into the shop,

away from the street. "We're in a place called Arcadia. In 1906, the Eternal Dawn attempted a ritual meant to bring more magick to our world, but they botched it. Instead of achieving what they wanted, they created this: a place sort of right behind Earth where magick is concentrated. That creation of Arcadia also caused the '06 earthquake, which all these ruins reflect." Dr. Conway pointed to one of the dead horses outside. "Time doesn't work the same way here as it does in our world. The *real* world. Some things are stuck, some aren't. That's why those horses don't look as if they've been dead more than a day or so."

"Huh?" This place caused the Great San Francisco Earthquake? *Time is different here*? If Dr. Conway told him that up and down had switched places, Brett would have to believe him, because right now he couldn't tell one from the other.

"Maybe it's easiest to think of it as a kind of pocket dimension. A place that looks like part of our world but has completely different rules."

"So . . ." Brett gestured around him. "This is like another San Francisco?"

Dr. Conway shook his head emphatically, and Brett got the impression the man was only keeping hold of his composure by the tips of his fingers. "This is *not* San Francisco. It isn't even the same reality. This is something much darker. A shadow city."

"You're saying—" Brett's heart sped up. Could it be possible? Had Jackson told him the truth after all? "We're not in the real world anymore?"

"No. This is a place where magick was concentrated, and now it's . . . *festered*. For better than a hundred years."

But Brett had stopped listening after Dr. Conway said no. His heart leaped. He was precisely where he wanted to be! The place he'd been trying to get to for a very long time.

Dr. Conway went to the front of the store and cautiously peered outside. "Okay, I think they're gone. We need to get moving again." He beckoned to Brett. "I might know where we can go."

Brett joined him, fighting to keep from bursting out in giggles. He was no longer on Earth. He was right where he wanted to be. Jackson had been telling the truth: there were other worlds. *This must be where Charlie is!*

As they walked, and as Brett's brain slowly grew accustomed to Arcadia's saturated colors and dreamlike shapes, Dr. Conway softly cleared his throat. "I need you to walk me through how you got here, Brett."

Brett squinched up his face. "Well, let's see. That creepy chick they were calling Primus had just stabbed you with a wicked-looking dagger, and I was trying to get the wound to quit bleeding—"

"No. I mean, start at the beginning. When did the rules of the world start to change for you?"

"Okay. Uh . . ." Brett took a deep breath. He didn't see how he'd be able to fill Uncle Steve in without making himself look pretty bad, but he figured he owed him *some* kind of explanation, what with having set into motion the series of events that got them sent to a shadow dimension. "I guess I'll go ahead and apologize in advance, but, uh . . . it started when I took the map out of your office." He cleared his throat. "Sorry."

Dr. Conway grasped Brett's shoulder and gently forced him to make eye contact. The look on the man's face told Brett what it'd feel like to be one of Dr. Conway's unprepared students. "You'd better tell me everything, Brett."

Brett told Dr. Conway a lot. He told him about the map and the tunnels and the Friendship Chamber and the Tablet.

But he didn't tell him everything. He didn't tell him about Jackson, and he definitely didn't tell him about Charlie. Brett's agreement with Jackson had gotten all fouled up, but he wasn't going to risk breaking his promises now. Not after everything he'd been through to see his brother.

Though he left out some details, the story was still a lengthy one. Brett wasn't sure how long they picked their way through the shattered, burned, collapsed wreckage of 1906-era *not*–San Francisco, but it felt as if he'd been talking for more than an hour before he finished his tale. Dr. Conway hadn't said much during the story, only asked a question here and there. But every time Brett glanced over at him, the tension in his face had screwed his features tighter and tighter.

"So, that's it. The weird blood balloon grabbed me, and next thing I knew I was waking up in that courtyard."

Dr. Conway massaged the back of his own neck. "So the four of you used your elemental powers to fight off an entire chapter of the Eternal Dawn?"

Brett shrugged. "And some of those hunter creatures."

Dr. Conway's knees seemed to get weak all of a sudden. He lowered himself onto a pile of fallen masonry and buried his face in his hands. "My whole adult life, this is exactly what I've been trying to prevent."

Brett sat down beside Dr. Conway. "So you always knew this stuff was real? Monsters and magick and everything?"

Dr. Conway went back to staring at the ground between his feet. "In a word, yes. Years ago, Gabe's parents and Greta Jaeger and I were bound together. In pretty much the same way you and Gabe and Lily and Kaz are now. We knew about this place. We knew the Dawn wanted to connect Arcadia to the real world. And we knew that if we *could* destroy Arcadia, we had to try."

Dr. Conway stood up and stretched, and gestured up the street with his thumb. Brett fell in beside him as they started walking again. "Things went wrong. What we tried to do didn't work. Blew up in our faces."

"But, wait, Dr. Conway. What's so bad about this place? Why would you try to destroy it?"

Dr. Conway gave Brett a look as if he'd asked "Why wouldn't you want several thousand black widow spiders sleeping in your bed?" But before he could come out with an answer,

Brett's toe kicked a small, loose cobblestone along the street, where it bounced, rolled, and fell into a six-foot-wide hole at the edge of the sidewalk.

With a piercing shriek, an animal the size of a golden retriever shot straight up out of the hole. It looked like a smaller version of a hunter, but then a pair of five-foot-long wings sprang out from its sides. Before Brett could ask "What the heck is that thing?" a dozen more just like it shot up out of the hole as if fired from a machine gun. Brett flinched as they all took up the first one's grating, fingernails-on-chalkboard screech, and their collective wingspan momentarily blotted out the sky.

"Abyssal bats!" Dr. Conway shouted. "Brett, get under that cart!"

Brett did, scrambling under a dirty, half-collapsed cart that lay near the corpse of the horse that had once drawn it. From there, peeking through gaps in the cart's floorboards, he got a better look at the creatures. Their bodies looked a lot like the hunters' had, at least as far as being vaguely canine and lacking skin and eyes and noses. But where the hunters had a lot in common with huge predators such as mountain lions, these things were half the size and ten times as aerodynamic. And their huge, translucent wings, shot through with visible veins, bore long, daggerlike claws at their tips. Claws that matched the ones on their feet, Brett noted. The bats circled above the hole they'd come out of, locked in on Dr. Conway, and attacked.

A stiff wind kicked up, blowing Brett's hair in his face,

and suddenly Dr. Conway just . . . wasn't there anymore. Brett blinked, looking around frantically—*Don't leave me alone here!*—but spotted Dr. Conway a dozen yards farther up the road, just standing there, calm as ever. The abyssal bats whirred through the empty air where he'd disappeared, banked like a flock of birds, and came after him again.

Dr. Conway threw up his arms and bared his teeth in a snarl, and a gust of wind came whistling through the street like a freight train. It blasted the first several abyssal bats straight back into the ones behind them, and half the pack—swarm—flock? Half the creatures lost their purchase in the air entirely and thudded into the street. The other half wheeled away, regrouped, and lined up for another dive-bomb attack.

Dr. Conway pointed up a side street. "Brett, run! We're almost there! Go to the second house on the left!"

Brett didn't want to leave. He and his friends had pulled some pretty cool stunts with their newfound abilities back in the theater, but Dr. Conway was a *master*. He wondered if Greta Jaeger could do the same kind of awesome moves with water that Gabe's uncle could with air.

But as the abyssal bats came rocketing back at Dr. Conway, their talons and teeth and God-awful screeching convinced Brett to do as he'd been told. He sprinted up the street, which opened into an upscale residential neighborhood. A series of fine Victorian homes lined the left side of the street. Or rather, they'd been fine at some point but were now half-collapsed or burned or both. Brett hurried toward them, even as he heard the distant sound of another abyssal bat splatting against the earth.

Second house on the left!

Brett vaulted over an ornate wrought-iron fence, ran through the tiny front yard of the second house, and bounded up the steps. He grabbed the front door handle, turned it, and pushed—and stumbled into a luxurious foyer.

Quickly he shut the door behind him, not wanting to attract the attention of whatever winged, fanged unpleasantness might be roaming the streets outside, and sagged against the doorframe.

For a moment he thought he'd entered a new kind of dream. The interior of the house didn't match the exterior in even the tiniest way.

The thick rugs on the floor had no dust on them. They weren't even threadbare. Could have been bought earlier that day, for all Brett could tell. The fancy chairs and love seat were likewise clean and in perfect shape, despite looking like the kind of stuff you'd see in some sort of historical exhibit. Brett looked up, trying to find the source of a faint hissing sound, and saw gas-burning lights set high on the walls, their flickering flames giving off the tiniest wisps of black smoke as they burned.

"How did you find me?"

Brett almost jumped out of his skin when he heard a woman's voice to his left. To make matters worse, he realized she'd been standing in a doorway, watching him, maybe since he came in from the street, but she'd kept so still that his brain hadn't recognized her as a person. Trying to get his heart to calm down, Brett asked, "Wh-wh-who're you?"

The woman took a couple of steps closer to him. The first thing Brett noticed was how astonishingly tall she was. She was also thin and graceful, with long, black hair and piercing blue eyes. She took yet another step, and in the illumination of the gaslights, Brett could see that her skin was *beyond* pale. A faint map of veins was visible beneath it, and when he squinted, he was pretty sure he could see the blood pump through them with every beat of her heart. Her clothes matched the house—old-fashioned, like something you'd see in a silent movie, he thought—but they were in a sad state, ripped and stained and scorched.

"You first." She leaned forward, peering at him. "What is your name? How dare you come here?"

She said it calmly, gently even, but there was an alien texture to her voice that made Brett consider turning around and heading back out to find Dr. Conway. He put up his hands in what he hoped would come across as a peaceful gesture. "I'm looking for my brother! He's here, somewhere. In Arcadia, I mean. I'm just trying to find him."

The woman cocked her head and smiled, and any trace of menace she might have presented vanished. "Ah. Family. Yes, I understand. Come with me." She took Brett's hand—hers was cool and oddly hard, as if made of living alabaster—and led him out of the foyer, down a short hallway, and into the kitchen.

"So, uh . . . have you seen him?" Brett was afraid to try to pull his hand free. "My brother. Charlie? Imagine me, except older and taller and better-looking."

She gave him the briefest of glances. "The bats are getting very bad around here, you know." She let go of his hand and went to a set of cabinets. They opened with a creak under her touch. "Here, let me get you something to drink. Something hot, to warm up your insides."

"Uh, okay. Thanks." There was something really *off* about this lady. Brett backed into a counter. "So, I'm looking for Charlie Hernandez," he tried again. "I was told he'd be here."

The woman had taken out a tea service, and at the word "here," she slammed it down onto the countertop so hard Brett was amazed none of the pieces shattered. He jumped, barely containing a yelp. The crash had made a terrific noise, and he winced at the thought of what it might attract from outside. "You don't know what it took!" the woman said, her voice rising with each word. "You don't know the *pain*!" Brett took a couple of steps backward, muscles tensing to run, but the storm seemed to pass as quickly as it had blown up. She calmed herself and smoothed the front of her dress with both hands. When she turned back to him, she had a bright and gentle smile in place. "It's just, I've been so *lonely* since your father left."

My father? *Who does she think I am?*

"Look," he started, trying to sound reasonable, "I realize, I mean, this being the afterlife and all, maybe if you've still got people on the other side, it *would* get lonely, but I'm really just trying to find my brother. Can you help me? Please?"

The woman turned back to the tea service. "Don't be silly. You're an only child." To Brett's growing concern—concern that threatened to tip over into horror—the woman poured *nothing* from an empty pitcher into equally empty teacups. *It's like a little kid's tea party.* It was the weirdest, creepiest thing Brett had ever seen. She picked up a smaller decanter, also empty, and tilted it over the cups. "Just the right touch of maple syrup. There, now. There we go."

Brett's breath caught somewhere right behind his breastbone. *Maple syrup in tea? That's . . . just like Gabe.*

"Ma'am, I really appreciate the, uh, the *tea*, but I've been through a lot, and I've come a long way to get here. If you'll just tell me whether you've seen my brother or not, I promise I'll get out of your hair."

The woman whirled and flung the crystal pitcher across the room. It smashed against a marble countertop so hard Brett flinched from the shrapnel. The woman curled her hands into claws, her brilliant-blue eyes boring into Brett's skull. She leaned toward him, and the bones of her face slid and cracked and *changed*. Suddenly the strange, pretty woman was gone, replaced by a howling, rage-filled creature that looked part human and part . . . *dinosaur*. Her voice boomed out like a massive fireworks display, every word an explosion.

"Do you not realize all I did for you? Do you not understand

the price I paid? The price we all paid?"

The woman crouched, eyes still fixed on Brett, razor-sharp teeth bared in a terrifying snarl, about to pounce on him like some kind of jungle predator—when Dr. Conway's voice rattled in from the front of the house.

"Brett? Brett! Where are you?"

The woman froze. Very, very slowly, she stood, and her face returned to normal. Or at least to "human." Her head turned, degree by degree, to look at the doorway to the kitchen. Dr. Conway came sprinting in, and skidded to a halt in the middle of the floor, staring at her. His hair was plastered to the side of his head, and one of the sleeves of his shirt had been ripped off, but other than that he appeared unhurt.

"Oh my God," Dr. Conway whispered. "Oh my God."

A genuine *sob* escaped the woman's lips, and tears fell from both eyes. Her voice sounded like a tiny child's: "Steve? Is that you?"

Dr. Conway crossed the kitchen in two huge steps and swept the woman up into his arms. She closed her eyes and returned the embrace, tears still flowing, but her mouth curved into a huge, heartfelt smile.

Brett stood, staring, as his jaw tried to thump against his chest.

"Uh . . . Dr. Conway? You *know* her?"

"Of course I do." He set the woman on her feet, gently smiling down at her. "This is Aria. She's Gabe's mother."

12

"*What did you do to Brett, you little creep?*" Lily yelled at Jackson.

Jackson Wright, aka Ghost Boy, didn't look too ghostly now. He was standing in the middle of the rain-washed floor, right under where the ceiling had collapsed. He turned his face up to it and a gigantic smile stretched his idiot face wide.

But the grin disappeared, along with what sounded like most of the air in Jackson's lungs, when Gabe rammed his shoulder into Ghost Boy's all-too-real stomach. Gabe wasn't very big—Brett had beaten him easily every time they'd ever arm wrestled—but his fury lent him a strength even he wasn't expecting. Gabe sat on Jackson's chest, pinned down his arms at his sides, and screamed into his face: *"Where's Brett? Where's my uncle?"*

"Ow! Let me go!" Jackson tried to squirm, but Gabe clamped his fingers on the boy's wrists like twin vises. "That hurts!" Jackson frowned, and abruptly the idiot grin came back. "It hurts! *It actually hurts!*" And he laughed like a crazy person.

That made Gabe even angrier. "Why'd the ritual work on Uncle Steve? He didn't unlock the stupid Tablet! *I* did! Why did it work if he wasn't who those crazies thought he was?"

Gabe might as well not have said any of that for all the effect it had on Ghost Boy. Jackson's laughter got louder and louder, and didn't stop until well after Kaz and Greta had dragged Gabe off him.

"Let go of me!" Gabe snapped, his eyes never leaving Jackson. "I'll rip his head off!"

"He can't tell us anything if he doesn't have a head," Greta Jaeger murmured. The soothing tone of her voice took the fight out of Gabe but did nothing for his feelings toward Jackson. Greta went on: "This boy might have benefited from what happened to Steven and your friend Brett, but he didn't cause it. That is the fault of the Dawn and the Dawn alone."

Kaz watched Greta Jaeger with narrowed eyes. "What are you doing here?"

The question seemed to amuse her. "You're welcome. I'm here because the rain told me you were in trouble. It seemed a good enough reason to leave Brookhaven."

That last sentence was casual enough to make Gabe wonder: *Does she just break out of the asylum whenever she feels like it?*

"You should listen to the old woman," Jackson said smugly, getting to his feet. "She speaks the truth. I didn't—" But before he could finish the sentence, Lily kicked the back of Jackson's left knee, dropping him to the debris-strewn floor again. He hadn't even finished his yelp of pain before she wrapped her arms around his head and throat. In two seconds, the utterly unprepared Jackson's face started turning purple.

"Answer the question," Lily hissed in Jackson's ear. "Tell me what happened to Brett."

With a thud in the pit of his stomach, Gabe realized Lily might have just lost her only remaining brother. Both brothers gone, in less than a year's time.

Jackson seemed to realize that Lily meant a lot more business than Gabe had and that if she didn't change her grip, he wouldn't be able to keep breathing. He slapped at her arms and made a weak nodding motion, and might have been trying to say "All right! All right!" with what limited air she was allowing him. But he didn't get the chance to talk, because the sound of multiple police sirens pierced the storm. They were getting closer in a hurry.

"Come, children." Greta Jaeger pointed toward the back exit. "We need to get away from this place." She looked pointedly at Lily, who made a disgusted sound and released Jackson. He slumped to the floor, gasping as his face returned to its normal color. Greta made an impatient gesture toward him. "On your feet, boy. The police are on their way, and it won't take long for the Dawn to return, either."

Kaz, not to be left out, prodded Jackson in the back with a broken length of rebar. "You heard the lady. Get a move on."

As they picked their way over the wreckage toward the back door, Gabe spoke up. "Won't the police have better things to do than look for us? I mean, there's a giant dragon thing out there in the city."

Greta shook her head. "The police have no connection to Arcadia. They won't be able to see the null draak for what it is. Though they *will* see the damage it has caused. Come on, we need to hurry."

Greta Jaeger took the lead, guiding Gabe and his friends—and Jackson Wright—through the streets. Despite having spent the last nine years in a mental hospital, she clearly knew San Francisco very well and led them on a winding path that not only guaranteed they'd shake any police pursuit, but also kept them mostly out of the rain. Along the way she spoke over her shoulder.

"I get the feeling young Mr. Wright already knows most of what I'm going to tell you, but I need the rest of you to understand. It will sound insane—especially coming from an escapee from a mental institution—but given what you've already witnessed, I believe you're ready to hear and accept it."

No one said anything. Well, no one except for Kaz, who poked Jackson in the back with the rebar and grumbled, "Keep up." Gabe was surprised to see Kaz doing anything that aggressive. Maybe Kaz's control over the earth had given him a new boost of confidence? Or maybe Kaz guessed that Jackson knew what had happened to Brett, and Jackson's unwillingness to cooperate was making him angry. Either way, Gabe didn't feel at all bad for the former ghost boy.

Greta cleared her throat. "What you saw back there in the theater—with the 'blood cocoon,' as you call it—that was Balance at work. In order for anyone here to get to Arcadia, or vice versa, someone of the same bloodline has to take that person's place. So, Lily, if your grandfather, let us say, were in Arcadia, you could swap places with him. But Gabe couldn't, because he's not related to you. Does that make sense?"

Lily and Kaz nodded. Gabe said, "I guess so, yeah."

"All right, good. So. The Dawn knew that only a descendant of the Great Founder, of Jonathan Thorne himself, could have unlocked the Tablet. Finding someone with this blood connection would have allowed them to exchange whoever this person is for the Great Founder, which they desperately want to do. Their mistake was in thinking that Steven had unlocked the Tablet, when it was actually Gabe." She pointed to the backpack holding the Tablet. Brett had passed the bag to Kaz moments before being sucked into the blood cocoon.

"Wait, wait." Gabe's brow wrinkled up. "You're saying

I'm related to this Thorne guy?" Uncle Steve had never told him much about Gabe's own family, but . . . *Jeez, if I'm the great-whatever-grandson of an evil cult leader, that's a pretty good reason not to.*

Greta stopped the group at a corner and glanced up and down the street. "I'll tell you the rest when we get somewhere safe." She started off again, and Gabe and the others hurried after her. Gabe didn't know where Greta was taking them. They were pretty far from his house and . . . *And I don't have a house to go to anymore, do I?* The realization hit him like yet another punch to the gut.

Gabe stepped up his pace until he was walking alongside Greta Jaeger. "Okay, I get that the Dawn screwed up with my uncle, but . . ." He jabbed a finger back at Jackson Wright. "How did *he* get here?"

"Your uncle also had ancestors who were members of the Dawn. I don't know how, but young Mr. Wright must be a blood relation to Steven. To some degree."

Wait a minute. If relatives get swapped between here and that other place . . .

And if Ghost Boy knew he was related to Uncle Steve . . .

Gabe whirled to face Jackson. "That's why you didn't want us to go into the theater! Isn't it? You wanted that sacrifice to happen! You knew you could come back here if the Dawn sent Uncle Steve to Arcadia! This was your plan the whole freaking time!"

Jackson Wright stared at Gabe coolly, his lips sealed.

The anger rose in Gabe again. "And that monster! Is that your fault, too?"

"It's called a null draak, dear boy," Jackson replied, so smug it made Gabe's teeth grind. "I have to admit, that was a bit unexpected."

Gabe had been walking backward, keeping up with Greta, but he suddenly wanted to do nothing more than punch Jackson's unbearable face right out of his skull. Gabe had already balled up both fists when Greta grabbed his shoulder. "In here. Come on. Off the street, now, all of you!"

Gabe let Greta usher him through a glass door and into a small café. It looked like a classic coffee-and-doughnuts shop, with a half-dozen customers seated at small round tables and a pleasant-looking college-age girl behind the counter. "Why are we here?" Gabe peered at the college girl, half-expecting her to levitate one of the coffee machines. "Is this, like, some kind of hangout for people like us? Elementalists, or whatever?"

Greta said, "Are you kidding? I haven't had a doughnut in nine years! Here, let's all have a seat." She led the group toward the table farthest from the door.

Halfway there, Gabe's disbelief got the better of him, and he shook her arm off his shoulder. "You brought us here so you can have a snack? Are you crazy for real? *We don't have time for this.*"

At the sound of Gabe's raised voice, every customer's head

turned toward them, but there were no knowing looks, no sense of threat. It was just ordinary people in an ordinary café sipping ordinary coffee, and Gabe realized Greta's words had been for the customers' benefit, not his. As if to prove that point, she put her arm around his shoulders again and gently turned him toward the broad picture window facing the street.

"See?" Greta asked quietly.

Gabe glanced out through the window, and his throat slammed shut. Right outside, at the edge of the sidewalk, three big, doglike creatures scratched around, sucking in great gulps of air. *Trying to find us.* They were creatures of the Dawn: skinless, pointed faces devoid of any features but gaping, fang-filled mouths. But unlike the hunters, these monstrosities had enormous wings in place of their front legs. Wings shockingly similar to the ones that had sprouted from the null draak's back.

Beside him, Kaz made a small, panicked sound, and the rebar he'd been holding clanged to the floor. Immediately he stooped and grabbed it up, looking embarrassed.

"Those are abyssal bats," Greta murmured. "More agents of the Dawn. Now can we please take our seats? I suggest we stay here until they move on."

Stunned, the group did as she asked, all crowding around one small table. They sat there, nervously making small talk, until the three nightmare creatures spread their wings and shot away into the sky. The downdraft knocked over a heavy trash can on the sidewalk, and Gabe heard the college girl say, "Somebody really ought to call animal control," before she hurried out to set it back upright.

"Animal control?" Kaz said sort of hollowly. "How—what do, uh, what do regular people see when they look at things like that?"

Greta Jaeger gave a tiny shrug. "Something more or less equivalent. It depends on the person. Always something easily accepted and dismissed."

"How did you know those things were out there?" Lily asked quietly.

"The rain warned me. The rain tells me many things, just as the wind may at some point begin talking to you, dear. The rain is protecting us now. We have to stay inside for a little while."

Jackson Wright made a noise like *pfff.* "You elementalists. Always jabbering on. 'The rain told me this,' or 'I saw this in the flames.' So tiresome."

Greta speared him with an icy stare. "You are hardly one to talk, young man."

Jackson's expression soured. He folded his arms across his chest, slumped in his seat, and fell silent. Gabe wished he could make the boy do that on command.

"Um . . ." Kaz sneaked a peek at the café's menu, written by hand on a small chalkboard on the counter. "How long is 'a little while'?"

Greta Jaeger's stare quickly shifted into a warm smile. "Long enough to order a few things. I really *haven't* had a doughnut in nine years."

Between them, Gabe, Kaz, and Lily had enough money to buy doughnuts for everyone and coffee for Greta. Ghost Boy eyeballed the display case, looking exactly like someone who hadn't eaten in over a hundred years.

Gabe's own stomach growled. He wasn't sure when he'd last had any food himself. Breakfast? It seemed as if a week had passed since then.

Despite getting his favorite, raspberry-jelly-filled, though, Gabe found himself only nibbling at it. He'd taken maybe a bite and a half before he let the doughnut plop back onto the small plate the college girl had served it on. Glancing around, he realized his friends weren't in much better shape than he was. Kaz didn't seem hungry, and though Lily had finished her doughnut, her leg bounced up and down with such nervous energy he was afraid she might crack the tile floor.

"Gabriel."

Gabe looked up sharply at the sound of Jackson's voice. "What?"

With such obvious reluctance that it made Gabe happy to hear it, Jackson asked, "Are you not going to finish yours?" Only crumbs remained of Jackson's vanilla-cream-filled.

Gabe sighed. "You know what?" He shoved the partially

eaten pastry at the younger boy. *Younger looking, anyway.* "Knock yourself out."

Gabe hadn't paid Jackson any attention when they'd first sat back down at the table with their doughnuts, but he did now. It was an odd kind of amusing to see the range of emotions on Jackson Wright's face as he bit into the raspberry-jelly-filled doughnut. For a second, only a second, all that smug, snarky, infuriating crap Jackson constantly spewed just vanished, and he looked . . . like a little boy. A little boy discovering something new and wonderful. Jackson even smiled as he chewed and swallowed.

That tiny, pleasant moment evaporated when Jackson grabbed Kaz's doughnut off his plate without asking.

"Hey!" Kaz tried to grab it back, but Jackson held it out of his reach. "That's mine!"

"You weren't eating it," Jackson said, his words garbled, spoken around another bite.

"But I might have! Give it back!"

In response, Jackson swallowed the remainder of the raspberry and crammed the entirety of Kaz's doughnut into his mouth. Kaz slumped back as Jackson dusted the powdered sugar off his hands.

Lily gave voice to Gabe's thoughts as she stared at Jackson: "God, you are *such* a creep."

"You endure a century without eating and see how polite you are." Jackson continued his bid for popularity by grunting at Greta Jaeger, pointing at her coffee, and miming taking a sip.

She sighed. "If you must."

Jackson took a big sip, swallowed, and gave them all a grin that was neither childlike nor charming. "Thank you all," he said, without a trace of sincerity. "You're too kind."

Gabe was about to say something decidedly *un*kind when he noticed Kaz had taken out his phone. Kaz's finger flicked up and down as he scanned headline after headline. "I guess you were right about no one else being able to see this stuff," he said in Greta's direction. "There is *nothing* online about any of it. And I'm pretty sure a giant dragon thing roaring around the Bay Area would get some coverage."

Greta took another sip, cautiously, as if to see if it had a bad taste now that Jackson had sampled it. Satisfied, she said, "That's correct. Those of us bound to the elements see a different world. Hunters may look like nothing more than stray dogs to the unbound. Those abyssal bats, perhaps vultures or large hawks. It depends on what the observer expects to see." She took another sip. "The Dawn members of this plane are unbound but wear glyphs that allow them to see things for what they truly are. The null draak is another Arcadian creature. Some believe that the null draaks were human once, but the corrupting influence of Arcadia overwhelmed them."

Kaz made a choking sound. "That giant six-winged freak show used to be a *man*?"

Greta continued calmly. "Or a woman. Yes. No one knows

for sure, but there's a theory that they were once members of the Dawn with no talent for magick. It's quite rare, you know: the ability to practice the Art."

Kaz's face had gone pale. "That's . . . that's horrible."

Greta nodded. "Becoming a null draak is a terrible fate, but not the worst one. For people like us—*elementalists*, as young Mr. Wright correctly said—far worse can happen."

Gabe waited for Greta to go on, but she just turned and stared out at the rain, her mind somewhere far away.

Apparently unconcerned with Greta Jaeger's thoughts, Jackson turned brazenly to Lily. "I don't suppose I could borrow another nickel or two? Those pastry concoctions were not half-bad, as it turns out, but now I fancy trying one of those"— he squinted at the menu—"*Icy Mocha Blast* items."

Lily narrowed her coal-black eyes at him. "Will it get you to shut up and leave us alone for a minute?" Jackson just held out his hand. Lily groaned and put a five-dollar bill in it.

While Jackson waited at the counter to get the college girl's attention, Gabe leaned over to Greta and spoke softly. "What about him? Is he like us?"

Greta shook out of her rain-focused haze. "Yes. And no. At first glance I would have said that he was another elementalist, but seeing what he did at the theater . . ." She frowned. "He seems to wield pure magick. I've never encountered that before. I didn't even know it was possible." She gestured for Gabe, Lily, and Kaz to lean in, and again spoke just loudly enough for them to hear her. "Magick was the glue that bound together the terrestrial elements at the moment of creation. Judging by what I observed, I believe young Mr. Wright's abilities are able to amplify your own terrestrial powers."

Gabe turned that over in his head. "Amplify them by how much?"

Greta shrugged. "Impossible to say as yet."

Lily cleared her throat. "I'm sorry, Dr. Jaeger, could we— I, uh . . . I still don't understand exactly what happened back there. I mean, I get that the Dawn wanted to exchange Gabe's uncle for this Founder guy, but why did that null draak thing show up?"

"A null draak is forced into our world when someone not belonging to one of the original bloodlines enters Arcadia. Someone like that is called a *null sanguis*. In this case, your brother Brett. The creatures must still have some small connection to humanity. And so they provide the counterbalance to the person entering Arcadia."

Gabe ran his hands through his hair. He wanted to pull it all out. "How do you *know* all this?"

"I've seen it happen once before." Greta's eyes clouded. "On the worst day of my life."

Gabe waited for her to continue, but she didn't. Those words just hung there, awkward in the silence. *Oh my God. Is that the day—did she really—did Greta Jaeger really kill my parents? Was Jackson telling the truth about that?* Gabe bit down hard on the thought. For one thing, he knew Jackson was a big fat liar. For another . . . right now Greta Jaeger was the only link he had to what was going on. He couldn't afford to alienate her.

"Hang on, hang on a minute." Gabe squinted at the ceiling. "If the null draak is here, that means Brett's in Arcadia?" Greta nodded solemnly. Gabe went on: "But I've *seen* Arcadia. Right after I unlocked the Tablet, I saw a vision of it. It looks like . . . well, it looks sort of like *hell*."

Greta's eyebrows twitched. "I'm sure there are some trapped there who would agree with you."

"Trapped?" Lily's voice rose. "No. Brett can't be *trapped* there! We're getting him back."

"Him and Uncle Steve both," Gabe said, maybe a touch defensively.

"Right." Kaz fixed his eyes on Greta Jaeger. "But how?"

Greta spread her hands. "It's all about Balance. To get someone *out*, you need to send something equivalent *in*. If you want them back, then we know our first order of business."

"And what's that?" Gabe demanded.

One corner of Greta Jaeger's mouth twitched upward. "We have to catch a dragon."

13

Brett tried his best to get a close look at the strange woman's face without obviously staring at her. He didn't want the . . . the dinosaur thing to come back out. It helped that she wasn't really paying any attention to him. All her concentration was focused on Dr. Conway. And yeah, now he could see it. The shape of the nose, the spacing of the eyes. This crazy lady could *totally* be Gabe's mom.

The knowledge made his heart pound. He knew Gabe's parents had died. And if his mother was here . . .

Dead isn't gone. That's what Jackson had told him.

He was on the right track!

Dr. Conway said, "Aria . . ." but the woman turned away

from him and started opening and closing cabinets as if searching for something. Brett had no idea what she could be looking for. All the cabinets and drawers appeared to be empty.

"It's so nice to have company!" She kept going, her hands fluttering as she moved around the kitchen. "Perhaps I shall bake a cake for the occasion!"

Dr. Conway sidled over to Brett, never taking his eyes off Aria. "I always thought this might have happened," he said softly. "We tried to destroy Arcadia nine years ago, but we botched it. Our Art is delicate and must be carefully balanced. There was some variable that we missed or got wrong. A null draak appeared, and it was total chaos. Henry—Gabe's dad, my best friend—died fighting it. I lost my leg. Greta was never the same, and we never found Aria's body. It was a disaster. But I believed there was a chance she'd be alive here."

Brett pulled himself out of the hurricane of thoughts swirling in his head enough to ask, "What's a null draak?"

Dr. Conway still didn't stop watching Aria, who'd begun humming a bizarre, off-key melody to herself as she puttered around the empty kitchen. "A creature. A huge, monstrous, destructive creature." He went on to describe how a null draak appeared in place of anyone who entered Arcadia but was not a blood relative of someone on the other side.

"I have ancestors who were members of the Eternal Dawn," Dr. Conway continued. "So one of them must have been exchanged for me. That's a pretty horrifying thought. The fact that a null draak appeared nine years ago was good evidence that Aria might have been sent here when our ritual went sour. And since you don't have a blood connection to anyone here, there's probably a null draak rampaging through San Francisco as we speak."

"Hang on. How do you know I'm not related to anybody in this place?" *My brother is here. Isn't he?* Brett nearly said that out loud but managed to keep it to himself.

"I know because everyone who came to Arcadia when it was created, everyone who got trapped here, was a member of the Eternal Dawn. And in addition to being crazy, they also weren't very . . . diverse."

Brett couldn't help it. He rolled his eyes. "Bunch of stuck-up *gringos*, is what you're saying?"

"White as milk, all of them, yes."

"I still don't get why you tried so hard to destroy this place."

Finally Dr. Conway dragged his eyes away from Aria, who was completely absorbed in whisking imaginary flour into fictitious sugar. He gave Brett a look that combined skepticism with genuine bafflement. "Because magick corrupts people. And Arcadia is made almost entirely out of magick." As if to provide an example, he gestured with one thumb toward Aria and lowered his voice. "I think that's why she's acting the way she is. It might have gotten to her. I'm hoping it hasn't, though."

Dr. Conway hadn't seen Aria's face change earlier. *Oh, I think it's gotten to her, all right.*

"But, listen, Brett, we tried to get rid of Arcadia so that Gabe would never have to hide from the Dawn the way the rest of his family has since 1906. His bloodline is particularly special to the cult, and they'd do anything to capture him. Plus, if the Dawn had its way, they'd actually *merge* Arcadia with our world, and if they did that, it would be—"

Brett tried to finish the sentence in his head. *Awesome? Fantastic to be reunited with people you've lost? Incredible to be part of a place with this much power?*

Instead, Dr. Conway said, "Catastrophic. I don't even know how many people would die. Maybe all of us. And that's why Greta Jaeger and Gabe's parents and I tried to do our own ritual. Tried to bring it all down. And it should have worked! We had all four elements represented! But something still went wrong. And what happened, happened . . . to Gabe's parents, and me, and poor Greta. She didn't even try to deny it when everything got blamed on her, which of course everyone took as an admission of guilt. It was only a good lawyer who got her into the asylum instead of prison. She's gotten better over the years, but she was a mess for a long time. Both of us were."

Brett tried his best to focus. "So this *null draak* that's running around the city now . . ."

"Try flying," Dr. Conway said glumly.

"*Holy cow.* Okay. That's *flying* around the city now. Is it looking for Gabe and Kaz and Lily?"

Dr. Conway shrugged. "Don't worry too much about them.

Gabe especially can handle himself. He may not realize it yet, but he can. It's in his blood. It's the *rest* of the city that's in danger." He waved his hands around the kitchen, but in a way that indicated Arcadia as a whole. "And let's not forget about ourselves. There are things crawling around Arcadia much, much worse than a null draak. We should stay here and gather our strength. You said you and your friends had talked with Greta, right? Well, she'll already be working on a way to get you back home."

Home?

Brett moved away from Dr. Conway, his hands shoved out in a gesture like *Stop!* "Are you crazy? I'm not going home! Not yet! After everything I've been through? Everything I've *done?*"

Gabe's uncle stared at Brett blankly. "What are you talking about?"

"My brother! Charlie!" Brett wasn't going to sit back and let this chance—this *one chance*—get away from him. "I can't come all this way and not see him!"

Aria kept puttering and clanking about the kitchen, oblivious to their conversation, but Dr. Conway frowned as he focused on Brett. "You're talking about your brother who *died?* Gabe told me about what happened. But I don't understand. Why would you think he'd be in Arcadia?"

"Because he *is.*" Brett wasn't sure he could make Dr. Conway understand, no matter how carefully he explained it.

"Listen. You need to hear this. Arcadia is another plane

of existence, yes, but it is *not* the afterlife. Your brother isn't here. He can't be."

"That's not true!" Brett's voice rose higher and higher. Aria finally stopped baking her imaginary cake and turned toward him. Brett kept talking, and even as the words poured out, he knew they sounded as if *he* were the one who belonged in a crazy house, not Greta Jaeger. "You're lying to me! I don't know why, but you are, because Jackson told me Charlie was here! He said, 'Dead isn't gone'! He *promised* me!"

Dr. Conway's eyebrows shot up. "Brett—"

But Brett couldn't stop the rush. "He told me what to do! All of it! I started seeing him in my dreams, right after I found the ring." He whipped the ring out of his shirt, where he kept it on a thin chain.

Dr. Conway gasped at the sight of the five-spoked wheel carved into the gold. "But that's—"

But Brett wasn't finished. "The map, the Tablet, the ritual, all of it—I did it all because Jackson *promised* me I could see my brother again! And you're saying it was all *garbage*?"

Dr. Conway made a calming gesture. "Hold on. Hold on. This is . . . this is *unprecedented*. You're saying someone from another plane made contact with you through your dreams?"

Brett emptied his lungs in a shrill scream: *"I don't care how it happened! I just need to see my brother!"* Before Dr. Conway could do anything about it, Brett bolted out of the kitchen. He sprinted down the hallway, banged through the front door, and charged headlong out into the street.

From behind him he heard running footsteps. "Brett, wait! It's too dangerous! You have to come back!"

But Brett had made up his mind. Dr. Conway was either lying or confused, because Charlie *was* here. He had to be. No other answer made sense. No other answer . . . would let Brett live with himself. With what he'd done. *If Dr. Conway's right, if I tricked Gabe into opening the Tablet for nothing—if I'm the one who might have made it possible for the Eternal Dawn to combine Earth with Arcadia and destroy the world . . .*

No. No! He pushed the thoughts away. Dr. Conway was wrong. *I just have to find Charlie!*

Brett tore off up the sidewalk, away from the house, heading deeper into the city. *Just have to figure out where all the people are! That's where I'll find Charlie!*

He glanced over his shoulder, and his eyes bugged out when he saw Dr. Conway gaining on him. Now that he had two flesh-and-bone legs, the man could have been a freaking track star. Brett poured everything he had into getting away, and might have begun to pull ahead just a bit—

—when the ground shook violently beneath his feet, and abruptly it no longer mattered. A group of four . . . Brett goggled at them. *What are those things?* A group of four creatures built like the hunters he and his friends had encountered on Earth burst out from a side street. Except these things were *so much bigger* than the hunters. They looked more like glistening, golden, skinless triceratops, massive horns and all. And all four of them were ignoring Brett and zeroing in on Dr. Conway

"Sorry, Dr. Conway," Brett whispered, massively relieved that the gigantic beasts hadn't noticed him. But then he saw something. Dark as a storm cloud, up a side street.

Whatever it was, it was hidden behind other buildings. Brett squinted, trying to see it clearly, but Arcadia's strange, blurred-edge distortion prevented him.

Something with . . . tentacles? The gold-tinted air swirled around the thing like heat waves.

Something *colossal.*

Brett stood rooted to the spot. Very dimly, as if from a mile away, he heard Dr. Conway screaming at him. It sounded like *"Get away"* or *"Run."* He couldn't really tell, because the tentacled thing gripped every last shred of his attention.

And it was coming closer.

Finally Brett's feet broke loose from their imaginary moorings, and he ran. Away from the massive tentacled storm cloud thundering its way through the city. Away from the horned super-hunters. Away from Dr. Conway. Brett ran and ran, through the twisted, desolate, shattered version of 1906 San Francisco. And as his legs and arms pumped, he realized he was faster than he'd ever been on Earth. When he jumped, he jumped higher and sailed farther through the yellow-orange-tinted air. Bit by bit, second by second, Brett forgot the terror of the Thing behind him and began to revel in the strength, the sensation of power as it steadily soaked into him.

Lily would love it here. I bet her asthma would be gone, just like Dr. Conway's leg regenerated.

Another thought struck him like a sledgehammer.

I bet Charlie loves it here, too! If he's okay. I have to get to him. I have to save him!

His heart filled back up with an impossible hope. Brett skidded to a stop at the crest of a steep hill. Below him, past the blasted buildings and broken streets and slaughtered horses, a shining sea stretched away, looking for all the world like molten gold. And thrusting up out of the shimmering, flashing liquid, far offshore, an immense rock outcropping . . . and a massive walled fortress.

Brett concentrated. Turned his head slightly to hear better and . . .

Yes. From across the water, carried to him by the waves, came the sounds of hundreds of tormented screams.

Arcadia had transformed it, just as it had transformed everything else about the city, but Brett would know that place anywhere:

Alcatraz.

14

Gabe almost had to push his own jaw shut. "Catch a dragon. You want *us* to capture the null draak?" When Greta nodded, Gabe sputtered, *"How?"* loudly enough to make the other customers turn and look at him. He ducked his head and slid down in his seat, and in a much lower tone said, "How are we supposed to do that?"

"It's not like we can call in the National Guard," Kaz said gloomily. "They'd get torn to bits."

"But you know a way, don't you?" Lily put her elbows on the table and leaned toward Greta. "What do we need to do?"

Greta took a sip from her coffee. "It's like this. That null draak doesn't belong here any more than Brett belongs in

Arcadia. And it's attracted to magick, because magick reminds it of home. So we can set a trap. But we can't dawdle. Ordinary people might not be able to see the null draak for what it is, but that doesn't mean it's any less dangerous to them."

"I fear we are ignoring a central issue here," Jackson said in pinched tones. He toyed with the straw sticking out of his Icy Mocha Blast. "If your goal is to retrieve 'Uncle Steve' and your friend Brett, that means exchanging the null draak *and myself.* And I did not accomplish all this just to be returned to Arcadia."

Gabe bristled, but before he could say anything, Greta Jaeger spoke. "Mr. Wright, dangerous though Arcadia is, Steven Conway can defend himself—and Brett as well, if they're together. The null draak, on the other hand, is only going to grow more and more deadly the longer it stays here. It has to be our first priority. Once we have Brett back, then we can figure out how to rescue Steven. And how to deal with your . . . predicament."

Jackson glared at her sullenly. "I suppose I am *slightly* better off staying with you lot than I would be striking out on my own at this point."

"Gosh," Lily said, oozing sarcasm. "That's so nice of you to say."

"Okay." Gabe straightened in his chair. "What do we need to do?"

"First we make a list. There are things we'll need." Greta

grabbed a napkin. "Anybody got a pen?" Kaz obligingly handed her one, and Greta started writing carefully on the flimsy paper. "There's a special chalk, laced with blood."

Gabe made a face. "Okay, *that's* gross. Where do we get it?"

One corner of Greta's mouth twitched upward. "In your uncle's office at the university."

"I should've known."

Greta went on writing. "There's a large shard of flawless amethyst in a museum on the other side of town. That's a must. We'll use that ritual blade you took from the Dawn, too." Gabe assumed she meant the silver dagger Primus had stabbed Uncle Steve with. "And we have to retrieve some equipment that your uncle and your father hid away, back when we all had our own elemental circle."

Kaz's face brightened. "Equipment? What kind of equipment?" Gabe figured Kaz was happy to latch on to the thought of anything technical in the midst of all this elemental, supernatural . . . *stuff.*

Greta looked up from the napkin. "You remember that show globe hanging from the ceiling in the theater? The one full of swirling, glowing energy?"

Lily nodded. "I didn't know it was called a 'show globe,' but yeah."

"That was energy siphoned from Arcadia. The Dawn used it to turn regular dogs into hunters. What we'll be looking for is a vial of the same energy, which we'll use to attract the null draak."

Kaz frowned. Gabe guessed he was disappointed that "equipment" involved more magick nonsense rather than electron microscopes or lasers. As if Kaz had read Gabe's mind, he said, "Couldn't have been anything *real*. Noooooo. Has to be more mumbo jumbo."

Jackson let out a nasty laugh. "I was aware you were all children, but it still surprises me when you prove yourselves to be such . . . *children*."

Gabe practically snarled, "Nobody asked you." Jackson shrugged and returned to his beverage.

Greta handed the pen back to Kaz and addressed the whole group. "Well, you can all take comfort in the knowledge that we have one big advantage here: the Emerald Tablet. That will definitely make things easier. It is perhaps the most powerful of all relics. Hideously powerful. If the Dawn ever acquire the Tablet, they will use it to merge Arcadia with this world. That is why they want it so badly."

Lily's forehead wrinkled up. "And we can't let that happen because . . ."

Tersely, Greta said, "Reality as we know it would cease to exist, and billions of people would likely die horrible, horrible deaths."

The words hung in the air.

Finally Gabe cleared his throat. "Then let's make sure they don't get the Tablet, huh?"

Greta put the napkin in the middle of the table and tapped

it with a knuckle. "We'll work faster if we separate into teams. I can find the hidden vial of energy. Lily and Kaz, can you get the amethyst shard from the museum?"

Kaz looked as if he was going to protest, but Lily immediately said, "Yup, no problem."

Greta turned to Gabe. "That leaves you and Jackson to get the chalk from your uncle's office. You two will make a great team, won't you, Gabe?" The ghost of a smile slid across her creased face.

Gabe glared at Jackson. Just about last on his list of things to do was "hang out with the weirdo creepy liar ghost boy." But at the same time, since Gabe trusted Jackson even less far than he could throw him, he'd prefer to keep an eye on him. "Yeah, that's fine with me. You got a problem with that, Wright?"

Jackson took the time to pull the very last bit of his drink through the straw, making a loud, obnoxious slurping sound, before he set down the cup and smiled. "Why no, of course not. Why would I?"

"We need to decide where to meet once we've acquired what we need." Greta stared at the tabletop. "The best place to trap a dragon would be . . ." She trailed off.

Condescendingly, Jackson finished her sentence. "Alcatraz. Without question. The walls of this reality are thinnest there. That is how I was able to step partially through when we first met."

Gabe exchanged quick glances with Lily and Kaz. He

thought they were all on the same page: none of them liked Jackson, and none of them trusted him, but they couldn't argue with what he'd just said.

"Fine," Lily said.

"Yeah," Kaz said. "Okay."

Greta nodded, making it official. "Alcatraz it is, then."

Gabe grumbled as he pushed his chair back from the table.

Jackson sat on the cable car with his legs splayed far apart, crowding into Gabe's space. It gave Gabe just one more reason to despise the boy.

"You realize," Jackson started, "your dislike of me is virtually palpable."

Gabe gritted his teeth. He didn't know what the word "palpable" meant, but he wasn't about to admit it. "Can't think of why I'd dislike you," he grumbled. "You've only lied to us all, got Brett and my uncle sent to some kind of shadow dimension, and dragged us into a giant mess that's probably going to get us all killed."

Jackson sighed. "Never mind all my attempts to save your lives, yes?"

Gabe ignored him.

Jackson said, "I hate the Eternal Dawn with an undying passion. No pun intended. I want to see them all suffer, and the best way to do that is to destroy Arcadia. I am *on your side*."

Gabe turned his head enough to give Jackson a skeptical look. "I think you're on *your* side. And I think I don't much care what else you have to say."

Jackson sighed again. A tense silence settled between them for several minutes.

The silence broke when a Maserati roared past them on the street outside. Jackson practically broke himself in half, twisting around to press his hands to the window, watching the sports car disappear around a curve. He sank slowly back into his seat once the Maserati was out of sight. "Astonishing. I had glimpses of such machines from where I was imprisoned, but the sleekness, the *power* of automobiles today. I never dreamed they would achieve such goals. No one did."

To Gabe's surprise, he found himself torn. A little part of him wanted to geek out with the kid over how cool Italian sports cars were.

It made him think. He turned over several thoughts in his head, just sort of examining them for a minute. Jackson Wright looked about ten, but if he was telling the truth—and who knew if he was or wasn't—he'd been stuck in some sort of *interdimensional limbo* for, like, over a hundred years. What would Gabe be like if that happened to him? What would it do to his personality? His *mind*? Would he be in any better shape than Jackson?

The very concept that maybe Jackson deserved at least a tiny little bit of sympathy irritated Gabe. He didn't *want* to be sympathetic. Gabe hunched his shoulders and folded his arms tightly across his chest, and when Jackson said "What troubles you now?" he didn't answer.

One thing Gabe did know for certain, though, sympathy or not. If it came to a choice between letting Jackson Wright stay here or getting Uncle Steve back from Arcadia, well, that was no choice at all. As soon as Greta Jaeger opened the connection between the worlds, Jackson was going back.

Neither boy said anything until the university came into view. Gabe stood up. "Come on, on your feet. This is our stop."

"Yes, sir," Jackson said mockingly.

Gabe's jaw clenched. *No choice at all.*

Gabe and Jackson both craned their heads to look up at the stately building where Uncle Steve had his office. "Rothenburg Hall?" Jackson said, reading the name carved into the stone facade.

"That's where we are." Gabe beckoned to him and started toward the side door. "Come on. Like Greta said, we can't waste time."

Jackson moved up shoulder to shoulder with him as they walked inside. "So, what manner of place is this?"

Gabe stopped just short of rolling his eyes at Jackson's "small talk." "This is a university. I know they had those in 1906."

Jackson narrowed his eyes at Gabe. "I was *eleven*. Forgive

me for not paying attention to higher education at that point."

Gabe shrugged. "And this particular building is part of the College of Humanities. Uncle Steve is a professor of mythology and folklore." A memory popped into Gabe's head, and he couldn't help but grin a little. "He said this was where they stuck all the shaggy-headed liberals. He heard one of the deans say that, and he took it as a compliment."

As they climbed the stairs toward Uncle Steve's third-floor office, and after a lengthy pause, Jackson asked, "You truly love your uncle, do you not? You miss him?"

"Of *course* I miss him." Gabe bit his tongue before he could add, "dumb ass."

Jackson paused again. "I only remember my father. I know I had other family, aunts and uncles. And I think I loved my mother, though I've forgotten her face. But *my father* . . ."

Gabe glanced over at Jackson's face. Jackson had put enough icy venom in those last two words to make Gabe wonder exactly what his father had done. Not that he was about to ask. He pushed open the door to the third floor. "It's right there. Second door on the left."

As Gabe fumbled in his pocket, Jackson spoke up again. "You have a key to your uncle's place of business? He trusts you that much?"

"It's not exactly his place of business." Gabe popped the key in the lock. "It's just where he keeps a bunch of books . . . and some weird chalk, I guess."

The door swung wide, and Jackson followed Gabe inside. It immediately felt strange to be there, in Uncle Steve's untouched office, given everything else he and his friends had been through in the last twenty-four hours. *At least none of the other professors has stopped us.* If any of them were looking for Uncle Steve, Gabe wondered what kind of explanation he'd give for his uncle's disappearance into a shadowy pocket dimension. Peering at the desk and the bookshelves and the worn fake-leather couch and the antique globe in the corner, Gabe could *almost* pretend nothing bad had happened. Almost.

"Where should we look?" Jackson asked.

"There's really only one place." Gabe sat down at his uncle's desk. "It's not like he could slip chalk in between the pages of a book, so it's got to be in here." He opened the center drawer and pushed on what looked like a knothole in the wood grain, and a false bottom popped up. Gabe grinned. "Ha! And he told me he never kept anything in here!"

Gabe reached in and pulled out a cloth-wrapped object about the size of a deck of playing cards, tied with old, rough hemp twine. Gabe could feel the outline through the cloth of several sticks of what had to be the chalk, and was about to untie it to be sure, when a jovial, British-accented voice boomed out, "What's that you've got there, Gabe?"

Gabe almost dropped the chalk—he was afraid he'd almost swallowed his tongue, too—but managed to tuck it quickly into his jeans pocket. "Oh, hi, Professor Juniper. I'm, ah, just picking something up for my uncle."

In the doorway, looking an awful lot like Santa Claus in a tweed jacket, stood a gloriously bearded man in his seventies: Professor Abram Juniper. Hovering at his right was a tall, lanky young woman with an enormous mass of red curls exploding from her head. Professor Juniper's teaching assistant, Mandy Carson. Gabe knew them both fairly well, since he'd been seated with them at one of Uncle Steve's horrendously boring faculty dinners six weeks ago.

Seems more like a lifetime ago.

"And where is Steven?" Professor Juniper asked, tucking his hands into his pockets. "He missed his afternoon classes. We've been in a bit of a crunch, filling up his schedule with no notice."

"Oh . . ." Gabe tried to seem casual about it. *Think fast!* "He got really sick. Sorry. I, uh, I was supposed to call and tell somebody, and I guess I forgot to."

Professor Juniper's face creased up in an expression of concern. He wandered into the office and slouched against one edge of the desk. "That's terrible news! Is there anything we can do to help?"

Mandy broke into a surprisingly pleasant smile. Her teeth were perfect, and suddenly she seemed tall and elegant rather than weird and gawky. "I could bring him some chicken soup," she said. "Help him get back on his feet." Her smile turned a tiny bit embarrassed. "I have to confess I've always had a little bit of a crush on him."

Gabe's heart surged. *Adults I know! Adults I can trust! People we can turn to for help!*

Unless they listened to his story and immediately shoved him into some place like Brookhaven.

I've at least got to try. If they did believe him, Juniper and Mandy could get them to Alcatraz safely, and maybe they could figure out how to get some *real* help. *Like, I don't know, maybe army help!* A few rocket launchers would take down a null draak, even if the soldiers didn't know exactly what they were shooting at, right? *Right?*

Then two things happened, at the exact same moment, that blew Gabe's hope to tiny pieces. First, in a soft, warning tone, Jackson said, *"Gabe . . ."* Second, the door of the office closed and locked under Mandy Carson's fingers. Gabe's eyes went wide as he looked back at Professor Juniper, whose grandfatherly expression had become a blunt, savage snarl.

"You're going to give me whatever you took from the desk," Juniper said. "And then you're going to take us to the rest of your little friends."

Any elegance Mandy might have shown disappeared with her smile, and she suddenly bore more resemblance to a scarecrow than to a normal human. Gabe sucked in a sharp, hissing breath as he caught sight of a tattoo on Mandy's forearm. Its design was that of a rising sun, the same symbol he'd seen woven onto the cultists' robes. *They're Eternal Dawn!* "And both of you will wish you'd never been born," she sneered.

Gabe barely had to concentrate at all. He thrust out a hand, his index finger pointing toward the lock on the office door, and envisioned a narrow beam of fire flashing out and melting the lock right out of its bracket.

Instead, lightning jumped out of every electrical socket in the room and blazed with blue-white brilliance around Gabe's hand. Juniper and Mandy immediately threw themselves out of the way, and in the blink of an eye a cone of flame four feet across blasted from Gabe's pointing finger and burned the entire door to dust.

Gabe's ears filled with deafening, staccato electric buzzing as every fire alarm in the building went off. Screams and running footsteps echoed up and down the corridor outside.

Gabe yelled at Jackson, *"Come on!"* The two boys bolted past the dazed forms of Juniper and Mandy, sprinted out of the office, hung a sharp right, and headed for the door to the stairwell—where two hunters slammed the door off its hinges, their weight bearing it to the floor. It crashed down hard enough to shake the walls. One of the hunters took a great bounding leap and threw itself straight at Gabe, but his electric fury flashed again, and a bolt of blazing power slammed the hunter back into its companion, its skinless exterior charred and smoking. Gabe whirled, about to shout to Jackson to run for it, but Jackson was rooted in place, his eyes flaring a brilliant gold.

Jackson made a lifting motion with one hand, and the door the hunters had torn down rose off the floor, wedged itself back into the doorway, and, golden light gleaming around its edge, sealed itself in place. Immediately a hunter crashed into it from the other side, but the door didn't budge.

"How long will that hold?" Gabe panted.

"Not long enough! Let us make haste away!"

As Gabe and Jackson tore down the hallway, Gabe risked one look over his shoulder. He saw Professor Juniper peeking out of Uncle Steve's office, a cell phone pressed to one ear. Gabe kept running.

"You know this building, Gabe, and I do not!" Jackson was breathing just as hard as Gabe was. "Which path should we take?"

Gabe pointed. "Turn left up there! It'll take us out the main entrance!"

"Is that *wise*? Will not the Dawn be waiting for us in such an obvious place?"

They took the corner and spilled into another long hallway, one side of which was lined with picture windows affording a top-notch view of the campus. At the end of the hall, Gabe knew, a set of double doors would open onto a large atrium, from which they could get outside. "It's the closest way out!" Gabe bellowed. "Run faster!"

From behind them, Gabe heard a shrill scream, followed by a man's voice: "Lock your doors! There're coyotes in the building!"

Coyotes. Of course. Nobody would see the hunters for what they were.

He and Jackson never reached the double doors. With a

tremendous grating, crunching sound, the ceiling just above the doors collapsed, and three abyssal bats crashed down into the hallway. Gabe and Jackson skidded to a stop, and Gabe *might* have peed in his pants a tiny bit. The bats squirmed, orienting themselves, and started practically *galloping* toward them, using their back feet and the tips of their wings to propel themselves like a couple of skinless, nightmare-inducing racehorses.

Gabe saw a brilliant flash of golden light in his peripheral vision. Jackson had just conjured a broad, gleaming golden disk, and as Gabe watched, Jackson thrust out his hands, sending the disk through one of the picture windows and smashing all the glass out of the frame. The disk hovered there, right outside the window, perfectly flat. Jackson shouted, "Jump on!"

Gabe didn't need to be told twice. He leaped onto the disk, and under Jackson's golden-eyed control, it glided away from the building and dropped them safely to the ground below.

As his feet touched the campus's manicured grass, Gabe tried to look in every direction at once. "Are they coming after us?"

Jackson stared up at the window they'd broken. "Oh, most assuredly," he said as the abyssal bats burst out after them, shrieking louder than the fire alarms.

15

Brett crouched down on a broad, flat stone at the edge of the sea and dipped a finger beneath the surface. A shiver ran through his body at the contact. *This is just water. So why's it this color?* The shiver intensified when the reason dawned on him: the water was filled with magick.

Was that why the sky looked the way it did? He thought about the glass globe in the theater, with the swirling golden energy inside it. *Is magick . . . gold?* If so, that meant that Arcadia was *saturated* with it. The water. The sky. The dirt, the buildings, the roads . . . that was why his vision had changed, or seemed to change. He wasn't looking through some sort of gold-hued filter.

He was seeing magick *everywhere.*

An entire world of magick. Brett stood and concentrated on the water lapping against the rocky shore at his feet. It only took the barest of effort, like the tiniest flick of the wrist, to make one of the waves freeze in place, twist like taffy, and *flow backward.* The terror of water that had consumed Brett for the last year fractured, dissolved, and melted away, replaced by . . .

What am I feeling?

It was a new sensation. Something he'd never experienced before. It took him a few moments to put a name to it.

Power.

Brett glanced around. He spotted an old, dented canteen lying nearby and carried it back to the water's edge. With the smallest bit of exertion, he caused a stream of water the thickness of a pencil to rise up out of the sea and pour itself into the canteen, which thrummed in his hand.

Brett lifted his eyes to . . . well, he couldn't simply call it Alcatraz Island anymore, because recognizable though it was, the place had changed drastically. At least quadrupling in size, it was now much closer to shore, which made the towering walls—he figured they rose at least three hundred feet above the water—that much more imposing.

"Citadel." That was the right word. Alcatraz Citadel.

The screams and moans of human voices emanating from the place still reached his ears. *If Charlie's in there* . . . No. Not "if." Charlie *had* to be in there. That must have been why

Jackson Wright wanted to meet there in the first place. And now it was up to Brett to break his brother out. And take him home.

Brett turned his attention to the surface of the water again. A broad disk, four feet across and with an upturned rim—*like an upside-down Frisbee*—froze solid and floated there, waiting for him. Brett took a careful step onto the disk, afraid that his feet would slip out from under him, but he didn't have to worry. The ice gripped the soles of his shoes as firmly as if he were walking on dry concrete.

"All right," Brett said to no one. "Let's raid a citadel."

The ice disk slid across the water's surface smoothly, as if gliding along on a track. The gold-tinted wind rushed past Brett's face, and slowly he lifted his arms, drinking in the exhilaration, the joy, the *sheer impossibility* of this. The water loved him. The water obeyed him. The water . . .

It *spoke* to him.

Not in actual words, but Brett heard its message just the same. *Rise higher*, it told him. *Step out onto the top of that wall like a king ascending to a throne.* Brett nodded. Yes. Yes, he needed to make an entrance here. An entrance fit for a king, because a king he was. He made a lifting motion with both arms, and the ice disk rose up from the sea's surface on a column of golden water.

Faster. The water's voice sang in his ears. *Higher.*

And it was *easy.* Riding atop his element, reveling in the

magick that permeated it, Brett elevated and widened the column until it became a wave. No, not just a wave. A *tsunami*. But not like a tsunami that had ever been recorded on Earth. The water rose up, speeding faster and faster, until it became a mammoth wave of destruction that would have obliterated any city in the real world. Up, and up, and up Brett rose, the crown on the head of this monstrous wave, rushing toward the walls of Alacatraz Citadel.

I'll be meeting Charlie soon! He could barely imagine it now, though that was all he'd done since he'd first met Jackson Wright in his dreams. He had *so much* to tell Charlie. Brett hoped his brother would be impressed that he'd literally walked between worlds to find him . . . but that wasn't the most important thing. What Brett had to do first, before everything else, was apologize.

He knew it was his fault that the boat had capsized.

That was why he *had* to get to Charlie. At all costs. At *any* cost.

Below him, the leading edge of the wave smashed against the base of the Citadel's soaring walls with a sound like a million cannons firing, but Brett's ice disk carried him up and onto the top of the wall as gently and precisely as if it were an elevator. Brett glanced behind him as the impossible wave broke and fell back into the sea, and abruptly wished he hadn't since that gave him a view *all* the way down to the rocky base of the island. Brett gulped and stepped quickly off the ice disk, onto the wall itself.

The first thing that struck him was the material under his feet: it wasn't concrete, or even stone. Instead, it seemed like the wall had been built from *bones*. He tried to identify what kinds of bones he was looking at. They seemed to come from a wide variety of creatures, all stuck together with some kind of gray, cement-like . . . *something*.

He knelt and touched it. "What *is* this stuff?"

As if in response, a skittering noise reached his ears. Brett straightened up in a hurry. A dozen insect-like creatures, each of them the size of a raccoon, scurried out of nooks in the wall and clicked their way down the side. It made him a little queasy, just looking at them. Each one combined the least pleasant aspects of army ants and centipedes. Brett eased over to the wall's rim and peered down. Dozens more of the creatures swarmed over the wall, as if emerging from a kicked anthill, and it took him a second to realize they were checking for damage. His enormous, city-destroying wave hadn't done much to the wall, but it had cracked it in a few places. And when the bug creatures found such a crack, they opened their mandibles wide and sprayed a vile gray slime into it.

That's what the wall is made of? Bones stuck together with bug snot?

But wait. Does that mean this whole place is . . .

. . . a hive?

Brett heard a clicking, skittering sound to his left, and had just enough time to turn his head before one of the insectile creatures sprayed him head to toe with the gray ooze.

He jumped to his feet and staggered backward, coughing and gagging, trying not to vomit. The creature didn't move. Just watched. Brett understood why as the ooze began to harden around him. *No no no no!*

Brett pulled the water out of his canteen and split it into multiple shimmering tentacles. He narrowed the tip of each of these into a blade, then sent them sliding along his skin, peeling and prying, until the gray ooze came loose and slapped to the ground in front of him like a molted shell.

The insectoid didn't seem to like that. It reared halfway up and *shrieked*.

Creature after skittering creature crawled up over the edge of the wall and headed for Brett, mandibles clacking. He turned and ran, and for the first time took a good look around him. The top of the gargantuan wall was incredibly broad; the walls must have been fifty feet thick at least. But then he realized that these weren't walls like those of a castle, as he'd been expecting. There was no courtyard on the other side of the wall. In fact, now that he was up here, Brett saw that what he stood on was more like a desert butte than a wall. Alcatraz Citadel itself was an immense block of black stone with no clear entrance, looming like a giant monument at the center of its platform of insects and bones. As Brett sprinted away from the insectoids clockwise around the Citadel, he realized how desperately, fatally limited his options were: an impenetrable black-stone edifice on one side and a three-hundred-foot drop into the bay on his other.

More and more creatures came clacking out of other nooks in the top of the wall. He slung water from the canteen at them, freezing the spray in midair and turning it into a series of lethal spikes. The insectoids were not very well armored, and the ice spikes punched through their exoskeletons, dropping them in their tracks.

But that only took care of about six of them. Brett couldn't tell how many were chasing him now, but it had to be . . . what, fifty? A hundred? Arcadia's strange gravity let him run in long, distance-eating bounds; but the Citadel was so huge, and the wall went on for so long, that soon his thighs and calves began to burn, and he knew he couldn't keep up that pace forever.

Except, if he slowed, they'd catch him.

And I'll become a part of the wall.

The ground beneath his feet vibrated, and Brett's heart sank when he realized the source: still more insects. Right below him, inside the wall. Skittering up from the dark. Hundreds. Maybe *thousands.*

Brett choked back a panicked sob.

But then, ahead, he finally noticed some kind of irregularity in the smooth black stone of the Citadel. *Yes! A door!* Brett pushed his aching muscles to their breaking point.

It wasn't just any door. What Brett saw when he drew closer was a pair of doors as tall as the tree he'd climbed at his aunt and uncle's house every summer. A pair of doors that would put any bank vault to shame. *Can I even open those? They look like they weigh a ton each!* But he had no choice. Putting on one last burst of speed, Brett dashed to the doors, threw his weight against one, and almost whooped with joy when it swung open easily, its unimaginable weight perfectly balanced on unseen hinges.

Inside, Brett saw nothing. Only darkness. He couldn't even tell if there was a floor to step onto. But the insectoids had almost caught up, and he knew he had no choice.

Brett flung himself into the fortress and shoved the giant door shut behind him.

16

Gabe threw both hands out, all his fingers stretched toward the abyssal bats rocketing at him and Jackson. Three different streetlamps nearby exploded, the plastic of their globes vaporizing as glaring blue-white bolts of lightning found their way to him. A vortex of flame burst from his hands and enveloped all three bats, which screamed and flailed and ultimately slammed into the ground around him, either dazed senseless or dead outright.

Students and faculty ran past, shouting at each other about wild animals and fire in the building.

Hope everybody's out. I'd hate for regular people to get caught in there with those hunters.

Then he wished he hadn't remembered the hunters, because two of them smashed through a ground-floor window and barreled toward him as though he'd summoned them just by thinking about them. Gabe raised his hands again, ready for another burst—and watched in shock as a manhole cover, glimmering with golden energy, flew across the ground like an oversize hockey puck and knocked both hunters nose over tail. Gabe darted a look at Jackson, whose eyes shone gold above his smug white grin.

"Do you think that was all of them?" Jackson's eyes returned to normal. "Might we make our escape now?"

"I don't know. There was still Mandy and Professor Juniper. And I saw him calling for help."

Jackson frowned. "Well, at least let us seek some less-exposed location." He gestured around them. They stood in a quad surrounded by College of Liberal Arts buildings. "Lingering out here in the open will surely invite nothing but trouble."

"Oh, it's too late to run," Professor Juniper barked as he slammed open the main doors of Rothenburg Hall. He strode out, Mandy Carson at his side, both of them wearing nasty, hungry grins. "At this point you're only prolonging the inevitable."

Gabe was about to *try* to run, at least, when he saw a dozen hunters slither around the two Dawn cultists, and two dozen more push their masses through ground-floor windows all along the building's length. They weren't in full-tilt pursuit. Instead, they spread out in a broad semicircle, moving to surround Gabe and Jackson.

"I can't blast this many at once," Gabe hissed.

Jackson put a hand on Gabe's shoulder. It surprised Gabe so much that he whipped his head around to look at the smaller boy, and found himself staring straight into shimmering, dangerous golden eyes. "Oh, I believe you can," Jackson said. "I shall make *sure* you can."

Starting at the place where Jackson's hand touched his shoulder, a wave of crackling, pulsing power flooded Gabe's entire body. He felt the heat emanating from his own eyes, which he knew must have ignited into twin infernos. Gabe raised his right hand, and instead of drawing electricity from the streetlamps, he reached *up*. Higher and higher.

All the way into the clouds.

A bolt of lightning as thick as a tree trunk stabbed down out of the heavens, and Gabe's body drew in every last volt like water into a sponge. Gabe swung his hand, finger pointing, in a wide arc, and a volcanic gout of flame slammed forth, raking over the hunters like the fury of an ancient Greek god. The fire reduced the twisted creatures to blackened dust as soon as it touched them, and when they were all gone, Gabe swung the infernal beam of destruction back to the building's main entrance.

Gabe couldn't tell if it hit Mandy and Professor Juniper or not. The glare from the column of flame hid the doorway from view . . . and grew even brighter.

He could feel fires starting inside the building.

He could feel *stone melting.*

"Gabe," Jackson said at his shoulder.

The flames kept pouring out of him. Hotter. Brighter. *Hungrier.*

A voice that spoke to him without words rejoiced inside his head. *"Yesssss."* It dragged out, popping and crackling and roaring, and Gabe laughed, delighted. The fire loved him. The fire *needed* him.

He was the fire. And fire burned.

Jackson shook him. "Gabe!"

"Burn . . . burn . . . burn . . ."

Gabe felt his lips pull back from his teeth in a savage snarl of destructive bliss.

"Burn more . . . burn it all . . . !"

"Gabriel!" Jackson balled up a fist and struck Gabe across the jaw.

Gabe staggered, the world spinning around him. The column of flame sputtered and went out. He shook his head, blinking hard, and rubbed his jaw. "Why'd you hit me?"

Jackson pointed at something. "Because of *that.*" Gabe couldn't see through the brightness that still seared his vision, but he did hear the sound of distant fire truck sirens growing closer. Jackson said, "And because of those. Come, we must depart."

As Gabe blinked, his world came back into focus, and with

a sickening clench in his stomach, he took a good look at what Jackson had been pointing at. Rothenburg Hall was completely engulfed in flames. Gabe might have started crying hysterically, except that he heard someone behind him say, "Yeah, everybody got out. Apparently there was a big gas leak and, like, some wild animals, too?"

Gabe turned. There, not ten feet away, stood a group of students, and he could tell just by looking at them that not one of them had seen a single bit of what he and Jackson had just done. *How could they, without any connection to Arcadia?* He took a staggering step, light-headed and exhausted, and didn't even try to fight Jackson off when the smaller boy steadied him.

"We have what we came for, yes? We need to go."

Gabe nodded, wordless, and let Jackson lead him away.

Half an hour later, Gabe and Jackson stood in a motorboat, trying not to lose their balance as they crossed the choppy waters of the bay. It had been a couple of years since Gabe had piloted a boat—not since the last time Uncle Steve had taken him fishing, back when they lived near Lake Lanier in Georgia—but he still remembered how. It made him miss his uncle that much more. He glanced over at Ghost Boy. He *would* get Uncle Steve back. No matter what.

Alcatraz loomed large in front of them, and overhead the stormy sky had turned an otherworldly, unsettling gold, not unlike Jackson's eyes when he . . . did whatever it was he did.

Gabe kept looking over his shoulder.

"You need to relax," Jackson said. "The Dawn lost our trail when you impersonated Mount Vesuvius."

Gabe frowned. It wasn't the Dawn he was worried about. "This isn't right."

"What isn't right?"

"We stole this boat! Do you know how serious that is? Uncle Steve's gonna kill me!"

Jackson peered at him from beneath lowered, intensely sarcastic eyelids. "Yes, your uncle will fret greatly over the theft of one boat. Especially after you just burned down his university."

Gabe's frown deepened. "Thanks. You're a real ray of sunshine."

As they approached the island, they passed the last ferry of the day. Gabe spotted tourists standing all along the top deck, taking photos of the bizarrely glowing sky. He wondered exactly what they saw when they looked up at it.

I wish things could go back to the way they were. Wish I could just see the world like everybody else again. . . . Wish I'd never heard of the stupid Tablet, and Ghost Boy here, and all of this other craziness.

"Gabe," Jackson said, just loud enough for him to hear. "Look."

Gabe followed the line of Jackson's pointing finger and saw, tiny at this distance, a multiwinged shape perched atop the TransAmerica Pyramid. "Holy crap. Is that the null draak?"

Jackson didn't have to answer. The massive creature threw back its head and *howled*. It was terrifying, to be absolutely sure, but as the sound carried across the water, Gabe realized it also sounded . . . lonely. It was trapped in a strange world where it didn't belong.

The way Brett is. The way Uncle Steve is.

"Don't worry, big fella," Gabe murmured. "We'll put all this right."

To Gabe's intense relief, he spotted Lily, Kaz, and Greta Jaeger on the dock, waiting as they pulled up. Lily hugged him as soon as he got out of the boat, and without giving it a second thought, Gabe returned the hug and kissed her on the cheek.

"It's really good to see you," he said, pulling back just far enough to look her in the eye. Lily's cheeks went a shade darker, and she turned away, but Gabe caught the glimmer of a smile on her lips.

Greta Jaeger cleared her throat. "Did you get the chalk?"

Gabe nodded and patted his pocket.

"I was concerned. It seemed as if you might have run into some obstacles." She jabbed her chin toward the mainland, where a line of dark smoke cut through the sky.

"Oh yeah." He didn't particularly want to go into detail about what happened back at the university. "You could say that."

"And did you and Jackson work well together?"

Gabe flashed a look at Ghost Boy, who was busy admiring

the glittering buildings downtown, an expression of dumb awe on his face. "Yeah, actually. He did help. And—" Gabe didn't quite know how to say it. "It's like I got more powerful around him, too." He'd never admit it, but Gabe wasn't sure he'd have made it off that campus without Jackson's help.

"Hmm," Greta looked Ghost Boy over with a slight frown. "Yes, he's a puzzle, isn't he?"

"What about the park rangers?" Gabe asked. He didn't want to talk about Jackson anymore. "Where are they? We can't just waltz in there after the place closes, can we?"

Greta smirked. "The water and I convinced them that it would be best if they left for the night." She patted her stomach. "Just a touch of, let us say, gastrointestinal distress, by way of a temporarily incapacitating water-borne virus."

"The rangers all have the runs!" Kaz explained helpfully.

Gabe chuckled, and pulled out the blood-infused chalk. "So what do we do now?"

As soon as Greta's eyes lit on the chalk, her face went pale. Her shoulders, normally squared and confident, slumped a fraction of an inch, and she chewed on one side of her lower lip.

Gabe slipped the chalk back into his pocket. "Greta, are you sure this is going to work?"

She examined her fingernails. "Of course. Of course it will."

"Really? I mean . . . really, *truly*?"

Instead of answering him, Greta turned back toward the other kids. "Come on. We don't have any time to waste." She gestured to the group and led all four of them up the steep steps to the prison.

As they climbed—and as a remote part of him registered that Lily had decided to walk right next to him—Gabe turned everything over in his head. *The last time Greta tried something like this, Uncle Steve lost a leg and both my parents died. What are we doing? Are we all about to get ourselves killed?* He paused, considering. *It's no wonder Greta looks nervous. Talk about traumatic memories.*

But he knew they had no choice. Not while Uncle Steve and Brett were stuck rotting in some gold-and-wrought-iron version of hell.

Greta strode out onto a broad, empty patch of ground and turned to face everyone. "All of you, listen to me. Once we start this, the Dawn and every otherworldly creature they can muster will descend on us. It's like lighting a beacon. But we need to keep them away until the null draak gets here. And then, once it's in the center of the circle, we have to stab it with the ritual dagger the Dawn used on Steven. Do you all understand?"

Gabe, Kaz, Lily, even Jackson all nodded solemnly. Gabe handed Greta the silver dagger he'd taken from the cultists at the theater, and Kaz pulled the Emerald Tablet out of Brett's backpack.

"All right. We need a circle from that point"—she gestured to a spot on the ground—"to that point. One I can draw on.

Kaz, some bare stone, if you would?"

Kaz's eyebrows shot up, but as soon as he realized he was being asked to help, he didn't hesitate. He concentrated, making a low, rumbling sound in his throat. His eyes turned solid slate gray, the ground beneath them vibrated and shifted, and a perfectly smooth circle of stone formed in the earth, exactly as wide as Greta had indicated.

"Thank you," she said, favoring Kaz with a smile. His eyes returned to normal, and he smiled back. "Good, good. Now. If you'll allow me to work for a moment." Gabe handed her the chalk. Greta Jaeger drew arcane symbols all over the broad, bare stone in much the same way Primus had back at the theater. Then she positioned the amethyst shard in the circle's center and held the glowing vial in one hand as she walked over to the circle's edge. "Kaz, you stand right there. Lily, over there, Gabe, right over here, and—"

"Move it, Ghost Boy," Gabe told Jackson as he began to traipse into position. "You're not needed here."

If Gabe hadn't known Ghost Boy better, he might have thought he looked genuinely hurt. "To have traversed dimensions only to be treated like common riffraff," he muttered as he turned away.

Greta came to a sudden halt. "Wait!" she yelled.

The tone of her voice demanded Gabe's attention. He turned to watch her, and saw the creases of Greta's face shift as she stared openmouthed at Ghost Boy.

After a few long seconds Gabe spoke up. "Um, Greta? Is something wrong?"

Greta Jaeger's eyes suddenly went wide. Gabe had seen the proverbial "lightbulb" moment before when someone had suddenly come to a thunderous realization, but never like this. The ground beneath them rumbled, and there was the groaning of bursting pipes underfoot as twin geysers of water tore through the grass and into the air, waving around like the wagging tails of excited dogs.

"Five," Greta whispered, but then abandoned the whisper for a full-voiced shout. "*Five!* FIVE! We only used *four!*"

"Okay," Lily said, sounding maybe a touch scared. "What does that mean?"

Greta Jaeger jabbed a finger at Jackson. "There are five! Don't you see? *Five elements!*"

Jackson Wright gaped at her, and then his face split into the biggest, most genuine smile Gabe had ever seen on him. "Magick!" Jackson bellowed. "Of course! *Magick is the fifth element!*"

Gabe glanced at Kaz and Lily. He didn't like where this was going at all. *Magick is an element?*

Greta waved her hands excitedly, and behind her, the water geysers mimicked her movements. "That's why we failed before! Why it all went so wrong! The creation of Arcadia back in 1906 changed everything! We only had four elements. *But now there are five!*"

Gabe scowled. Greta was looking at Jackson as if he was

superimportant or something. And yes, he had saved Gabe's life, and if somebody wanted to get technical about it, maybe he wasn't entirely, *completely* bad. But he was still getting shoved back into Arcadia where he belonged.

Gabe spoke up. "All right, okay. Can we get on with it? I'm sure Brett would rather be here arguing with us than doing whatever he's doing right now."

Greta beamed at him. "Of course. Not only can we get on with *this*, but once we take care of our little dragon problem, we can take care of our *big* Arcadia problem. And we can get it *right* this time!" She took a deep breath and looked at Lily. "But first things first. Gabe is right—let's get your brother back. Then we can worry about everything else."

Lily nodded seriously and gestured at the circle. "Let's do this."

Gabe took his place along with everyone else.

Holding the Tablet in both hands, Greta started chanting in that same weird, alien-sounding language he'd heard the cultists use. It made the insides of his ears itch.

As Greta chanted, vibrations pulsed out from the Tablet. Gabe felt them ripple across the island and the bay like huge rocks dropped into water. Everything they touched seemed to be affected.

The waves crashing along the shore grew until they became towering. What had been a simple breeze accelerated into a gale that howled all around them. The ground pulsed and throbbed like a gigantic, beating heart. Torrents of rain poured from the golden clouds overhead.

Greta Jaeger threw the vial of swirling, golden energy at the amethyst shard in the middle of the circle. It shattered, and the energy—the *magick*—flowed out from the point of impact, sinking into the stone.

"Look," Lily breathed.

Gabe glanced down at their feet. The perimeter of the circle pulsed with more golden light—but this light came straight from Jackson. Just as he had at the university, Gabe felt power flood through him, and judging by the gasps he heard from Lily and Kaz, they must have felt the same thing.

Fiery red lightning flickered overhead. Gabe could feel that, too. Every bolt, branching and forking through the clouds.

In the distance, the Golden Gate Bridge swayed ominously in the clutches of an earthquake. That's when he heard it: the howl of the null draak. *Growing closer.*

"The null draak!" Gabe shouted. "It's headed this way! Get ready!"

"All right, it's time to finish this." Greta pulled the silver dagger out of her sleeve. "You have to keep them all off me until it's done!" She closed her eyes and started chanting again.

"Keep what off her?" Kaz squinted around the island. "I don't see anything."

Her face paling, Lily gestured skyward. "I think she means them."

Gabe followed Lily's pointing finger. Despite the fire of his magick, his blood ran cold.

Winging their way across the water, a massive flock of abyssal bats shrieked toward them. And in their taloned feet, every bat held a member of the Eternal Dawn—or one of their terrifying, skinless hunters.

17

I t took several minutes, but Brett's eyes finally adjusted to the interior of the Citadel. Glass globes like the one in the theater gave off dim golden light high above him. He couldn't see if they were attached to the walls or hanging from the ceiling or what. It was like looking at fireflies on a moonless night.

Brett took a hesitant step forward. The stone beneath his feet felt familiar somehow. *Like the real Alcatraz?* Maybe the inside of this place was an echo of the prison in the real world? A much bigger, twisted, darker shadow of that favorite tourist destination but at its core the same? If that were the case, and if Brett kept walking, he should start passing prison cells.

Then a sound. Somewhere ahead of him—a human voice.

Whimpering. Brett had heard so many anguished cries from this place, carrying to him across the water, he could only guess at how many prisoners there must be here. *And if Charlie's one of them, I've got to get him out.* Brett took a deep breath, tightened his stomach, and started walking. Slowly, carefully, yes, but forward. *Gotta go forward.*

Bit by bit, as he drew closer to the distant light globes, he began to orient himself in the darkness. He was standing on a sort of balcony, a long, long balcony that dropped off over the rail into . . . nothing. No, not nothing, because looking down *and* up, he saw more balconies, above him and below him. Too many to count, fading into the darkness in either direction.

A bestial hiss sounded from the cell right behind him—a cell Brett had thought was empty. When he whirled, he saw a lizard-like face pressed against the bars, a long, forked tongue flicking out at him. Golden eyes with slitted red pupils blinked independently of each other, but both studied Brett like a cat poised to pounce on a mouse. Brett edged away from the creature, his back to the balcony's rail, ice water in his gut.

The next cell was no better. Worse, in fact, as a multijointed insectile leg passed between the bars, pincers on the end of it clacking and snapping . . . followed by another leg just like the first one, and another, and another. Brett couldn't see the owner of those legs. Whatever it was stood too far back from the bars, too far into the darkness. He was glad he didn't *have* to see it.

The lizard creature made a noise. A *wail.* Long and

sorrowful and savage, a sound of powerless rage. The noise also sounded like . . .

"*Boy* . . ."

The multilegged creature joined the lizard: "*Heeeere* . . . *boy* . . ."

Brett scurried away from both cells, but the inhabitants of the first two had gained the attention of the rest. Tongues and limbs and antennae and tentacles all waved and pawed and clutched at Brett as he walked faster and faster past cell after cell, and he had just decided to break into a run when he all but stumbled onto a set of stairs.

The stairs led down to a lower level. Brett stepped out onto them. His new vantage point gave him a better look at the balconies below him, and he had to clap one hand over his mouth to keep from crying out.

On terraces and walkways below were more nightmarish *things*. He couldn't make out much more than their shadows, but they were huge, and moving, patrolling like some sort of demonic prison guards.

"Charlie," Brett whispered, in a desperate attempt to remind himself why he was there.

What happened next almost sent him scrambling back for the door, and the army of insectoids waiting for him on the wall.

It started as an echo. A whisper, slithering along the floor and out of dark corners. But instead of fading, the echo grew louder, until it seemed as if the entire Citadel took a great breath and *began talking to him.*

The voices came from everywhere. Not just from the cells, and not just from the inhuman creatures prowling the lower levels. It sounded as though the walls themselves took up the same awful, terrifying theme.

"He's looking for Charlie."

Brett understood the words though they were issued from inhuman mouths and lungs. They buzzed and scratched in his head like a nest of hornets.

"He lost him."

"Couldn't help him."

"Let him drown."

"Killed his own brother."

Tears sprang to Brett's eyes. He fiercely wiped them away with his shirtsleeve. "It was an accident," he said, his words catching in a sob.

"He killed him."

"Drowned him."

"Split his skull open."

"Killed your brother. Killed your brother!"

The voices took that up as a chorus, until they all blended together into one deafening wall of accusation:

"Youkilledhimyoukilledhimyoukilledhimyoukilledhim!"

A single sound pierced through the roar. A scream. *His brother's scream!* Brett's insides twisted into a knot of pain as he recognized it: the scream that had escaped from Charlie's throat in the instant before he died.

It was coming from below him.

Brett charged down the steps, caring nothing for the immense, impossible beasts he rushed past.

I should have tacked left like you said! If I had, we wouldn't have capsized. You wouldn't have hit your head. You wouldn't have drowned!

Brett reached the end of the stairs and sprinted down a corridor, following the lingering, horrible sound of his brother's agonized cry. He couldn't tell how many levels he'd descended. It didn't matter. His brother was there. Charlie was *there*!

Leaving the balconies and the cells behind him, Brett ran as fast as he could, using every bit of extra strength and speed Arcadia gave him. That speed almost killed him when he nearly rocketed off the edge of an abyss that abruptly opened at the end of the corridor.

Brett crawled to the edge and looked over. He had to blink and touch his eyes to make sure they were open, the darkness was so absolute. There were no glass globes here. Only a void darker than outer space itself.

"Charlie?" Brett got to his knees. His brother's scream had stopped. He couldn't tell what direction it had come from. "Charlie, where are you?"

The voice that hissed out of the darkness wasn't like the

taunting of the monsters from the cells. Each word it spoke caressed Brett's brain, gripping and exploring, like the tentacles of some horrible deep-sea creature.

"Long and long has it been since anyone from the outer world came here."

Brett shook his head, got to his feet, and backed away a few steps. The voice whispered to him, but that whisper vibrated in his chest like an avalanche. A dim green light appeared, out there in the abyss, some distance from the edge, and rapidly grew brighter. In the strange illumination, Brett saw something and wanted to look away, but as his eyes filled with angry, involuntary tears, he *couldn't*.

Vast tentacles coiled and uncoiled, sliding across each other like a nest of snakes.

The body they belonged to defied description. Defied *comprehension*. Brett so lacked the ability to understand the shape that his mind trembled. Threatened to crack. Something warm and wet flowed down over his lips, and Brett realized it was a salty, coppery mixture of tears and the blood that had begun pouring out of his left nostril.

The creature in the abyss moved, and Brett *recognized* it. This was the shape he had seen behind the buildings, when the giant horned hunters had gone after Dr. Conway. The creature like a living, moving thundercloud.

He hadn't escaped it. He had served himself up to it. On a platter.

The source of the green radiance slowly turned and finally focused on Brett. The strange lights weren't lanterns but a pair of eyes. Green eyes. *Human* eyes, though much, much larger.

Brett moved somewhere beyond fear. He was afraid he had moved beyond sanity, as well, even as a tiny voice in his mind said, *You can't be crazy if you know you're crazy!* He felt a sudden urge to giggle and fought it, strangled it, because he knew if he started he might never stop.

"I want to see my brother." Brett's hands clenched and unclenched. Sweat dripped off them. "Give him to me. *Now.*"

The hissing laughter echoed from every surface in the Citadel. *"You do not walk the halls of the dead here."* The green eyes moved closer to him, each one easily the size of a compact car. *"Though if you wish to visit the dead . . ."*

The eyes narrowed. Grew *hungry.*

" . . . I can make that happen."

Brett sank to his knees. The vast shape's voice . . .

It's not speaking.

The knowledge made Brett shiver to his bones.

It's pushing those words straight into my brain.

He slumped onto the floor. He lay sideways on the cold stone as he stared at the creature. *Through* the creature. Unfocused. Brett could feel the monster in his head. He could sense an evil beyond all measure.

He understood finally that Charlie wasn't here. He'd never been here. Jackson had lied to him.

Controlling the water, riding that wave to the top of the Citadel wall, Brett had thought he knew what it meant to be powerful. But with the sinister hiss of this voice in his head, he understood how wrong he'd been. This shape, this being, here in the heart of Arcadian Alcatraz . . . *this* was power.

The grotesque, alien thoughts scratched and wormed themselves farther into his mind, and Brett realized something. Knew it, with as much certainty as he knew his own name.

This creature lured me here. Made me think I was strong enough to handle this place. It played me, just like Jackson played me. . . .

He felt like the biggest idiot who'd ever lived. The poor little boy who wanted to see his dead brother. The dumb pawn who did exactly what he was told, who believed exactly what he was made to believe. Ghost boys from dreams, and monstrous green eyes staring from the abyss. He'd done everything they'd hoped he'd do.

I tried, Charlie.

He reached a hand into the void.

I tried.

As Brett curled into a ball, there on the floor in front of the Citadel's master, the buzzing laughter echoed around him and through him and filled him up.

He could *never* bring Charlie back. It had never even been a possibility. Instead . . .

The baleful green eyes drew ever closer.

Instead, in Charlie's name . . .

What had he unleashed?

Brett had just enough energy left for one coherent thought.

I am so sorry, my brother. So sorry.

18

Clustered together at one edge of the circle, Gabe, Kaz, Lily, and Jackson faced the swarm of cultists and skinless beasts winging their way toward the island. Gabe wondered if he could pull off the same calling-down-lightning trick he had at the university. He didn't really want Jackson to grab him by the shoulder again, but he might have to since they were seconds away from getting mobbed.

Except that wasn't what happened. To Gabe's surprise, the abyssal bats set the cultists and the hunters down about twenty yards away . . . and waited. Gabe counted thirty bats, and about fifteen each of the humans and the hunters.

"What's happening?" Kaz asked quietly. "Why aren't

they jumping all over us?"

Before anyone could answer him, a single figure stepped out from the throng and glided toward them, her feet hidden beneath the long robe all the cultists wore.

"Primus," Gabe murmured.

"Be ready for anything," Greta told them from the center of the circle. Then she continued her chanting.

Primus stopped just far enough away to be able to talk to them without shouting. Slowly she raised her hands and pushed back her hood, revealing a woman of about forty. Gabe thought she might have been beautiful, if she hadn't looked so cruel. Primus smiled at them. Gabe shuddered.

"You fly in the face of inevitability." Primus's voice carried easily, clear and crisp. "In the face of destiny. Arcadia and this world are meant to be joined. Nothing can prevent that."

"Nothing, my butt," Lily all but growled. The air around her danced and spun, miniature tornadoes kicking up tiny plumes of dust.

Primus continued as if no one had spoken. Gabe wasn't even sure she'd heard Lily. "The five of you have demonstrated an enviable command of the Art. Give me the Emerald Tablet and join us, and you shall reap the benefits of such talent and skill. Aid us, and the new world will treat you like royalty."

"Lies." Jackson stated the word flatly. He wasn't talking to Primus, but he didn't bother keeping his volume down. "The Dawn doesn't care about us. They only want to use us." He sneered even more than usual. "Even from the Umbra, I saw enough to know that much."

Kaz nodded. So did Lily. Greta Jaeger stepped forward to stand alongside Gabe. "The circle is set. The ritual is ready," she whispered. Then in a louder voice, "Jackson's right. There's no cooperating with these zealots."

Gabe drew a deep breath. "Then I guess it's settled."

"I'm afraid we'll have to reject your offer," Greta called out. Behind Primus, the hunters growled, and the abyssal bats shifted and rustled their wings.

Primus cocked one eyebrow. "There is no need for you to die, here on this desolate chunk of rock. You could make your lives worthwhile. You could *whoulff—*"

A focused battering ram of water struck Primus squarely in the torso and drove her off her feet. The impact was so hard the woman flipped end over end, limbs flailing like a rag doll, until she landed in a senseless heap halfway between the ritual circle and the assembled Eternal Dawn.

"Consider that our answer," Greta Jaeger said, and every bit of hell broke loose.

The hunters sprang toward them at the same instant the abyssal bats launched up in the air. That left the human cultists alone, but they had apparently learned a few lessons since their thorough dismantling at the theater. Every one of them drew a gun from their robe and took aim at Gabe and his friends.

There won't be anything left for the bats and hunters to tear apart if we all get shot to pieces!

"Jackson!" Gabe barked. The smaller boy looked at him, surprised. "Time for another boost! For all of us!"

Jackson nodded, closed his eyes, and extended his hands from his sides. A fine, glowing web of golden energy shot through the air, first touching Kaz and Lily, then Greta Jaeger, and finally Gabe. Jackson opened his eyes again, their brilliant golden glow bright enough to cast shadows across the grass.

This time Gabe was ready for the rush of power. His own eyes blazed with light and terrible heat as the electric veins of Alcatraz Island revealed themselves to him. Electricity ran through wires, along cables all across the island . . . and through one conduit only a few inches beneath their feet. Gabe latched on to that energy, wrenched it free, and absorbed every kilowatt. His infernal gaze swept across the firearms in the cultists' grips, and in the quarter second of concentration he gave each one, every bit of the gunpowder in their magazines exploded.

It sounded like the loudest string of firecrackers ever, and the cultists shrieked and cursed and staggered, clutching burned and bloody hands.

A grin crept onto Gabe's face as a tiny voice in the center of his brain whispered, *"Burn . . . burn . . . burn . . . !"*

The grin vanished and the voice receded when an abyssal bat crashed to the ground beside him, its skinless body soaked with water—water with hints of Jackson's golden energy flickering through it. Gabe tore his attention from the wounded cultists and spun in place, trying to make sense of the whirling chaos.

While he'd been busy with the cultists' guns, the hunters had surged forward and surrounded them. Every second two or three dashed in, jaws savagely snapping and lunging. But Kaz had pulled at least two dozen head-sized stones from a nearby retaining wall and set them spinning in a protective barrier. As Gabe watched, one of the hunters tried to slip through it, and a great, heavy stone dipped out of its course and smashed against its skull. The beast flopped to the ground, shrieking in pain.

The abyssal bats fared no better. Her eyes a gorgeous silver-white, Lily had both hands raised toward the sky, and as the winged creatures swooped and dived, the multitude of tiny vortices dancing around her shot up in the air, one after another, growing and yawning wide. The miniature tornadoes enveloped the bats, spun them senseless, and smashed them against the ground or trees or buildings.

Any bats that Lily missed Greta tried to take out with directed blasts of water, but Gabe saw at a glance that the older woman was already tiring. He put an arm around her, supporting her. "What's wrong? Are you hurt?"

"No," she panted. "Just old. Setting up the ritual and hitting Primus hard enough to take her out of the fight . . . well, it almost took *me* out of the fight." She looked past him. "Kaz could use your help with the hunters."

She was right. Gabe saw at least ten of the creatures approaching Kaz in a single mass, clumped up closely enough that the ones on the inside would be protected from his flying stones by the bodies of the ones on the outside. Gabe was at Kaz's shoulder in a heartbeat. "That's not working anymore! You've got to try something else!"

Kaz's eyes were a solid slate gray. "If I try something else, some of them will get through while I'm shifting!"

Gabe could see what he meant. The protective ring of stones was slowing down the hunters, but if Kaz changed gears, that split second would give them time to pounce. "Don't worry," Gabe told him. "I got this."

The electricity in the huge conduit beneath them still flowed, channeling near-limitless power from the mainland, and once again Gabe drew from it until every cell in his body vibrated with power. He thrust out one hand, fingers splayed, and concentrated on the five hunters in the center of the lethal, slowly approaching pack.

A roar like a forest fire almost deafened him. Gabe's skin tightened from the heat, and Kaz yelped as he recoiled from the glare. The protective ring of stones fell inert to the ground; but that didn't matter, because the five hunters in the center of the pack suddenly exploded in balls of fire, reduced in a heartbeat to nothing more than elongated scorch marks. The rest of the hunters screamed, their skinless bodies burning, and staggered out of sight.

Even the abyssal bats abandoned their attack. For a few long, silent moments Gabe and his friends stood alone on the impromptu battlefield.

It took Gabe half that time to realize everyone was staring at him—followed by the further realization that the fire-hungry grin had again appeared on his face.

"My God, Gabe." Lily's beautiful, coal-black eyes held an emotion he'd never seen before. Not when she was looking at *him*. He didn't want to admit it, but he had to: her eyes were filled with fear. "What'd you just *do*?"

"I— The hunters . . ." Why were they all looking at him like that? "They were coming, and I thought— I had to—"

He was interrupted by a bone-jarring impact that shook the entire island. The null draak had slammed into the ground right behind the cluster of wounded cultists and, amid their abruptly-even-more-terrified screams, it began tossing them aside, their bodies crumpling like wet leaves. The null draak roared—even at that distance the force of it blew Gabe's hair back—and charged straight for the ritual circle.

No.

It charged straight for *Gabe*.

"Why's it coming after me?" he bellowed.

"Your connection to the Tablet!" Greta Jaeger answered. "It must sense the strongest trace of Arcadia on you! You have to get it into the circle!"

Time seemed to slow down as Gabe faced the eyeless,

interdimensional behemoth. *How are we supposed to get it inside the circle and* keep *it there? Better yet, how are we supposed to do that without it eating me?* Gabe had no chance to think about it at that moment, though, because the null draak rushed straight through the circle without even slowing down, its mighty jaws stretched wide and coming straight for him.

Gabe shouted and took a running leap to the side—not enough to get away, but maybe enough to survive—and shouted even louder when a burst of wind carried him completely out of the null draak's bite zone. The beast skidded to a stop, pitchfork-sized claws digging trenches in the dirt, and flailed as it turned its vast bulk for another charge.

Gabe got to his feet, his breathing ragged. "I know one way to get it to stay in the circle," he said, grinning.

With the fingers of his mind he reached deep into the electrical grid of the island. *More.* The lights of skyscrapers on the mainland dimmed. *MORE.* His hands became furnaces of white-blue energy. He was hotter than any fire. He was more focused than a laser. But it wasn't enough. He could pull in enough power to be a nuclear explosion. A *sun*! *A SUPERNOVA—*

Then Lily grabbed his shoulder.

"You can't kill it!"

Gabe frowned at her, feeling a crippling disappointment as the power flowed back into the world around him. "What?"

She sighed in frustration. "We need it alive to exchange it

for Brett, Gabe! You can't just roast it!"

Gabe stared at her. He wanted to say, "Don't be ridiculous! I wasn't going to kill it!" But as Lily looked him straight in the eyes, he knew that she knew he was. And that he *could*.

Shame filled him. That was exactly what he'd intended to do: open himself up to the fire. Listen to the hissing voice. Heed its words. *Burn . . . burn . . . burn . . . !*

If anyone but Lily had tried to stop me, he wondered, *what would I have done to them?* He shuddered.

"Guys!" Kaz's voice came from somewhere to their left. "Look out!" Gabe and Lily both turned in time to see the null draak come thundering toward them, and Lily carried them to safety on another gust of wind.

They landed right beside Kaz, Greta, and Jackson. Partly from self-preservation, but largely out of shame at his own lack of self-control, Gabe spoke up. "We're gonna have to work together to get this thing where we need it without getting chomped. I'll lure it back across the circle. Kaz, be ready to box it in. Throw up some walls but leave openings a person could get through. Lily, once it's in place, I doubt even stone will hold it for long, so you're going to have to get me to it really fast—and maybe to a part of it that's not covered with teeth and claws? Jackson, you've got to juice us all up with as much power as you can. And Greta . . ."

Greta shook her head. "I've got my breath back now. Don't worry. I'll make sure you aren't interrupted by any beasties or hooded maniacs." As if to emphasize this, the temperature abruptly dropped by forty degrees, and a violent storm of hail-stones began smashing into the ground in a broad, circular array, isolating the five of them. The null draak roared, shook out its wings, and lowered its head as if it was about to charge. "Any of them try to get through this, it'll knock their heads in."

Gabe held out his hand. Without a word, Greta gave him the slim silver dagger.

Before he could change his mind, Gabe nodded and dashed away from the group, shouting and waving his arms at the null draak. "Hey! Hey, you bargain-basement dragon knockoff! You want me? Try and take me!"

Gabe didn't think a creature as huge as the null draak was built for tight maneuvers, and its ungainly charges up to this point had borne that out. But as the creature's immense head swung around at his words, its claws and all six of its wing tips dug into the ground, and it launched itself at Gabe like an Olympic sprinter out of the starting block. Gabe yelped and poured on more speed.

He couldn't run directly away from it. That would just make the null draak chase him toward the cellblock, not over the ritual circle. So Gabe sprinted to the left at an angle across the chalk edge of the circle. He ran through the center, his lungs feeling as if they were on the brink of bursting. As soon as he crossed the far border of the circle, the null draak's breath hot and horrible on his back, he screamed, "NOW, KAZ!"

A new vibration shook the ground so hard that Gabe's feet went out from under him, and he slid to a painful stop on his chin and belly. Rolling over, he saw that Kaz had raised a fifteen-foot-high ring of pillars around the perimeter of the ritual circle. The null draak was trapped within it. The stones had stopped its charge short, but the creature's neck stretched over the barricade of columns, its jaws snapping at the air not two feet from the soles of Gabe's shoes.

The distance between each pillar was just wide enough for Gabe to fit through. As the null draak slammed against the columns, cracks began to fracture across their rough surfaces.

"Get me in there!" Gabe bellowed, scrambling away from the null draak's razor-sharp teeth. "Lily! Get me close to it, before it breaks loose!" Gabe couldn't see Lily, but another forceful gust of wind lifted him off his feet, and he sailed through the gap between two of the quickly crumbling pillars. When Gabe's feet touched the ground again, he was staring at the null draak's flank, a broad expanse of gray. . . . *What is this stuff? Hide? Scales?* He couldn't tell.

And he didn't really care. Gabe plunged the dagger into the beast all the way up to its hilt.

Tiny though it was in comparison to the beast's mass, the dagger must have hurt like crazy, because the null draak roared and thrashed and would have crushed Gabe to a pulpy mess against the inside of one of the walls—if someone hadn't grabbed him by the neck and the shoulder and hauled him back out through one of the gaps.

"Holy crap," Gabe panted. "Thanks, it almost—" He broke off when he found himself looking at Jackson Wright. "You—you just saved my life."

"Do not mention it," the smaller boy said. "But now I suggest we give this large fellow a bit of room, yes?"

The null draak thrashed again. All four stone walls split apart and crumbled, revealing that a blood cocoon—just like the one that had covered Uncle Steve and Brett back at the theater—was swiftly enveloping its body. *It's working! It's working!* Gabe looked around but couldn't see anyone else. *They must all be on the other side.* He glanced at Jackson. *Now's my only chance.*

"Thanks." Gabe struggled to maintain his balance as another tremor shook the island. Jackson had just saved him. Saved all of them, really, with his magick.

"I owe you," Gabe said, turning to the other boy. "And for what it's worth, I'm sorry."

"Sorry for what?"

"This is the only way to get my uncle back."

Jackson's eyes crinkled with confusion, then widened with alarm, but it was too late.

Gabe pushed Jackson into the cocoon.

Jackson screamed as the membrane flowed over his body, just as it had over Brett's when he'd tried to help Uncle Steve.

But Greta Jaeger reached past Gabe and, with one definitive

motion, yanked Jackson free, slicing the sheet of blood away with blades of water. The cocoon slid off him, sucking back into itself with an awful *plop*.

"What are you doing?" Greta shouted, inches away from Gabe's face. "You'll disrupt the ritual!" She thrust Jackson off to one side, one arm thrown across him protectively. In her other hand, the Emerald Tablet seemed to shudder. The air filled with strange, dissonant vibrations that Gabe didn't remember from the Dawn ritual back at the theater. Something was going wrong.

"I have to get Uncle Steve back!" Gabe's throat hurt with the force of the words. "That lying little jerk isn't worth his life!"

The blood cocoon began to tremble and darken like a dying star.

"Gabe, you need Jackson to destroy Arcadia! It's the only way any of us will ever be free. It's the thing your parents most wanted for you. Not to spend your life in hiding like your father did. The element of magick—the missing element—it's crucial. With Jackson, we can finally—"

Sschunk.

It happened in an instant. The long, knife-sharp claws of an abyssal bat burst through Greta's chest, dark with her blood.

Gabe stood there, frozen in disbelief.

The abyssal bat hurtled away, shrieking, yanked away from Greta Jaeger's back by the hurricane force of one of Lily's winds.

Soaked with blood, Greta dropped to her knees. Gabe stepped forward and caught her, knelt and cradled her in his lap, pain and guilt crushing his heart.

She came to stop me. She ended the hailstorm to stop me.

A tiny, distant part of him was aware that the blood cocoon had finished enveloping the null draak, and that the giant creature had begun to shrink, and that the island lurched beneath them as it did. But he didn't care. He only held Greta.

"I didn't mean—" he said, before a sob cut him off. "I didn't."

Weakly, she raised a finger and shushed him. "Just remember." Talking seemed to hurt her. "You need Jackson."

Gabe raised his head to see Jackson slowly backing away from them, an unreadable expression on his pale face. He didn't look like a boy at all just then. If anything, he seemed more like a tiny, tired old man.

Behind them, Lily screamed, *"Brett!"*

Gabe looked over his shoulder. The cocoon had shrunk down to human size, and as he watched, Brett struggled out of the middle of the enormous, empty membrane. Lily ran forward and threw her arms around her brother, laughing and crying at the same time. And after a second, Kaz joined in for an awkward group hug.

But Gabe had no chance to share in the joy. Still cradling Greta, he shouted, "Guys! Guys, *over there!*"

At the head of the steep road leading up from the docks,

the Eternal Dawn forces had marshaled. The battered cultists stood behind the surviving hunters, while abyssal bats perched all around them in trees and on rooftops. Every one of them stared at Gabe and his friends with murder in their eyes.

Primus, back on her feet, stood front and center, a long, elegant finger pointed at them like a hunter's claw. "Hand over the Tablet right now or your suffering will know no end!"

"I guess it's time for round two." Kaz clenched his fists. "Jackson, you ready with some more oomph?"

Jackson drew a breath, about to speak, but Brett's voice cut across everyone else's. It sounded as if it echoed around the entire island. "No need to worry, guys." Brett's eyes turned a deep blue-green, filled with unfathomable, glimmering power. He made a beckoning gesture. "I got this."

Something in the air changed.

Gabe couldn't tell why his breath caught in his throat. It could have been that all the oxygen around them had just radically shifted somehow. It could have been because of the grief that threatened to choke him as he held Greta Jaeger in his arms.

Or it could have been the shock of seeing a towering, city-destroying wave rise up out of the ocean, curl over the docks and the service road, and crash down on the assembled masses of the Eternal Dawn. It swept every trace of the cultists, the hunters, and the abyssal bats up in its savage, churning waters and dragged them all down the slope and into the bay.

As if they had never been there at all.

It was Brett's turn to be stared at. But only for about three seconds, before Lily rushed to Greta's side, gaping at her terrible wound. "We've got to get you to a hospital!" Lily held Greta's hand. "I think I can do it! I can lift you up, get you across the bay!"

Greta shook her head. "They . . . couldn't have saved me . . . even if this had happened in the emergency room." She tried for a weak smile and almost made it. "I don't have long. Listen. It will take all five of you to do what . . . has to be done."

Gabe wiped the tears from his cheeks. "To destroy Arcadia."

Greta nodded toward the ritual circle. Gabe looked and saw, hanging in the air at the circle's center, a tiny vertical crack of golden light. "The ritual was disrupted," she whispered. "The walls between Arcadia and our world have been breached. *That* is the power you five possess. You can bridge the two worlds . . . or destroy Arcadia . . . permanently."

Gabe didn't know what to say. He looked up from Greta and saw Jackson Wright staring at him, his eyes glowing with a mix of hatred and fear. Gabe felt another stab of shame. *I guess I can't blame him.*

"They will . . . come after you." Greta's eyes slid closed. "They will use you . . . to merge the worlds . . . unless you stop them." Her eyes fluttered back open, and the force of her stare almost made Gabe recoil. *"Together."*

Greta Jaeger went limp.

Gabe didn't bother trying to hide his sobs as he laid her down on the ground.

For a few moments, Gabe wasn't sure how long, they stood around her in a circle. Gabe kept staring at her body. He couldn't believe she was really gone.

No one said anything as Kaz's eyes turned stony gray. They backed away from Greta's body and watched as the ground opened up and gently pulled her down.

Gabe was the first to speak. "Make sure she's deep, Kaz."

Kaz nodded. "Taken care of."

Lily stared at the hair-thin golden fracture still hanging in the air. A crack in the world. "What're we going to do about that?"

"I will tell you what you cannot do," Jackson said, in an unusually not-so-smart-ass tone. "You cannot simply hang about and moon over it. Greta was correct. The Eternal Dawn will sense this breach's presence, and they will return here to try to exploit it."

Lily shot back, "But then we *have* to stay here! We have to stop them!"

Jackson shook his head and pointed at the Emerald Tablet, which rested in Kaz's stubby-fingered clutch. "They shan't be able to do much without that. Which means it is in our best interests to get the Tablet as far away from here as possible."

"Why do you care so much?" Gabe was physically and emotionally exhausted, and didn't bother trying to keep the anger out of his voice. Deep down, he knew it was anger at himself. "You're just in this for yourself, aren't you?"

"I spent over a century trying to get back to this world." The sneer made its way into Jackson's voice again. "I am not about to allow it to be destroyed. And like it or not, the five of us are strongest when we work together." He pointed a thumb at his own chest. "Thanks to *me*, lest you've forgotten."

Lily broke the silent tension hanging between Gabe and Jackson. "But where are we going to go?"

Kaz joined in. "If the Dawn's coming after us, the last place we should be is with our families. It'd just put a great big target on them."

Brett, Lily, and Kaz still had families here to worry about. Gabe did not. That was something he and Ghost Boy had in common.

"We'll have to think of something to tell our parents," Brett said. "I mean, it won't hold for long, but still. We gotta tell them *something*. And I guess we can go back to the tunnels under the city. We know our way around down there. We've still got the map, and we can sneak out and get food and supplies."

Kaz sighed. "Just what I always wanted. To live in the sewer. I bet we'll all catch tuberculosis. Or malaria. Or hantavirus."

Gabe stared at the ground, thinking. "We can stay in the tunnels. While we're there we've got to figure out how to seal that breach and destroy Arcadia for good. Then we'll come back here and fix things. We've got to do at least that much.

I've got to. I owe it to Greta." He glanced up and saw Jackson giving him the mother of all accusatory stares. No one but Greta and Jackson knew that Gabe had disrupted the ritual by trying to force Jackson back to Arcadia. That breach was Gabe's fault and Gabe's alone. He wondered how long Ghost Boy would keep that bit of information to himself. "And I owe it to my parents."

"Oh, destroy an evil shadow dimension—is that all?" Kaz muttered. "Awesome. Should be lots of fun trying to get back here, considering how fast the government's going to lock this place down."

Lily nodded in agreement. "Yeah. Weird shining crack in the world that won't go away? It's not like the National Park Service is going to just add that to Alcatraz's list of attractions."

Brett cleared his throat. "I wouldn't be in such a hurry to destroy Arcadia, Gabe."

Gabe's eyebrows shot up. "Huh? Why not?"

"Look, I've got a lot to tell you guys. Somewhere else, sometime later, when we're not fleeing the scene of the world's weirdest case of vandalism and . . . y'know. Mourning a loss." Brett reached out and put a hand on Gabe's arm. "Gabe, listen, this is gonna be kind of a shock. But I met your *mom* over there. Your uncle Steve's with her now. She's still alive, man. And that breach might be your only shot at getting her back."

All the blood drained from of Gabe's face, and for a second he couldn't breathe. Brett and Kaz grabbed his arms to help him stay on his feet. Of all the things that had happened to him since everything began—the rituals, the magick, the monsters, the alternate dimensions—his mom was *alive and in Arcadia*?

The ground seemed to lurch under his feet, and this time it wasn't a trick of the elements. It was the last shred of his old reality disintegrating around him.

He struggled for words. The ones he finally found were "Let's get off this island."

He numbly put one foot in front of the other as they made their way down the hill to the dock.

EPILOGUE

The five of them stood comfortably on a broad, flat ice raft, skimming across the bay's surface on their way back to San Francisco. They needed to cooperate now, that much was true . . . but the boy called Brett Hernandez knew their little cluster of elementalists was a time bomb, ticking merrily toward its detonation. He eyed his fellow fugitives one by one.

Lily. Always so fearless . . . but she feared Gabe now, didn't she?

Jackson Wright. The Ghost Boy. Brain scrambled by a century of isolation.

Gabe himself, wrecked by inescapable guilt.

Only Kaz seemed unchanged. Dependable. Generous. One to watch.

Not one of them suspected anything was different about their dear friend and brother Brett Hernandez. *Good.* Brett considered the ice raft he had created on Alcatraz's shore. He'd barely even had to think about it, thanks to the power that flowed through his veins now. True power. Majestic. Inescapable.

Brett turned his gaze skyward. The storm had finally broken, and a vast swath of stars sparkled overhead. Their radiance illuminated a twisting, coiling mass deep within Brett's eyes . . .

. . . down, down in the darkness . . .

. . . where tentacles like storm clouds curled around brilliant twin pinpoints of ravenous green light.